The critics love *Without a Hero*

"Sharp, rueful, malevolently funny . . . Mr. Boyle's wry sense of the unnatural is so highly developed that it shows up everywhere . . . these stories are lean and focused, with slender, eccentric premises that need no further elaboration."   —Janet Maslin, *The New York Times*

"Gloriously comic . . . vintage Boyle . . . [these] stories are more than funny, better than wicked. They make you cringe with their clarity."
          —*The Philadelphia Inquirer*

"Boyle mixes entertainment and insight with words that will delight readers with a richness and intensity of their own . . . his sharply defined, varied group of characters don't fall short of heroic status for lack of trying."
          —*St. Louis Post-Dispatch*

"In *Without a Hero* once more there is nothing casual or tired; the literary performances here retain Mr. Boyle's astonishing and characteristic verve, his unaverted gaze, his fascination with everything lunatic and queasy . . . his stories fill a reader with the giddy nausea of our cultural and theological confusions."   —Lorrie Moore, *The New York Times Book Review*

"Wildly inventive . . . darkly satiric . . . Boyle churns along at his hyperbolic best . . . he writes with a breathless vigor and stylistic panache . . . that makes you suspend, for a moment, any cares about the terra firma where more conventional stories are rooted."
          —*The Hartford Courant*

PENGUIN BOOKS

WITHOUT A HERO

T. Coraghessan Boyle is the author of the novels *A Friend of the Earth*, *Riven Rock*, *The Tortilla Curtain*, *The Road to Wellville*, *East Is East*, *World's End* (winner of the PEN/Faulkner Award), *Budding Prospects*, and *Water Music*. His short story collections include *T.C. Boyle Stories*, *Descent of Man*, *Greasy Lake*, *If the River Was Whiskey*, and *Without a Hero*. His short fiction regularly appears in major American magazines, including *The New Yorker*, *Harper's*, *The Paris Review*, *Playboy*, *Esquire*, and *The Atlantic Monthly*. Boyle was the recipient of the 1999 PEN/Malamud Award for Excellence in Short Fiction. He lives in Santa Barbara, California.

ALSO BY T. CORAGHESSAN BOYLE

NOVELS

The Road to Wellville

East Is East

World's End

Budding Prospects

Water Music

SHORT STORIES

If the River Was Whiskey

Greasy Lake

Descent of Man

WITHOUT A HERO

Stories by

T. CORAGHESSAN BOYLE

PENGUIN BOOKS

PENGUIN BOOKS
Published by the Penguin Group
Penguin Books USA Inc., 375 Hudson Street, New York, New York 10014, U.S.A.
Penguin Books Ltd, 27 Wrights Lane, London W8 5TZ, England ·
Penguin Books Australia Ltd, Ringwood, Victoria, Australia
Penguin Books Canada Ltd, 10 Alcorn Avenue, Toronto, Ontario, Canada M4V 3B2
Penguin Books (N.Z.) Ltd, 182–190 Wairau Road, Auckland 10, New Zealand

Penguin Books Ltd, Registered Offices: Harmondsworth, Middlesex, England

First published in the United States of America by Viking Penguin,
a division of Penguin Books USA Inc., 1994
Published in Penguin Books 1995

7 9 10 8 6

PUBLISHER'S NOTE
These are works of fiction. Names, characters, places, and incidents either are the product of
the author's imagination or are used fictitiously, and any resemblance to actual persons, living
or dead, events, or locales is entirely coincidental.

Grateful acknowledgment is made to the following magazines, in which these stories first
appeared: *Antaeus*, "The 100 Faces of Death, Volume IV"; *Gentleman's Quarterly*, "Back in
the Eocene," "The Fog Man," and "Without a Hero"; *Granta*, "Little America" and "Sitting
on Top of the World"; *Harper's*, "Hopes Rise" and "Top of the Food Chain"; *The New
Yorker*, "Filthy with Things"; *Playboy*, "Beat," "Carnal Knowledge," "56–0" and "Respect";
Rolling Stone, "Big Game"; and *Wigwag*, "Acts of God."

Excerpt from "Poem Without a Hero" by Anna Akhmatova from *Poems of Akhmatova*,
translated by Stanley Kunitz and Max Hayward. © 1972 by Stanley Kunitz and Max Hayward.
By permission of Darhansoff & Verrill Literary Agency.

THE LIBRARY OF CONGRESS HAS CATALOGUED THE HARDCOVER AS FOLLOWS:
Boyle, T. Coraghessan.
Without a hero: stories/by T. Coraghessan Boyle.
p. cm.
ISBN 0-670-84963-4 (hc.)
ISBN 0 14 01.7839 2 (pbk.)
I. Title
PS3552.O932W58   1994
813'.54—dc20   93–35919

Printed in the United States of America
Set in Adobe New Caledonia

For Mitchell Burgess and Robin Green

... all that remained to hope was that on the day of my execution there should be a huge crowd of spectators and that they should greet me with howls of execration.

—ALBERT CAMUS, *The Stranger*

To her horror, . . . Dottie found herself having second thoughts: what if she had lost her virginity to a man who scared her and who sounded, from his own description, like a pretty bad hat?

—MARY MCCARTHY, *The Group*

Contents

BIG GAME   *1*

HOPES RISE   *25*

FILTHY WITH THINGS   *41*

WITHOUT A HERO   *65*

RESPECT   *83*

ACTS OF GOD   *95*

BACK IN THE EOCENE   *117*

CARNAL KNOWLEDGE   *123*

THE 100 FACES OF DEATH, VOLUME IV   *145*

56–0   *157*

TOP OF THE FOOD CHAIN   *173*

LITTLE AMERICA   *179*

BEAT   *193*

THE FOG MAN   *209*

SITTING ON TOP OF THE WORLD   *221*

WITHOUT
A HERO

BIG GAME

The way to hunt is for as long as you live against as long as there is such and such an animal.

—ERNEST HEMINGWAY, *Green Hills of Africa*

YOU COULD SHOOT ANYTHING you wanted, for a price, even the elephant, but Bernard tended to discourage the practice. It made an awful mess, for one thing, and when all was said and done it was the big animals—the elephant, the rhino, the water buff and giraffe—that gave the place its credibility, not to mention ambiance. They weren't exactly easy to come by, either. He still regretted the time he'd let the kid from the heavy-metal band pot one of the giraffes—even though he'd taken a cool twelve thousand dollars to the bank on that one. And then there was the idiot from MGM who opened up on a herd of zebra and managed to decapitate two ostriches and lame the Abyssinian ass in the process. Well, it came with the territory, he supposed, and it wasn't as if he didn't carry enough insurance on the big stuff to buy out half the L.A. Zoo if he had to. He was just lucky nobody had shot himself in the foot yet. Or the head. Of course, he was insured for that, too.

Bernard Puff pushed himself up from the big mahogany table and flung the dregs of his coffee down the drain. He wasn't exactly overwrought, but he was edgy, his stomach sour and clenched round the impermeable lump of his breakfast cruller, his hands afflicted with the little starts and tremors of the coffee shakes. He lit a cigarette to calm himself and gazed out the kitchen window on the dromedary pen, where one of the moth-eaten Arabians was methodically peeling the bark from an elm tree. He looked at the thing in amazement, as if he'd never seen it before—the flexible lip and stupid eyes, the dully working jaw—and made a mental note to offer a special on camels. The cigarette tasted like tin, like death. Somewhere a catbird began to call out in its harsh mewling tones.

The new people were due any minute now, and the prospect of new people always set him off—there were just too many things that could go wrong. Half of them didn't know one end of a rifle from the other, they expected brunch at noon and a massage an hour later, and they bitched about everything, from the heat to the flies to the roaring of the lions at night. Worse: they didn't seem to know what to make of him, the men regarding him as a subspecies of the blue-collar buddy, regaling him with a nonstop barrage of lickerish grins, dirty jokes and fractured grammar, and the women treating him like a cross between a maître d' and a water carrier. Dudes and greenhorns, all of them. Parvenus. Moneygrubbers. The kind of people who wouldn't know class if it bit them.

Savagely snubbing out the cigarette in the depths of the coffee mug, Bernard wheeled round on the balls of his feet and plunged through the swinging doors and out into the high dark hallway that gave onto the foyer. It was stifling already, the overhead fans chopping uselessly at the dead air round his ears and the sweat prickling at his new-shaven jowls as he stomped down the hall, a big man in desert boots and khaki shorts, with too much belly and something overeager and graceless in his stride. There was no one in the foyer and no one at the registration desk. (Espinoza was out feeding the animals—Bernard could hear the hyenas whooping in the distance —and the new girl—what was her name?—hadn't made it to work on time yet. Not once.) The place seemed deserted, though he knew Orbalina would be making up the beds and Roland sneaking a drink somewhere—probably out behind the lion cages.

For a long moment Bernard stood there in the foyer, framed against a bristling backdrop of kudu and oryx heads, as he checked the reservation card for the tenth time that morning:

Mike and Nicole Bender
Bender Realty
15125 Ventura Blvd.
Encino, California

Real estate people. Jesus. He'd always preferred the movie crowd
—or even the rock-and-rollers, with their spiked wristbands and
pouf hairdos. At least they were willing to buy into the illusion that
Puff's African Game Ranch, situated on twenty-five hundred acres
just outside Bakersfield, was the real thing—the Great Rift Valley,
the Ngorongoro Crater, the Serengeti—but the real estate people
saw every crack in the plaster. And all they wanted to know was how
much he'd paid for the place and was the land subdividable.

He looked up into the yellow-toothed grin of the sable mounted
on the wall behind him—the sable his father had taken in British
East Africa back in the thirties—and let out a sigh. Business was
business, and in the long run it didn't matter a whit who perforated
his lions and gazelles—just as long as they paid. And they always
paid, up front and in full. Bernard saw to that.

"What was it, Nik, six months ago when we went to Gino Par-
ducci's for dinner? It was six months, wasn't it? And didn't I say
we'd do the African thing in six months? Didn't I?"

Nicole Bender was curled up in the passenger seat of the white
Jaguar XJS her husband had given her for Valentine's Day. A pile
of knitting magazines lay scattered in her lap, atop a set of bamboo
needles trailing an embryonic garment in a shade so pale it defied
categorization. She was twenty-seven, blond, a former actress/model/
poet/singer whose trainer had told her just two days earlier that she
had perhaps the most perfectly sculpted physique of any woman he'd
ever worked with. Of course, he was paid to say things like that, but
in her heart she suspected they were true, and she needed to hear
them. She turned to her husband. "Yes," she said. "You did. But I
pictured us in Kenya or Tanzania, to tell the truth."

"Yeah, yeah," he fired back impatiently, "yeah, yeah, yeah," the
words coming so fast they might have been bullets squeezed from

one of the glistening new big-bore rifles in the trunk, "but you know I can't take six weeks off from work, not now when the new Beverly Hills office is about to open up and the Montemoretto deal is all but in the bag . . . and besides, it's dangerous over there, what with the next revolution or war or whatever coming down every six minutes, and who do you think they're going to blame when the roof caves in? White people, right? And where do you think you'll want to be then?"

Mike Bender was a barely contained factory of energy, a steam-roller of a man who had risen from receptionist to king and despot of his own real estate empire in the space of twelve short years. He was given to speechifying, the precious words dropping from his lips like coins from a slot machine, his fingertips alighting on his tongue, his hair, his ears, the crotch of his pants and his elbows as he spoke, writhing with the nervous energy that had made him rich. "And plus you've got your tsetse flies and black mambas and beriberi and the plague and god knows what all over there—I mean, picture Mexico, only a hundred times worse. No, listen, trust me—Gino swore this place is as close as it gets to the real thing, only without the hassles." He lowered his sunglasses to give her a look. "You're telling me you really want to get your ass chewed off in some lopsided tent in, in"—he couldn't seem to think of a place sufficiently grim, so he improvised—"Zambeziland?"

Nicole shrugged, giving him a glimpse of the pouty little half-smile she used to work up for the photographers when she was nineteen and doing the summerwear ads for JCPenney.

"You'll get your zebra-skin rug yet, you wait and see," Mike assured her, "and a couple lions' heads and gazelles or whatever for the wall in the den, okay?"

The Jaguar shot across the desert like a beam of light. Nicole lifted the knitting needles from her lap, thought better of it, and set them down again. "Okay," she said in a breathy little whisper, "but I just hope this place isn't too, you know, *tacky.*"

A sudden harsh laugh erupted from the back seat, where Mike Bender's twelve-year-old daughter, Jasmine Honeysuckle Rose Bender, was stretched out supine with the last ten issues of *Bop* and a sixpack of New York Seltzer. "Get real, will you? I mean like shooting lions in Bakersfield? Tacky city. Tacky, tacky, tacky."

Up front, behind the wheel, his buttocks caressed by the supple kid leather of the seat and visions of bontebok leaping before his eyes, Mike Bender was mildly annoyed. He'd had an itch to hunt lion and elephant and rhino since he was a kid and first read *Confessions of a White Hunter* and the Classic Comics version of *King Solomon's Mines*. And this was his chance. So maybe it wasn't Africa, but who had the time to go on safari? If he could spare three days he was lucky. And you couldn't shoot anything over there anyway. Not anymore. Everything was a preserve now, a game park, a conservancy. There were no more white hunters. Just photographers.

He wanted to say "Give me a break, will you?" in his most imperious voice, the voice that sent his sales force scurrying for cover and his competitors into shock, but he held his peace. Nothing was going to ruin this for him. Nothing.

It was midafternoon. The sun hung overhead like an egg shirred in a cup. The thermometer in the feed shed was pushing a hundred and fifteen degrees, nothing was moving but for the vultures aloft in the poor bleached expanse of the sky, and the whole world seemed to have gone to sleep. Except for Bernard. Bernard was beside himself—the Benders had been due at 10:00 A.M. and here it was quarter past two and still they hadn't arrived. He'd had Espinoza let the Tommies and eland out of their pens at nine, but he was afraid they'd all be lying up in the heat, and by noon he'd sent him out to round them up again. The giraffes were nowhere to be seen, and the elephant, tethered to a live oak Bernard had pruned to resemble an umbrella thorn, was looking as rumpled and dusty as a heap of Taiwanese luggage abandoned at the airport.

Bernard stood in the glare of the dried-up yard, squinting out on the screen of elephant grass and euphorbia he'd planted to hide the oil rig (if you knew it was there you could just detect the faintest motion of the big steel arm as it rose and fell and rose and fell again). He felt hopeless. For all the effort he'd put into it, the place looked like a circus camp, the bombed-out remains of a zoo, a dusty flat baking former almond ranch in the sun-blasted southeast corner of the San Joaquin Valley—which is exactly what it was. What would the Benders think? More important, what would they think at six hundred dollars a day, payable in advance, plus prices that ranged from a thousand a pop on the gazelles on up to twelve thousand for a lion and "priced as available" for the elephant? Real estate people had balked on him before, and business hadn't exactly been booming lately.

The vultures wheeled overhead. He was running sweat. The sun felt like a firm hand steering him toward the cool of the kitchen and a tall glass of quinine water (which he drank for effect rather than therapeutic value: there wasn't a malarial mosquito within a thousand miles). He was just about to pack it in when he caught the distant glint of sun on safety glass and saw the Benders' car throwing up dust clouds at the far end of the drive.

"Roland!" he bellowed, and every mortal ounce of him was in motion now, "Let the monkeys out into the trees! And the parrots!" Suddenly he was jogging across the dusty lot and up the path to where the elephant lay collapsed beneath the tree. He was working at the slip of the tether to set her loose and wondering if Roland would have the sense to stir up the lions and hyenas for the sake of sound effects, when suddenly she rose to her feet with a great blowing snort and gave a feeble trumpet.

Well. And that was a break—at least now he wouldn't have to use the ivory goad.

Bernard looked up at the old elephant in wonder—she still had a bit of showmanship in her, after all. Either that, or it was senile dementia. She was old—Bernard didn't know quite how old, though he did know she was a veteran of thirty-eight years with the Ringling Bros. and Barnum & Bailey Circus who'd performed under the name "Bessie Bee" and responded to "Shamba"—that is, if you happened to have the ivory goad in your hand. Bernard shot a glance up the drive, where a white Jaguar sedan was beginning to define itself against a billowing backdrop of dust, and then he heard the screech of the monkeys as they shot out of their cages and up into the trees, and he began to compose himself. He forced a smile, all red-cheeked and long-toothed, cinched the leopard-skin belt, squared his pith helmet and marched forward to greet his guests.

By the time the Benders rolled up to the veranda, the parrots were in the trees, the marabou stork was pecking at a spot of offal in the dirt, and the lions were roaring lustily from their hidden pens out back. Roland, decked out in his Masai toga and lion's-tooth neck-lace, bounded down the steps with alacrity to hold open the door for Bender, while Bessie Bee shambled around in the near distance, flapping her ears and blowing about in the dust. "Mr. Bender," Ber-nard cried, extending his hand to a fortyish man in sunglasses and polo shirt, "welcome to Africa."

Bender sprang out of the car like a child at the zoo. He was tall, lean, tanned—why did they all have to look like tennis pros? Bernard wondered—and stood there twitching a moment in the heat. He pumped Bernard's hand professionally and then launched into a lip-jerking, ear-tugging, foot-thumping apology: "Sorry we're late, Bernard, but my wife—have you met my wife?—my wife just had to get a couple rolls of film and we wound up buying out half of Reynoso's Camera in Bakersfield—you know it?—good prices. Real good prices. Hell, we needed a new video camera anyway, especially with"—he gestured to take in the house, the outbuildings, the elephant, the monkeys in the trees and the sun-blasted plains beyond—"all this."

Bernard was nodding, smiling, murmuring agreement, but he was on autopilot—his attention was fixed on the wife, whom Roland was fussing over now on the far side of the car. She raised her lovely white arms to fluff her hair and imprison her eyes behind a pair of sunglasses and Bernard called out a greeting in his best British-colonial accent (though he was British by ancestry only and had never in his life been east of Reno). The second wife, of course, he was thinking as she returned his greeting with a vague little pouting smile.

"Yes, yes, of course," Bernard said in response to some further idiocy from the husband's lips, his watery blue eyes shifting to the daughter now—as black-headed as an Indian, and nearly as dark—and he saw right away that she was trouble, the sort of child who cultivates ugliness as a weapon.

Nicole Bender gave him a long slow appraisal over the hood of the car, and in the next moment he was ducking round the grille to squeeze her hand as if he were trying on a glove for size. "Beastly day," he said, proud of the Britishism, and then he was leading her up the broad stone steps and into the house, while her husband fumbled with an armload of guns and the daughter slouched along behind, already complaining about something in a nagging querulous little whine of a voice.

"I'm not saying that, Mike—you're not listening to me. I *said* the gazelles are very nice and they'll be perfect for the office, but I wanted something, well, *bigger* for the front hall and at least three of the zebra—two for the den, I thought, and we're going to need one for the ski lodge . . . you know, to hide that ugly paneling behind the bar?"

Mike Bender was deep into his fourth gin and tonic. Already the elation he'd felt over his first kill had begun to dissipate, replaced now by a gnawing sense of frustration and anger—why couldn't Nikki shut her face, even for a second? No sooner had they changed clothes and got out there on the savannah or veldt or whatever you wanted to call it, than she'd started in. He'd squeezed off a clean shot at a Thomson's gazelle at two hundred yards and before the thing's head had hit the ground, she was running it down. *Oh*, she gasped, as if she'd been surprised on the toilet, *but it's so small, isn't it?* And then she struck a pose for Puff and the colored guy who carried the guns and skinned out the carcasses. *Almost like a rabbit with horns.*

And now the great white hunter was leaning across the table to reassure her, his gut drawn tight against the khaki safari shirt, his accent so phony it was like something out of a Monty Python routine. "Mrs. Bender, Nicole," he began, mopping his blood blister of a face with a big checked handkerchief, "we'll go out for zebra in the morning, when it's cool, and if it's three you want, we'll get them,

there's no problem with that. Four, if you like. Five. If you've got
the bullets, we've got the game."

Mike watched as the canny crewcut head swiveled toward him.
"And Mike," Puff said, as amenable as any tour guide but with just
the right hint of stagery in his voice, "in the evening, it's the big
stuff, the man-maker, old Simba himself."

As if in response, there was a cough and roar from somewhere
out beyond the darkened windows, and Mike Bender could feel the
wildness of it on the thin night air—lion, the lion he'd dreamed
about since his aunt had taken him to the Central Park Zoo as a boy
and the roar of the great shaggy yellow-eyed things had shaken him
to his primordial root. To be out there, in that African night that
was haunted with predators, big-headed and thick-skinned, the
pounce, the slash, the crack of sinew and bone—it was at once
terrifying and wonderful. But what was that smell of oil?

"What do you say, old man? Are you game?" Puff was leering
at him now, and behind Puff's blocky leonine figure, the faces of his
wife and daughter, arrayed like tribal masks.

Nothing fazed Mike Bender, the King of Encino. No seller
could hold out against him, no buyer hope for more. His contracts
were vises, his promotions sledgehammers, his holdings as solid as
a mountain of iron. "I'm game," he said, touching his lips, running
his fingers through his hair, jabbing at his elbows and underarms in
a rising plume of metabolic excess. "Just oil up my H&H Magnum
and point me toward 'em; it's what I've wanted all my life—"

There was a silence and his words seemed to hang in the air,
empty of conviction. His daughter crouched over her plate, looking
as if she were sucking on something rotten; his wife had that alert,
let's-go-shopping look in her glittering little eyes. "Really. I mean,
ever since I was a kid, and—how many are out there, anyway? Or
do you keep count?"

Puff stroked the graying stubble of his head. There was another
roar, muted this time, followed by the stabbed-in-the-belly whoop
of the hyena. "Oh, we've got a good-sized pride out there—twelve
or fourteen, I'd say, and a few rogue males."

"Are there any big ones, with manes? That's what we want."

He shifted his gaze to Nicole. "Maybe the whole thing, stuffed, standing up on its hind legs, what do you think, Nik? For maybe the reception room at the Beverly Hills office?" And then he made a joke of it: "Hey, if Prudential can get away with it—"

Nicole looked satisfied. So did Puff. But his daughter wasn't about to let him off so easily. She let out a snort of contempt, and the three of them turned toward her. "And so you go and kill some poor lion that isn't hurting anybody, and what's that supposed to prove?"

Puff exchanged a look with him, as if to say, *Now isn't that adorable?*

Jasmine Honeysuckle Rose pushed aside her salad plate. Her hair hung in her eyes in greasy black coils. She'd eaten nothing, having separated the tomatoes from the greens and the greens from the croutons and the croutons from the garbanzo beans. "Sting," she spat, "Brigitte Bardot, the New Kids, all of them say it's like animal death camps, like Hitler, and they're doing this special concert to save the animals in France, in Paris—"

"One lion more or less isn't going to hurt anybody," Nicole said, cutting the child off, and her mouth was drawn tight against the swell of her collagen-enhanced lips. "And I think your father's idea is super. An erect lion standing there as people come in the door— it's, it's symbolic is what it is."

Mike Bender couldn't tell if he was being ribbed or not. "Listen, Jasmine," he began, and his leg started to thump under the table as he tugged at his ear and fooled with his cutlery.

"Jasmine Honeysuckle Rose," she fired back.

Mike knew she'd always hated her name, an inspiration of her mother, the sort of crackbrained woman who saw spirits in the sunset and believed that he was the reincarnation of John D. Rockefeller. To throw it up to him, and to remind him of his ex-wife and all the mistakes he'd ever made or contemplated, his daughter insisted on her full name. Always.

"Okay: Jasmine Honeysuckle Rose," he said, "listen to me. All of this hippie-dippy save-the-environment crap might be all right if

you're twelve, but you've got to realize hunting is as natural a part
of man as, as—"

"Eating or drinking," Puff put in, rounding off the participle
with a pseudo-Etonian ring.

"Right!" Jasmine cried, on her feet now, her eyes like sinkholes,
her mouth twitching at the corners. "And so's shitting, farting and,
and *fucking!"* And then she was gone, stamping down the trophy-
hung hallway to her room, where she flung the door to with a
thunderous crash.

A moment of silence descended on the table. Puff's eyes lingered on Nicole as she raised her arms to stretch and show off her
breasts and the prim white pockets of shaved flesh under her arms.
"Cute kid, huh?" he said. There was no mistaking the sarcasm this
time.

"Real cute," Nicole said, and they were in league.

Turning to Mike as the colored guy came through the door with
a platter of gazelle steaks and mesquite-roasted ears of corn, Puff
let his voice grow warm and confidential. "Zebra in the morning,
Mike," he said. "You'll like that." He leveled his watery gaze on him.
"And then"—the gazelle steaks hitting the table, little dollops of
blood-running flesh—"and then we load up for lion."

It wasn't that he bolted, actually—Bernard had seen worse,
much worse—but he was on the verge of it. Either that or he was
about to pass out. Any way you sliced it, it was a bad situation, the
kind of encounter that made Bernard wish he'd never heard of Africa, lions, game parks or real estate people.

They'd come on the lion in the old almond grove. The trees
there were like twisted antlers, leafless and dead, set out in rows as
far as you could see, and the ground beneath them was littered with
fallen branches. "Not too close now," Bernard had warned, but
Bender wanted to be sure of the shot, and he got himself in a bind.
In the next moment he was standing there knee-deep in the litter,
jerking and shrugging like a spastic, the gun to his shoulder and
nowhere to go, and the lion was coming at him with as much pure

malice as Bernard had seen in his fourteen years as proprietor of Puff's African Game Ranch. And while Bernard didn't like to intervene—it always caused hard feelings after the fact—Mrs. Bender was a heartbeat away from being an aggrieved widow and his own insurance rates were about to go through the roof, never mind the lawsuits. It was a moment, no doubt about it.

The night before, after the Benders had gone off to bed, Bernard had had Espinoza go out and stir up the lions a bit and then set them loose—without their supper. That always put them in a mood, no matter how old, toothless and gimpy they might be. Let them go a night without horse meat and they were as savage as anything you'd encounter anywhere on earth. For Bernard, it was standard practice. Give the guests their money's worth, that was his motto. If they suspected that the lions were penned up ninety-nine percent of the time, none of them let on—for all they knew the beasts lived out there among the drought-ravaged almond trees and camouflaged oil rigs. And besides, it wasn't as if they had anywhere to go—the entire property was circumscribed by a twenty-foot-deep dry moat with a twelve-foot-high electrified fence rising up behind it. The ones the guests didn't put holes in would just wander back to their cages in a day or so, roaring their bellies out for horse meat and offal.

In the morning, after a breakfast of kippers and eggs and while the daughter slept in, Bernard had taken the Benders out after their zebra. They'd driven out to the water hole—an abandoned Olympic-sized swimming pool Bernard had planted up to look natural—and, after some discussion of price, the Benders—or, rather, the wife—decided on five. She was something, the wife. As good-looking a woman as Bernard had ever laid eyes on, and a better shot than her husband. She took two of the zebra at a hundred and fifty yards, barely a mark on the hides. "You can shoot, little lady," Bernard said as they sauntered up to the nearest of the fallen zebra.

The zebra lay there on its side beneath the knifing sun, and already the first flies had begun to gather. Bender was crouched over one of the carcasses in the near distance, inspecting it for bullet holes, and Roland was back in the Jeep, whetting his skinning knife.

From the hills beyond, one of the starved lions let loose with an irascible roar.

Nicole smiled at him, pretty—awfully pretty—in her Banana Republic shorts and safari shirt. "I try," she said, unbuttoning her shirt to reveal a peach-colored halter top decorated with a gold pin in the shape of a rifle. He had to bend close to read the inscription: *Nicole Bender, Supermarksman Award, N.R.A., 1989.*

Then it was lunch and siesta, followed by gin and bitters and a few hands at canasta to while away the waning hours of the afternoon. Bernard did everything he could to amuse the lady, and not just in the interest of business—there was something there, something beating hot and hard beneath the mask of blusher and eyeliner and the puffed-up lips, and he couldn't help feeling the tug of it. It had been tough since Stella Rae had left him, and he took his tumbles where he could find them—after all, *that* came with the territory too.

At any rate, they took the Jeep Wrangler, a cooler of beer, Bender's .375 Holland & Holland, the lady's Winchester .458 Mag and his own stopper—the .600 Nitro—and headed out to where the twisted black branches of the orchard raked the flanks of the hills in the far corner of the ranch. It was where the lions always went when you set them loose. There was a little brook there—it was a torrent in season, but now it wasn't much more than a trickle. Still, they could lap up some water and roll in the grass and find a poor striped shade beneath the naked branches of the trees.

From the start, even when they were still on the gin and bitters and waiting out the heat, Bender had seemed edgy. The man couldn't sit still, rattling on about escrows and titles and whatnot, all the while tugging at his lips and ears and tongue like a third-base coach taking signals from the dugout. It was nerves, that's what it was: Bernard had taken enough dudes out there to recognize a fellow measuring out his own manhood against that big tawny thing stalking his imagination. One guy—he was a TV actor; maybe a fag, even—had got himself so worked up he'd overloaded on the gin and pissed his pants before they got the Jeep started. Bernard had seen him a hundred times since on the flickering tube, a hulking muscular character with a cleft chin and flashing eyes who was forever smashing crooks in the face and snaring women by the waist, but he could never forget the way the guy's eyes had vanished in his head as the piss stain spread from his crotch to his thighs and beyond. He took one look at Bender and knew there was trouble on the horizon.

They'd agreed on $11,500 for a big male with a mane, Bernard knocking off the odd five hundred because they'd taken the two extra zebra and he figured he'd give them a break. The only male he had of any size was Claude, who must have been something in his day but was now the leonine equivalent of a nonagenarian living on a diet of mush in a nursing home. Bernard had picked him up for a song at a flea-bitten circus in Guadalajara, and he must have been twenty-five years old if he was a day. He was half-blind, he stank like one of the walking dead and the molars on the lower left side of his jaw were so rotten he howled through his food when he ate. But he looked the part, especially at a distance, and he still carried some of the flesh he'd put on in his youth—and the pain in his jaw made him cranky; savage, even. He would do, Bernard had thought. He would do just fine.

But there was Bender, stuck in a morass of dead black branches, trembling all over like a man in an ice bath, and the lion coming at him. The first shot skipped in the dirt at two hundred feet and took Claude's left hind paw off at the joint, and he gave out with a roar of such pure raging claw-gutting bone-crunching nastiness that the idiot nearly dropped his rifle. Or so it seemed from where Bernard was standing with the Mrs. and Roland, fifteen yards back and with the angle to the right. Claude was a surprise. Instead of folding up into himself and skittering for the bushes, he came on, tearing up the dirt and roaring as if he'd been set afire—and Bender was jerking and twitching and twittering so much he couldn't have hit the side of a beer truck. Bernard could feel his own heart going as he lifted the Nitro to his shoulder, and then there was the head-thumping blast of the gun and old Claude suddenly looked like a balled-up carpet with a basket of ground meat spread on top of it.

Bender turned to him with a white face. "What the——?" he

stammered, and he was jerking at his fingers and flailing his arms.
"What do you think you're doing?"

It was Bernard's moment. A jetliner rode high overhead, bound
for the northwest, a silver rivet in the sky. There was an absolute,
unutterable silence. The wife held her peace, the remaining lions
cowered somewhere in the grass and every bird on the ranch was
holding its breath in the dying wake of that rolling cannonade. "Sav-
ing your bloody life," Bernard snarled, hot and disgusted and royally
pissed off, but proud, as always, of the Britishism.

Mike Bender was angry—too angry to eat his kippered whatever and the deep-fried toast and runny eggs. And where was the
coffee, for god's sake? They were in Bakersfield, after all, and not
some canvas tent in Uganda. He barked at the colored guy—all
tricked up to look like a native, but with an accent right out of
Compton—and told him he wanted coffee, black and strong, even
if he had to drive to Oildale for it. Nicole sat across the table and
watched him with mocking eyes. *Her* zebra had been perfect, but
he'd fouled up two of the three he'd shot: *But Mike,* she'd said, *we
can't hang these—they'll look like colanders.* And then the business
with the lion. He'd looked bad on that one, and what was worse, he
was out eleven and a half thousand bucks and there was nothing to
show for it. Not after Puff blew the thing away. It was just meat and
bone, that's all. Shit, the thing didn't even *have* a head after the
great white hunter got done with it.

"C'mon, Mike," Nicole said, and she reached out to pat his
hand but he snatched it away in a rage. "C'mon, baby, it's not the
end of the world." He looked at her in that moment, the triumph
shining in her eyes, and he wanted to slap her, choke her, get up
from the table, snatch a rifle from the rack and pump a couple slugs
into her.

He was about to snap back at her when the swinging doors to
the kitchen parted and the colored guy came in with a pot of coffee
and set it on the table. Roland, that was his name. He was surprised
they didn't call him Zulu or Jambo or something to go along with
the silly skirts that were supposed to make him look like a native.

Christ, he'd like to get up and drill him too, for that matter. About the only break he'd had on this trip was that Jasmine Honeysuckle Rose had taken to sleeping till noon.

"Mike," Nicole pleaded, but he wouldn't hear her. Brooding, burning, plotting his revenge on every lender, shopkeeper and homeowner from the San Fernando Valley to Hancock Park, Mike Bender sipped moodily at his tepid instant coffee and awaited the great white hunter.

Puff was late to breakfast, but he looked rejuvenated—had he dyed his hair, was that it?—beaming, a fountain of energy, as if he'd stolen the flame from the King of Encino himself. "Good morning," he boomed in his phony West End accent, practically inhaling his mustache, and then he gave Nicole a look that was unmistakable and Mike felt it all pouring out of him, like lava from a volcano.

"No more lions, right?" Mike said, his voice low and choked.

"Afraid not," Puff answered, sitting himself down at the head of the table and smearing a slab of toast with Marmite. "As I told you yesterday, we've got all the females you want, but the males are juveniles, no manes at all to speak of."

"That stinks."

Bernard regarded Bender for a long moment and saw the child who'd never grown up, the rich kid, the perennial hacker and duffer, the parvenu stifled. He looked from Bender to the wife and back again—what was she doing with a clown like that?—and had a fleeting but powerful vision of her stretched out beside him in bed, breasts, thighs, puffy lips and all. "Listen, Mike," he said, "forget it. It happens to everybody. I thought we'd go for eland today—"

"*Eland.* Shit on eland."

"All right, then—water buff. A lot of them say Mbogo is the most dangerous animal in Africa, bar none."

The sunny eyes went dark with rage. "This isn't Africa," Bender spat. "It's Bakersfield."

Bernard had tried hard, and he hated it when they did that, when they punctured the illusion he so carefully nurtured. It was the illusion he was selling, after all—close your eyes and you're in Africa—and in a way he'd wanted the place to *be* Africa, wanted to make the old stories come alive, wanted to bring back the thrill of the great days, if only for a moment at a time. But it was more than that, too: Puff's African Game Ranch stood as a testament and memorial to the towering figure of Bernard's father.

Bernard Puff, Sr., had been one of the last great white hunters of East Africa—friend and compatriot of Percival and Ionides, host to some of the biggest names of American cinema and European aristocracy. He married an American heiress and they built a place in the White Highlands, dined with Isak Dinesen, ate game the year round. And then the war turned the place on its head and he sought refuge in America, losing himself in the vastness of the Southwest and the pockets of his in-laws. As a boy, Bernard had thrilled to the stories of the old days, fingering the ragged white scar a bush pig's tusks had left on his father's forearm, cleaning and oiling the ancient weapons that had stopped rhino, elephant, leopard and lion, gazing for hours into the bright glass eyes of the trophies mounted on the wall in the den, the very names—sable, kudu, bushbuck, kongoni—playing like an incantation in his head. He'd tried to do it justice, had devoted his life to it, and now here was this sorehead, this condominium peddler, running it all down.

"All right," he said. "Granted. What do you want me to do? I've got more lions coming in at the end of the month, prime cats they've trapped and relocated from Tsavo East . . ." (He was fudging here: actually, he had an emaciated sack of bones lined up at the San Francisco Zoo, a cat so old the public was offended by it, and another that had broken its leg three times jumping through a hoop with a West German circus.) "Eland we have, water buff, oryx, gazelle, hyena—I've even got a couple ostrich for you. But unless you want a female, no lion. I'm sorry."

And then, a light shining up from the depths, the glitter came back into the dealmaker's eyes, the smile widened, the tennis pro and backyard swimmer climbed out from behind the mask of the petulant real estate wonder boy. Bender was grinning. He leaned forward. "What about the elephant?"

"What about it?" Bernard lifted the toast to his lips, then set it down carefully again on the edge of his plate. The wife was watching him now, and Roland, refilling the coffee mugs, paused to give him a look.

"I want it."

Bernard stared down at the plate and fussed a moment with the coffeepot, the sugar, the cream. He hated to part with her, though he was pretty sure he could replace her—and the feed bills were killing him. Even in her dotage, Bessie Bee could put away more in an afternoon than a herd of Guernseys would go through in a winter. He gave the wife a cool glance, then shot his eyes at Bender. "Eighteen grand," he said.

Bender looked uncertain, his eyes glittering still, but sunk in on themselves, as if in awe at the enormity of the deal. "I'll want the head," he said finally, "the whole thing, stuffed and mounted—and yes, I know it's big, but I can deal with that, I've got the space, believe me . . . and the feet, I want the feet, for those, uh, what do you call them, umbrella stands?"

They found her in a brushy ravine, just beyond the swimming-pool-cum-water-hole. She was having a dust bath, powdering her pitted hide with fine pale dirt till she looked like an enormous wad of dough rolled in flour. Bernard could see where she'd trampled the high grass that hid the blue lip of the pool and uprooted half a ton of water lily and cattail, which she'd mounded up in a festering heap on the coping. He cursed under his breath when he saw the stand of eucalyptus she'd reduced to splinters and the imported fever tree she'd stripped of bark. It was his policy to keep her tethered—precisely to avoid this sort of wholesale destruction—but when there were guests on the ranch, he let her roam. He was regretting it now, and thinking he'd have to remember to get Espinoza to call the landscaping company first thing in the morning, when Bender's voice brought him back to the moment. The voice was harsh, petulant, a rising squawk of protest: "But it's only got one tusk!"

Bernard sighed. It was true—she'd broken off half her left tusk somewhere along the line, but he'd gotten so used to her he hardly noticed. But there was Bender, sitting beside him in the Jeep, the wife in the back, the guns stacked up and the cooler full, and Bender was going to try to gouge him on the price, he could see it coming.

"When we said eighteen, I assumed we were talking a trophy animal," Bender said, and Bernard turned to him. "But now, I don't know."

Bernard just wanted it over with. Something told him he was making a mistake in going after Bessie Bee—the place wouldn't seem the same without her—but he was committed at this point, and he didn't want any arguments. "Okay," he sighed, shifting the weight of his paunch from left to right. "Seventeen."

"Sixteen."

"Sixteen-five, and that's as low as I'm going to go. You don't know what it's like to skin out something like this, let alone disposing of the carcass."

"You're on," Bender said, swiveling his head to give the wife a look, and then they were out of the Jeep and checking their weapons. Bender had a .470 Rigby elephant rifle and Bernard his Nitro —just in case the morning brought a reprise of the lion fiasco. The wife, who wasn't doing any shooting, had brought along a video camera. Roland was back at the house with a truck, a chain saw and a crew of Mexicans to clean up the mess once the deed was done.

It was still early, and the heat hadn't come up full yet—Bernard guessed it must have been eighty, eighty-five or so—but he was sweating already. He was always a little edgy on a hunt—especially with a clown like Bender twitching at his elbow, and most especially after what had happened with the lion. Bender was writhing and stamping up a storm, but his eyes were cool and focused as they strolled through the mesquite and tumbleweed and down into the ravine.

Bessie Bee was white with dust, flapping her ears and blowing up great clouds of it with her trunk. From a hundred yards you couldn't see much more than flying dirt, as if a tornado had touched down; at fifty, the rucked and seamed head of the old elephant began to take on shape. Though there was little more risk involved than in potting a cow in its stall, Bernard was habitually cautious, and he stopped Bender there, at fifty yards. A pair of vultures drifted overhead, attracted by the Jeep, which they knew as the purveyor of bleeding flesh and carrion. The elephant sneezed. A crow called out somewhere behind them. "This is as far as we go," Bernard said.

Bender gaped at him, popping his joints and bugging his eyes like a fraternity boy thwarted by the ID checker at the door of a bar full of sorority girls. "All I can see is dust," he said.

Bernard was deep inside himself now. He checked the bolt on the big gun and flipped back the safety. "Just wait," he said. "Find a spot—here, right here; you can use this rock to steady your aim —and just wait a minute, that's all. She'll tire of this in a minute or so, and when the dust settles you'll have your shot."

And so they crouched in the dirt, hunter and guide, and propped their guns up on a coarse red table of sandstone and waited for the dust to clear and the heat to rise and the vultures to sink down out of the sky in great ragged swoops.

For her part, Bessie Bee was more than a little suspicious. Though her eyes were poor, the Jeep was something she could see, and she could smell the hominids half a mile away. She should have been matriarch of a fine wild herd of elephants at Amboseli or Tsavo or the great Bahi swamp, but she'd lived all her fifty-two years on this strange and unnatural continent, amid the stink and confusion of man. She'd been goaded, beaten, tethered, taught to dance and stand on one leg and grasp the sorry wisp of a tail that hung from the sorry flanks of another sorry elephant like herself as they paraded before the teeming monkey masses in one forbidding arena after another. And then there was this, a place that stank of the oily secrets of the earth, and another tether and more men. She heard the thunder of the guns and she smelled the blood on the air and she knew they were killing. She knew, too, that the Jeep was there for her.

The dust settled round her, sifting down in a maelstrom of fine white motes. She flared her ears and trumpeted and lifted the standing timber of her right front foot from the ground and let it sway before her. She was tired of the goad, the tether, the brittle dry tasteless straw and cattle feed, tired of the sun and the air and the night and the morning: she charged.

She let her nose guide her till the guns crashed, once, twice, three times, and a new sort of goad tore into her, invasive and hot, but it just made her angry, made her come on all the harder, invincible, unstoppable, twelve feet at the shoulder and eight standing tons, no more circuses, no more palanquins, no more goads. And then she saw them, two pitiful sticklike figures springing up from behind a rock she could swallow and spit up three times over.

It wasn't panic exactly, not at first. Bender shot wide, and the heavy shock of the gun seemed to stun him. Bessie Bee came straight for them, homing in on them, and Bernard bit down on his mustache and shouted, "Shoot! Shoot, you idiot!"

He got his wish. Bender fired again, finally, but all he managed to do was blow some hair off the thing's back. Bernard stood then, the rifle to his shoulder, and though he remembered the lion and could already hear the nagging whining mealy-mouthed voice of Bender complaining over lunch of being denied *this* trophy too, the situation was critical; desperate, even—who would have thought it of Bessie Bee?—and he squeezed the trigger to the jerk and roar of the big gun.

Nothing. Had he missed? But then all at once he felt himself caught up in a landslide, the rush of air, the reek of elephant, and he was flying, actually flying, high out over the plain and into the blue.

When he landed, he sat up and found that his shoulder had come loose from the socket and that there was some sort of fluid—blood, his own blood—obscuring the vision in his right eye. He was in shock, he told himself, repeating it aloud, over and over: "I'm in shock, I'm in shock." Everything seemed hazy, and the arm didn't hurt much, though it should have, nor the gash in his scalp either. But didn't he have a gun? And where was it?

He looked up at the noise, a shriek of great conviction, and saw Bessie Bee rubbing her foot thoughtfully, almost tenderly, over Mike

Bender's prostrate form. Bender seemed to be naked—or no, he didn't seem to be wearing any skin, either—and his head had been vastly transformed, so much more compact now. But there was something else going on too, something the insurance company wouldn't be able to rectify, of that he was sure, if only in a vague way—"I'm in shock," he repeated. This something was a shriek too, definitely human, but it rose and caught hold of the tail of the preceding shriek and climbed atop it, and before the vacuum of silence could close in there was another shriek, and another, until even the screams of the elephant were a whisper beside it.

It was Mrs. Bender, the wife, Nicole, one of the finest expressions of her species, and she was running from the Jeep and exercising her lungs. The Jeep seemed to be lying on its side—such an odd angle to see it from—and Mrs. Bender's reedy form was in that moment engulfed by a moving wall of flesh, the big flanks blotting the scene from view, all that movement and weight closing out the little aria of screams with a final elephantine roll of the drums.

It might have been seconds later, or an hour—Bernard didn't know. He sat there, an arm dangling from the shoulder, idly wiping the blood from his eye with his good hand while the naked black vultures drifted down on him with an air of professional interest. And then all at once, strange phenomenon, the sun was gone, and the vultures, and a great black shadow fell over him. He looked up dimly into the canvas of that colossal face framed in a riot of ears. "Bessie Bee?" he said. "Bessie Bee? Shamba?"

Half a mile away, fanned by the gentle breeze of the air conditioner, Jasmine Honeysuckle Rose Bender, two months short of her thirteenth birthday and sated with chocolate and dreams of lean spike-haired adolescents with guitars and leather jackets, shifted her head on the pillow and opened her eyes. She was, in that waking moment, sole inheritor of the Bender real estate empire, and all the monies and houses and stocks and bonds and properties that accrued to it, not to mention the beach house and the Ferrari Testarossa, but she wasn't yet aware of it. Something had awakened her, some ripple on the great pond of life. For just a moment there, over the drone of the air conditioner, she thought she'd heard a scream.

But no. It was probably just some peacock or baboon or whatever. Or that pitiful excuse for an elephant. She sat up, reached into her cooler for a root beer and shook her head. Tacky, she thought. Tacky, tacky, tacky.

HOPES RISE

I TOOK MY ACHING BACK to my brother-in-law, the doctor, and he examined me, ran some X-rays, and then sat me down in his office. Gazing out the window on the early manifestations of spring—inchoate buds crowning the trees, pussy willows at the edge of the marsh, the solitary robin probing the stiff yellow grass—I felt luxurious and philosophical. So what if my back felt as if it had been injected with a mixture of battery acid and Louisiana hot sauce? There was life out there, foliate and rich, a whole planet seething with possibility. It was spring, time to wake up and dance to the music of life.

My brother-in-law had finished fiddling with his unfashionable beard and pushing his reading glasses up and down the bridge of his nose. He cleared his throat. "Listen, Peter," he said in his mellifluous healing tones, "we've known each other a long time, haven't we?"

A hundred corny jokes flew to my lips, but I just smiled and nodded.

"We're close, right?"

I reminded him that he was married to my sister and had fathered my niece and nephew.

"Well, all right," he said. "Now that that's been established, I think I can reveal to you the first suppressed axiom of the medical cabal."

I leaned forward, a fierce pain gripping the base of my spine, like a dog shaking a rat in its teeth. Out on the lawn, the robin beat its shabby wings and was sucked away on the breeze.

My brother-in-law held the moment, and then, enunciating with elaborate care, he said, "Any injury you sustain up to the age of twenty-one, give or take a year, is better the next day; after twenty-one, any injury you sustain will haunt you to the grave."

I gave a hoot of laughter that made the imaginary dog dig his claws in, and then, wincing with the pain, I said, "And what's the second?"

He was grinning at me, showing off the white, even, orthodontically assisted marvel of his teeth. "Second what?"

"Axiom. Of the medical cabal."

He waved his hand. It was nothing. "Oh, that," he said, pushing at his glasses. "Well, that's not suppressed really, not anymore. I mean, medical men of the past have told their wives, children, brother-in-laws—or is it brothers-in-law? Anyway, it's 'Get plenty of rest and drink plenty of fluids.' "

This time my laugh was truncated, cut off like the drop of a guillotine. "And my back?"

"Get plenty of rest," he said, "and drink plenty of fluids."

The pain was there, dulling a bit as the dog relaxed its grip, but there all the same. "Can we get serious a minute?"

But he wouldn't allow it. He never got serious. If he got serious he'd have to admit that half the world was crippled, arthritic, suffering from dysplasia and osteoporosis; he'd have to admit that there were dwarves and freaks and glandular monsters, not to mention the legions of bandy-legged children starving in the streets even as we spoke. If he got serious he'd have to acknowledge his yawning impotence in the face of the rot and chaos that were engulfing the world. He got up from his desk and led me to the door with a brother-in-lawly touch at the elbow.

I stood at the open door, the waiting room gaping behind me. I was astonished: he wasn't going to do anything. Not a thing. "But, but," I stammered, "aren't you going to give me some pills at least?"

He held his flawless grin—not so much as a quiver of his bearded lip—and I had to love him for it: his back didn't hurt; his knees were fine. "Peter," he said, his voice rich with playful admonition, "there's no magic pill—you should know that."

I didn't know it. I wanted codeine, morphine, heroin; I wanted the pain to go away. "Physician," I hooted, "heal thyself!" And I swung round on my heels, surfeited with repartee, and nearly ran down a tiny wizened woman suspended like a spider in a gleaming web of aluminum struts and wheels and ratchets.

"You still seeing Adrian?" he called as I dodged toward the outer door. My coat—a jab of pain; my scarf—a forearm shiver. Then the gloves, the door, the wind, the naked cheat of spring. "Because I was thinking," the man of healing called, "I was thinking we could do some doubles at my place"—thunderous crash of door, voice pinched with distance and the interposition of a plane of impermeable oak—"Saturday, maybe?"

At home, easing into my chair with a heating pad, I pushed the playback button on my answering machine. Adrian's voice leapt out at me, breathless, wound up, shot through with existential angst and the low-threshold hum of day-to-day worry. "The frogs are disappearing. All over the world. Frogs. Can you believe it?" There was a pause. "They say they're like the canary in the coal mine—it's the first warning, the first sign. The apocalypse is here, it's now, we're doomed. Call me."

Adrian and I had been seeing each other steadily for eleven years. We shopped together, went to movies, concerts, museums, had dinner three or four nights a week and talked for hours on the phone. In the early years, consumed by passion, we often spent the night together, but now, as our relationship had matured, we'd come increasingly to respect each other's space. There'd been talk of marriage, too, in the early years—talk for the most part generated by parents, relatives and friends tied to mortgages and diaper services —but we felt we didn't want to rush into anything, especially in a world hurtling toward ecological, fiscal and microbial disaster. The concept was still on hold.

I dialed her number and got her machine. I waited through

three choruses of "Onward, Christian Soldiers"—her joke of the week—before I could leave my message, which was, basically, "I called; call me." I was trying to think of a witty tag line when she picked up the phone. "Peter?"

"No, it's Liberace risen from the dead."

"Did you hear about the frogs?"

"I heard about the frogs. Did you hear about my back?"

"What did Jerry say?"

" 'Get plenty of rest and drink plenty of fluids.' "

She was laughing on the other end of the line, a gurgle and snort that sounded like the expiring gasps of an emphysemic horse, a laugh that was all her own. Two days earlier I'd been carrying a box of old college books down to the basement when I tore everything there is to tear in the human back and began to wonder how much longer I'd need to hold on to my pristine copy of *Agrarian Corsica, 800 B.C. to the Present.* "I guess it must not be so bad, then," she said, and the snorting and chuffing rose a notch and then fell off abruptly.

"Not so bad for you," I said. "Or for Jerry. I'm the one who can't even bend down to tie his shoes."

"I'll get you a pair of loafers."

"You spoil me. You really do. Can you find them in frog skin?"

There was a silence on the other end of the line. "It's not funny," she said. "Frogs, toads and salamanders are vital to the food chain—and no jokes about frogs' legs, please—and no one knows what's happening to them. They're just disappearing. Poof."

I considered that a moment, disappearing frogs, especially as they related to my throbbing and ruined back. I pictured them—squat, long of leg, with extruded eyes and slick mucus-covered skin. I remembered stalking them as a boy with my laxly strung bow and blunt arrows, recalled the sound of the spring peepers and their clumsy attempts at escape, their limbs bound up in ropy strings of eggs. Frogs. Suddenly I was nostalgic: what kind of world would it be without them?

"I hope you're not busy this weekend," Adrian said.

"Busy?" My tone was guarded; a pulse of warning stabbed at

my spine through its thin tegument of muscle fiber and skin. "Why?"

"I've already reserved the tickets."

The sound of my breathing rattled in my ear. I wasn't about to ask. I took a stoic breath and held it, awaiting the denouement.

"We're going to a conference at NYU—the Sixth Annual International Herpetology and Batrachiology Conference. . . ."

I shouldn't have asked, but I did. "The what?"

"Snakes and frogs," she said.

On Saturday morning we took the train into Manhattan. I brought along a book to thumb through on the way down—a tattered ancient tome called *The Frog Book*, which I'd found wedged in a corner of one of the denuded shelves of the Frog and Toad section at the local library. I wondered at all that empty space on the shelves and what it portended for the genuses and species involved. Apparently Adrian wasn't the only one concerned with their headlong rush to extinction—either that, or the sixth grade had been assigned a report on amphibians. I wasn't convinced, but I checked the book out anyway.

My back had eased up a bit—there was a low tightness and an upper constriction, but nothing like the knifing pain I'd been subjected to a few days earlier. As a precautionary measure I'd brought along a Naugahyde pillow to cushion my abused vertebrae against the jolts and lurches of the commuter train. Adrian slouched beside me, long legs askew, head bent in concentration over *Mansfield Park*, which she was rereading, by her own calculation, for the twenty-third time. She taught a course in the novels of Jane Austen at Bard, and I never really understood how she could tolerate reading the same books over and over again, semester after semester, year after year. It was like a prison sentence.

"Is that really your twenty-third time?"

She looked up. Her eyes were bright with the nuances of an extinguished world. "Twenty-fourth."

"I thought you said twenty-third?"

"Reread. The first time doesn't count as a reread—that's your original read. Like your birthday—you live a year before you're one."

Her logic was irrefutable. I gazed out on the vast gray reaches of the frogless Hudson and turned to my own book: *The explosive note of the Green Frog proceeds from the shallow water; the purring trill of "the Tree Toad" comes from some spot impossible to locate. But listen! The toad's lullaby note comes from the far margin, sweeter than all the others if we except the two notes in the chickadee's spring call. We could never have believed it to be the voice of a toad if we had not seen and heard on that first May Day.* I read about the love life of toads until we plunged into the darkness at Ninety-seventh Street, and then gave my eyes a rest. In the early days, Adrian and I would have traded witticisms and cutting portraits of our fellow passengers all the way down, but now we didn't need to talk, not really. We were beyond talk.

It might have been one of those golden, delicately lit spring mornings invested with all the warmth and urgency of the season, bees hovering, buds unfolding, the air soft and triumphant, but it wasn't. We took a cab down Park Avenue in a driving wintry rain and shivered our way up two flights of steps and into a drafty lecture hall where a balding man in a turtleneck sweater was holding forth on the molting habits of the giant Sumatran toad. I was feeling lighthearted—frogs and toads: I could hold this one over her head for a month; two, maybe—and I poked Adrian in the ribs at regular intervals over the course of the next two stultifyingly dull hours. We heard a monograph on the diet and anatomy of *Discoglossus nigriventer*, the Israeli painted frog, and another on the chemical composition of the toxin secreted by the poison-arrow frog of Costa Rica, but nothing on their chances of surviving into the next decade. Adrian pulled her green beret down over her eyebrows. I caught her stifling a yawn. After a while, my eyes began to grow heavy.

There was a dry little spatter of applause as the poison-arrow man stepped down from the podium, and it roused me from a morass of murky dreams. I rose and clapped feebly. I was just leaning into Adrian with the words "dim sum" on my lips, words that were certain to provoke her into action—it was past one, after all, and we hadn't eaten—when a wild-looking character in blond dreadlocks and tinted glasses took hold of the microphone. "Greetings," he said,

his hoarse timbreless voice rustling through the speakers and an odd
smile drifting across his lips. He was wearing a rumpled raincoat
over a T-shirt that featured an enormous crouching toad in the act
of flicking an insect into its mouth. The program identified him as
B. Reid, of UC Berkeley. For a long moment he merely stood there,
poised over the microphone, holding us with the blank gaze of his
blue-tinted lenses.

Someone coughed. The room was so still I could hear the distant hiss of the rain.

"We've been privileged to hear some provocative and stimulat-
ing papers here this morning," B. Reid began, and he hadn't moved
a muscle, save for his lips, "papers that have focused brilliantly on
the minute and painstaking research crucial to our science and our
way of knowledge, and I want to thank Professors Abercrombie and
Wouzatslav for a job well done, but at the same time I want to ask
you this: will there be a Seventh Annual International Herpetology
and Batrachiology Conference? Will there be an eighth? Will there
be a discipline, will there be batrachiologists? Ladies and gentlemen,
why play out a charade here: will there be frogs?"

A murmur went up. The woman beside me, huge and amphib-
ious-looking herself, shifted uneasily in her seat. My lower back announced itself with a distant buzz of pain and I felt the hackles rise
on the back of my neck: this was what we'd come for.

"Cameroon," B. Reid was saying, his voice rasping like dead
leaves, "Ecuador, Borneo, the Andes and the Alps: everywhere you
look the frogs and toads are disappearing, extinction like a plague,
the planet a poorer and shabbier place. And what is it? What have
we done? Acid rain? The ozone layer? Some poison we haven't yet
named? Ladies and gentlemen," he rasped, "it's the frogs today and
tomorrow the biologists . . . before we know it the malls will stand
empty, the freeways deserted, the creeks and ponds and marshes
forever silent. We're committing suicide!" he cried, and he gave his
dreadlocks a Medusan swirl so that they beat like snakes round his
head. "We're doomed, can't you see that?"

The audience sat riveted in their seats. No one breathed a word.
I didn't dare look at Adrian.

His voice dropped again. *"Bufo canorus,"* he said, and the name was like a prayer, a valediction, an obituary. "You all know my study in Yosemite. Six years I put into it, six years of crouching in the mud and breathing marsh gas and fighting leeches and ticks and all the rest of it, and what did it get me? What did it get the Yosemite toad? Extinction, that's what. They're gone. Wiped from the face of the earth." He paused as if to gather his strength. "And what of Richard Wassersug's albino leopard frogs in Nova Scotia? White tadpoles. Exclusively. What kind of mutation is that?" His voice clawed its way through the speakers, harsh with passion and the clangorous knelling of doom. "I'll tell you what kind: a fatal one. A year later they were gone."

My face was hot. Suddenly my back felt as if it were crawling with fire ants, seared by molten rain, drawn tight in a burning lariat. I looked at Adrian and her eyes were wild, panicky, a field of white in a thin net of veins. We'd come on a lark, and now here was the naked truth of our own mortality staring us in the face. I wanted to cry out for the frogs, the toads, the salamanders, for my own disconnected and rootless self.

But it wasn't over yet. B. Reid contorted his features and threw back his head, and then he plunged a hand into the deep pocket of his coat; in the next instant his clenched fist shot into the air. I caught a glimpse of something dark and leathery, a strip of jerky, tissue with the life drained from it. "The Costa Rican golden toad," he cried in his wild burnished declamatory tones, "R.I.P.!"

The woman beside me gasped. A cry went up from the back of the room. There was a shriek of chairs as people leapt to their feet.

B. Reid dug into his breast pocket and brandished another corpse. *"Atelopus zeteki,* the Peruvian variegated toad, R.I.P.!"

Cries of woe and lamentation.

"Rana marinus, R.I.P.! The Gambian reed frog, R.I.P.!"

B. Reid held the lifeless things up before him as if he were exorcising demons. His voice sank to nothing. Slowly, painfully, he shook his head so that the coils of his hair drew a shroud over his face. "Don't bother making the trip to Costa Rica, to Peru or Gambia," he said finally, the shouts rising and dying round him. "These"—and his voice broke—"these are the last of them."

The following day was my sister's birthday, and I'd invited her, Jerry and the children to my place for dinner, though I didn't feel much like going through with it after B. Reid's presentation. The lecture hall had echoed like a chamber of doom with the dying rasp of his voice and I couldn't get it out of my head. Stunned silent, our deepest fears made concrete in those grisly pennants of frog flesh, Adrian and I had left as soon as he stepped down from the podium, fighting our way through the press of stricken scientists and heartsick toad lovers and out into the rain. The world smelled of petroleum, acid, sulfur, the trees were bent and crippled, and the streets teemed with ugly and oblivious humanity. We took a cab directly to Grand Central. Neither of us had the stomach for lunch after what we'd been through, and we sat in silence all the way back, Adrian clutching Jane Austen to her breast and I turning *The Frog Book* over and over again in my hands. Each bump and rattle of the Hudson Line drove a burning stake into the small of my back.

The next morning I debated calling Charlene and telling her I was sick, but I felt guilty about it: why ruin my sister's birthday simply because the entire planet was going to hell in a handbasket? When Adrian showed up at ten with three bags of groceries and acting as if nothing had happened, I took two aspirin, cinched an apron round my waist and began pulverizing garbanzo beans.

All in all, it was a pleasant afternoon. The rain drove down outside and we built a fire in the dining room and left the door to the kitchen open while we cooked. Adrian found some chamber music on the radio and we shared a bottle of wine while she kneaded dough for the pita bread and I folded tahini into the garbanzo mash, sliced tomatoes and chopped onions. We chatted about little things—Frank Sinatra's hair, whether puree was preferable to whole stewed tomatoes, our friends' divorces, lint in the wash—steering clear of the fateful issue burning in both our minds. It was very nice. Tranquil. Domestic. The wine conspired with the aspirin, and after a while the knot in my back began to loosen.

Jerry, Charlene and the kids were early, and I served the hum-
mus and pita bread while Adrian braised chunks of goat in a big
black cast-iron pan she'd brought with her from her apartment. We
were on our second drink and Jay and Nayeli, my nephew and niece,
were out on the porch catching the icy rainwater as it drooled from
the eaves, when Adrian threw herself down in the chair opposite
Jerry and informed him in a clarion voice that the frogs were dying out.

The statement seemed to take him by surprise. He and Charlene had been giving me a seriocomic history of their yacht, which
had thus far cost them something like $16,000 per hour at sea and
which had been rammed, by Jerry, into a much bigger yacht on its
maiden voyage out of the marina. Now they both paused to stare at
Adrian. Jerry began to formulate his smile. "What did you say?"

Adrian smelled of goat and garlic. She was lanky and wide-eyed,
with long beautifully articulated feet and limbs that belonged on a
statue. She drew herself up at the edge of the chair and tried out a
tentative smile. "Frogs," she said. "And toads. Something is killing
them off all over the world, from Alaska to Africa. We went to a
conference yesterday. Peter and I."

"Frogs?" Jerry repeated, stroking the bridge of his nose. His
smile, in full efflorescence now, was something to behold. My sister,
who favored my late mother around the eyes and nose, emitted a
little chirp of amusement.

Adrian looked uncertain. She gave out with an abbreviated version of her horsey laugh and turned to me for encouragement.

"It's not a joke," I said. "We're talking extinction here."

"There was this man," Adrian said, the words coming in a rush,
"a biologist at the conference, B. Reid—from Berkeley—and he had
all these dried frogs in his pockets . . . it was horrible. . . ."

I could hear the rain on the roof, cold and unseasonal. Nayeli
shouted something from the porch. The fire crackled in the hearth.
I could see that we weren't getting it right, that my brother-in-law,
the doctor, was making a little notation of our mental state on the
prescription pad of his mind. Why were we telling him all this? Was

he, the perennial jokester who couldn't even salvage my lower back, about to take on loss of habitat, eternal death and the transfiguration of life as we know it?

No, he wasn't.

"You're serious, aren't you?" he said after a moment. "You really believe in all this environmental hysteria." He let the grin fade and gave us his stern off-at-the-knee look. "Peter, Adrian," he said, drawing out the syllables in a profound and pedagogical way, "species conflict is the way of the world, has been from the beginning of time. Extinction is natural, expected: no species can hope to last forever. Even man. Conditions change." He waved his hand and then laughed, making a joke of it. "If this weather doesn't let up I think we're in for a new ice age, and then where will your frogs be?"

"That's not the point," I said.

"What about the dinosaurs, Peter?" Charlene interjected. "And the woolly mammoth?"

"Not to mention snake oil and bloodletting." Jerry's smile was back. He was in control. All was right with the world. "Things move on, things advance and change—why cry over something you can't affect, a kind of fairy-tale Garden of Eden half these environmentalists never knew? Which is not to say I don't agree with you—"

"My god!" Adrian cried, springing from her seat as if she'd been hot-wired. "The goat!"

Late that night, after everyone had gone home—even Adrian, though she'd gotten amorous at the door and would, I think, have spent the night but for my lack of enthusiasm—I eased into my armchair with the newspaper and tried to wipe my mind clean, a total abstersion, tabula rasa. I felt drained, desolate, a mass of meat, organ and bone slipping inexorably toward the grave along with my distant cousins the frogs and the toads. The rain continued. A chill fell over the room and I saw that the fire had burned down. There was a twinge in my back as I shifted my buttocks to adjust the heating pad, and then I began to read. I didn't feel up to war in the Middle East, AIDS and the homeless or the obituaries, so I stuck to the movie reviews and personal-interest stories.

It was getting late, my mind had gone gratifyingly numb and I was just about to switch off the light and throw myself into bed, when I turned to the science section. A headline caught my eye:

HOPES RISE AS NEW SPECIES MOVE INTO SLUDGE OFF COAST

And what was this? I read on and discovered that these rising hopes were the result of the sudden appearance of tubeworms, solemya clams and bacteria in a formerly dead stretch of water in the Hudson Canyon, used from time immemorial as a repository for the city's sewage and refuse. Down there, deep in the ancient layers of sludge, beneath the lapping fishless waves, there was life, burgeoning and thriving in a new medium. What hope. What terrific uplifting news.

Tubeworms. They had to be joking.

After a while I folded up the newspaper, found my slippers and took this great and rising hope to bed with me.

The week that followed was as grim and unrelenting as the week that had given rise to it. Work was deadening (I shifted numbers on a screen for a living and the numbers had never seemed more meaningless), my back went through half a dozen daily cycles of searing agony and utter absence of feeling, and the weather never broke, not even for an hour. The skies were close and bruised, and the cold rain fell. I went directly home after work and didn't answer the phone at night, though I knew it was Adrian calling. All week I thought of frogs and death.

And then, on Saturday, I woke to an outpouring of light and a sudden sharp apprehension of the world that was as palpable as a taste. I sat up. My feet found the floor. Naked and trembling, I crossed the room and stood at the window, the cord to the glowing blinds caught up in my hand, the stirrings of barometric change tugging at the long muscles of my lower back. Then I pulled the cord and the light spilled into the room, and in the next moment I was shoving the blinds aside and throwing open the window.

The air was pregnant, rich, thick with the scent of renewal and the perspicacious hum of the bees. All that moping, all those fears, the named dread and the nameless void: it all evaporated in the face

of that hosanna of a morning. I felt like Ebenezer Scrooge roused
on Christmas Day, Lazarus reanimated, Alexander the Great heading
into Thrace. I opened every window in the house; I ate a muffin,
read the paper, matched the glorious J. S. Bach to the triumph of
the morning. It was heady, but I couldn't sustain it. Ultimately, inevitably, like a sickness, the frogs and toads crept back into my head,
and by 10:00 A.M. I was just another mortal with a bad back sinking
into oblivion.

It was then, at the bottom of that trough, that I had an inspiration. The coffee was cold in the cup, the newsprint rumpled, Bach
silenced by the tyranny of a mechanical arm, and suddenly a notion
hit me and I was up and out of the kitchen chair as if I'd been
launched. The force of it carried me to the bedroom closet, where
I dug around for my hiking boots, a sweatshirt, my Yankees cap and
a denim jacket, and then to the medicine cabinet, where I unearthed
the tick repellant and an old aerosol can of Off! Then I dialed
Adrian.

"Adrian," I gasped, "my heart, my love—"

Her voice was thick with sleep. "Is this an obscene phone call?"

"I've been gloomy lately, I know it—"

"Not to mention not answering the phone."

"I admit it, I admit it. But have you seen the day out there?"
She hadn't. She was still in bed.

"What I'm thinking is this: how can we take B. Reid's word for
it? How can we take anybody's?"

I didn't know where to begin looking for the elusive toad, *Bufo
americanus*, let alone the spring peeper or the leopard frog, but I
was seized with a desire to know them, touch them, observe their
gouty limbs and clumsy rituals, partake once more of the seething
life of pond, puddle and ditch, and at least temporarily lay to rest
the nagging memory of B. Reid and his diminutive corpses. It was
irrational, I knew it, but I felt that if I could see them, just this once,
and know they were occupying their humble niche in the hierarchy
of being, everything would be all right.

We parked along the highway and poked desultorily through

the ditch alongside it, but there was nothing animate in sight. The old cane was sharp and brittle, and there was Styrofoam, glass and aluminum everywhere. Trucks stole the air from our lungs, teenagers jeered. Adrian suggested a promising-looking puddle on the far verge of the rutted commuter lot at the Garrison station, but we found nothing there except submerged gum wrappers and potato-chip bags ground into the muck by the numbing impress of steel-belted radials. "We can't give up," she said, and there was just the faintest catch of desperation in her voice. "What about the woods off the Appalachian Trail? You know, where it crosses the road down by K mart?"

"All right," I said, and the fever was on me, "we'll give it a try."

Twenty minutes later we were in the woods, sun glazing bole and branch, tender new yellow-green leaves unfolding overhead, birds shooting up from the path as if jerked on a string. There was a smell here I'd forgotten, the dark wet odor of process, of things breaking down and springing up again, of spore and pollen and seed and mulch. Bugs hovered round my face. I was sweating. And yet I felt good, strong in back and leg, already liberated from the cloud that had hung over me all week, and as I followed Adrian up the long slow incline of the path, I thought I'd never seen such a miracle as the way the muscles of her thighs and buttocks flexed and relaxed in the grip of her jeans. This was nature.

We'd gone a mile or so when she suddenly stopped dead in the middle of the path. "What's the matter?" I said, but she waved her hand to shush me. I edged forward till I stood beside her, my pulse quickening, breath caught high in my throat. "What?" I whispered. "What is it?"

"Listen."

At first I couldn't hear it, my ears attuned to civilization, the chatter of the TV, high fidelity, the blast of the internal-combustion engine, but then the woods began to speak to me. The sound was indistinct at first, but after a while it began to separate into its in-dividual voices, the smallest rustlings and crepitations, the high-pitched disputations of the birds, the trickle of running water—and something else, something at once strange and familiar, a chirping fluid trill that rose strong and multivoiced in the near distance. Adrian turned to me and smiled.

All at once we were in a hurry, breathless, charging through the frost-burned undergrowth and sharp stinging branches, off the path and down the throat of a dark and sodden ravine. I thought nothing. B. Reid, Jerry, herniated discs, compound fractures, the soft green glow of the computer monitor: nothing. We moved together, with a fluid balletic grace, the most natural thing in the world, hunched over, darting right, then left, ducking this obstruction, vaulting the next, shoving through the tangle as easily as we might have parted the bead curtains in a Chinese restaurant. And as we drew closer, that sound, that trill, that raucous joyous paean to life swelled round us till it seemed to vibrate in our every cell and fiber. "There!" Adrian cried suddenly. "Over there!"

I saw it in that moment, a shallow little scoop of a pond caught in the web of the branches. The water gave nothing back, dead black under the buttery sun, and it was choked with the refuse of the trees. I saw movement there, and the ululating chorus rang out to the treetops, every new leaf shuddering on every branch. The smell came at me then, the working odor, rank and sweet and ripe. I took Adrian's hand and we moved toward the water in a kind of trance.

We were up to our ankles, our boots soaked through, when the pond fell silent—it happened in a single stroke, on the beat, as if a conductor had dropped his baton. And then we saw that there was no surface to that pond, that it was a field of flesh, a grand and vast congress of toads. They materialized before our eyes, stumpy limbs and foreshortened bodies clambering over one another, bobbing like apples in a barrel. There they were—toads, toads uncountable—humping in a frenzy of webbed feet and seething snouts, humping blindly, stacked up three and four high. Their eggs were everywhere, beaded and wet with the mucus of life, and all their thousands of eyes glittered with lust. We could hear them clawing at one another, grunting, and we didn't know what to do. And then a single toad at the edge of the pond started in with his thin piping trill and in an instant we were forgotten and the whole pullulating mass of them took it up and it was excruciating, beautiful, wild to the core.

Adrian looked at me and I couldn't help myself: I moved into her arms. I was beyond reason or thought, and what did it matter? She pushed away from me then, for just a moment, and stepped back, water swirling, toads thrilling, to strip off her shirt and the black lace brassiere beneath it. Holding me with her eyes, she moved back another step and dropped them there, in the wet at the edge of the pond, and eased herself down as if into a nest. I'd never seen anything like it. I shrugged out of my denim jacket, tore off my shirt, sailed the Yankees cap into oblivion. And when I came for her, the toads leapt for their lives.

FILTHY WITH THINGS

HE DREAMS, amidst the clutter, of sparseness, purity, the wheeling dark star-haunted reaches beyond the grasp of this constrained little world, where distances are measured in light-years and even the galaxies fall away to nothing. But dreams get you nowhere, and Marsha's latest purchase, the figured-mahogany highboy with carved likenesses of Jefferson, Washington and Adams in place of pulls, will not fit in the garage. The garage, designed to accommodate three big chromium-hung hunks of metal in the two-ton range, will not hold anything at all, not even a Japanese fan folded like a stiletto and sunk to the hilt in a horizontal crevice. There are no horizontal crevices—nor vertical, either. The mass of interlocked things, the great squared-up block of objects, of totems, of purchases made and accreted, of the precious and unattainable, is packed as tightly as the stones at Machu Picchu.

For a long moment Julian stands there in the blistering heat of the driveway, contemplating the abstract sculpture of the garage while the boy from the Antique Warehouse rolls and unrolls the sleeves of his T-shirt and watches a pair of fourteen-year-old girls saunter up the sidewalk. The sun and heat are not salutary for the colonial hardwood of which the highboy is composed, and the problem of where to put it has begun to reach critical proportions. Julian thinks of the storage shed behind the pool, where the newspapers are stacked a hundred deep and Marsha keeps her collection of Brazilian scythes and harrows, but immediately rejects it—the last time he was back there he couldn't even get the door open. Over the course of the next ten seconds or so he develops a fantasy of draining the pool and enclosing it as a sort of step-down warehouse, and it's a rich fantasy, richly rewarding, but he ultimately dismisses it, too. If they were to drain the pool, where would Marsha keep her museum-quality collection of Early American whaling implements, buoys and ship's furniture, not to mention the two hundred twelve antique oarlocks currently mounted on the pool fence?

The boy's eyes are vapid. He's begun to whistle tunelessly and edge back toward the van. "So where'd you decide you want it?" he asks listlessly.

On the moon, Julian wants to say. Saturn. On the bleak blasted ice plains of Pluto. He shrugs. "On the porch, I guess."

The porch. Yes. The only problem is, the screened-in porch is already stacked to the eaves with sideboards, armoires, butter churns and bentwood rockers. The best they can do, after a fifteen-minute struggle, is to wedge the thing two-thirds of the way in the door. "Well," says Julian, and he can feel his heart fluttering round his rib cage like some fist-sized insect, "I guess that'll have to do." The laugh he appends is curt with embarrassment. "Won't have to worry about rain till November, anyway."

The boy isn't even breathing hard. He's long-lipped and thin, strung together with wire, and he's got one of those haircuts that make his head look as if it's been put on backwards. For a long moment he leans over the hand truck, long fingers dangling, giving Julian a look that makes him feel like he's from another planet. "Yeah, that's right," the boy finally murmurs, and he looks at his feet, then jerks himself up as if to drift back to the van, the freeway, the warehouse, before stopping cold again. He looks at Julian as if he's forgotten something, and Julian digs into his pocket and gives the boy three dollars for his efforts.

The sun is there, a living presence, as the boy backs the van out of the driveway, and Julian knows he's going to have to do something about the mahogany highboy—drape a sheet over it or maybe a plastic drop cloth—but somehow he can't really seem to muster the energy. It's getting too much for him—all these things, the addition that was filled before it was finished, the prefab storage sheds on the back lawn, the crammed closets, the unlivable living room—

and the butt end of the highboy hanging from the porch door seems a tangible expression of all his deepest fears. Seeing it there, the harsh light glancing off its polished flanks, its clawed feet dangling in the air, he wants to cry out against the injustice of it all, his miserable lot, wants to dig out his binoculars and the thin peeling ground cloth he's had since he was a boy in Iowa and go up to the mountains and let the meteor showers wash him clean, but he can't. That ancient handcrafted butt end represents guilt, Marsha's displeasure, a good and valuable thing left to deteriorate. He's begun to move toward it in a halfhearted shuffle, knowing from experience that he can squeeze it in there somehow, when a horn sounds breathlessly behind him. He turns, condemned like Sisyphus, and watches as Marsha wheels into the drive, the Range Rover packed to the windows and a great dark slab of furniture lashed to the roof like some primitive landing craft. "Julian!" she calls, "Julian! Wait till you see what I found!"

"I've seen worse," the woman says, and Julian can feel the short hairs on the back of his neck begin to stiffen—she's seen worse, but she's seen better, too. They're standing in the living room—or rather on the narrow footpath between the canyons of furniture that obscure the walls, the fireplace, even the ceiling of what was once the living room—and Julian, afraid to look her in the eye, leans back against a curio cabinet crammed with painted porcelain dolls in native costume, nervously turning her card over in his hand. The card is certainly minimalistic—*Susan Certaine*, it reads in a thin black embossed script, *Professional Organizer*, and it gives a telephone number, nothing else—and the woman herself is impressive, brisk, imposing, even; but he's just not sure. Something needs to be done, something radical—and, of course, Marsha, who left to cruise the flea markets an hour ago, will have to agree to it, at least in substance—but for all his misery and sense of oppression, for all the times he's joked about burning the place down or holding the world's biggest yard sale, Julian needs to be reassured, needs to be convinced.

"You've seen worse?" he prompts.

"Sure I have. Of course I have. What do you take me for, an amateur?"

Julian shrugs, turns up his palms, already on the defensive.

"Listen, in my business, Mr. Laxner, you tend to run across the hard cases, the ones anyone else would give up on—the Liberaces, the Warhols, the Nancy Reagans. You remember Imelda Marcos? That was me. I'm the one they called in to straighten out that mess. Twenty-seven hundred pairs of shoes alone, Mr. Laxner. Think about that."

She pauses to let her eyes flicker over the room, the smallest coldest flame burning behind the twin slivers of her contact lenses. She's a tall, pale, hovering presence, a woman stripped to the essentials, the hair torn back from her scalp and strangled in a bun, no cheeks, no lips, no makeup or jewelry, the dress black, the shoes black, the briefcase black as a dead black coal dug out of the bottom of the bag. "There's trouble here," she says finally, holding his eyes. "You're dirty with things, Mr. Laxner, filthy, up to your ears in the muck."

He is, he admits it, but he can't help wincing at the harshness of the indictment.

She leans closer, the briefcase clamped like a breastplate across her chest, her breath hot in his face, soap, Sen-Sen, Listerine. "And do you know who I am, Mr. Laxner?" she asks, a hard combative friction in the back of her throat, a rasp, a growl.

Julian tries to sound casual, tries to work the hint of a smile into the corners of his mouth and ignore the fact that his personal space has suddenly shrunk to nothing. "Susan Certaine?"

"I am the purifying stream, Mr. Laxner, that's who I am. The cleansing torrent, the baptismal font. I'll make a new man of you."

This is what she's here for, he knows it, this is what he needs, discipline, compulsion, the iron promise, but still he can't help edging away, a little dance of the feet, the condensing of a shoulder. "Well, yes, but"—giving her a sidelong glance, and still she's there, right there, breathing out her Sen-Sen like a dental hygienist—"it's a big job, it's—"

"We inventory everything—*everything*—right down to the paper clips in your drawers and the lint in your pockets. My people are the best, real professionals. There's no one like us in the business, believe me—and believe me when I tell you I'll have this situation under control inside of a week, seven short days. I'll guarantee it, in fact. All I need is your go-ahead."

His go-ahead. A sudden vista opens up before him, unbroken beaches, limitless plains, lunar seas and Venusian deserts, the yawning black interstellar wastes. Would it be too much to ask to see the walls of his own house? Just once? Just for an hour? Yes, okay, sure, he wants to say, but the immensity of it stifles him. "I'll have to ask my wife," he hears himself saying. "I mean, consult with her, think it over."

"Pah! That's what they all say." Her look is incendiary, bitter, the eyes curdling behind the film of the lenses, the lipless mouth clenched round something rotten. "Tell me something, Mr. Laxner, if you don't mind my asking—you're a stargazer, aren't you?"

"Beg pardon?"

"The upstairs room, the one over the kitchen?" Her eyes are jumping, some mad electric impulse shooting through her like a power surge scorching the lines. "Come on now, come clean. All those charts and telescopes, the books—there must be a thousand of them."

Now it's Julian's turn, the ball in his court, the ground solid under his feet. "I'm an astronomer, if you want to know."

She says nothing, just watches him out of those burning messianic eyes, waiting.

"Well, actually, it's more of a hobby really—but I do teach a course Wednesday nights at the community college."

The eyes leap at him. "I knew it. You intellectuals, you're the worst, the very worst."

"But, but"—stammering again despite himself—"it's not me, it's Marsha."

"Yes," she returns, composing herself like some lean effortless snake coiling to strike, "I've heard that one before. It takes two to tango, Mr. Laxner, the pathological aggregator and the enabler. Either way, you're guilty. Don't *ask* your wife, tell her. Take command." Turning her back on him as if the matter's been settled, she props her briefcase up against the near bank of stacked ottomans, produces a note pad and begins jotting down figures in a firm microscopic hand. Without looking up, she swings suddenly round on him. "Family money?" she asks.

And he answers before he can think: "Yes. My late mother."

"All right," she says, "all right, that's fine. But before we go any further, perhaps you'd be interested in hearing a little story one of my clients told me, a journalist, a name you'd recognize in a minute. . . ." The eyes twitch again, the eyeballs themselves, pulsing with that electric charge. "Well, a few years ago he was in Ethiopia—in the Eritrean province—during the civil war there? He was looking for some refugees to interview and a contact put him onto a young couple with three children, they'd been grain merchants before the war broke out, upper-middle-class, they even had a car. Well, they agreed to be interviewed, because he was giving them a little something and they hadn't eaten in a week, but when the time came they hung back. And do you know why?"

He doesn't know. But the room, the room he passes through twenty times a day like a tourist trapped in a museum, seems to close in on him.

"They were embarrassed, that's why—they didn't have any clothes. And I don't mean as in 'Oh dear, I don't have a thing to wear to the Junior League Ball,' but literally no clothes. Nothing at all, not even a rag. They finally showed up like Adam and Eve, one hand clamped over their privates." She held his eyes till he had to look away. "And what do you think of that, Mr. Laxner, I'd be interested to know?"

What can he say? He didn't start the war, he didn't take the food from their mouths and strip the clothes from their backs, but he feels guilty all the same, bloated with guilt, fat with it, his pores oozing the golden rancid sheen of excess and waste. "That's terrible," he murmurs, and still he can't quite look her in the eye.

"Terrible?" she cries, her voice homing in, "you're damned right it's terrible. Awful. The saddest thing in the world. And do you know what? Do you?" She's even closer now, so close he could be breathing for her. "That's why I'm charging you a thousand dollars a day."

The figure seizes him, wrings him dry, paralyzes his vocal apparatus. He can feel something jerking savagely at the cords of his throat. "A thousand—*dollars*—a day?" he echoes in disbelief. "I knew it wasn't going to be cheap—"

But she cuts him off, a single insistent finger pressed to his lips. "You're dirty," she whispers, and her voice is different now, thrilling, soft as a lover's, "you're filthy. And I'm the only one to make you clean again."

The following evening, with Julian's collusion, Susan Certaine and her associate, Dr. Doris Hauskopf, appear at the back gate just after supper. It's a clear searing evening, not a trace of moisture in the sky—the kind of evening that would later lure Julian out under the stars if it weren't for the light pollution. He and Marsha are enjoying a cup of decaf after a meal of pita, tabbouleh and dolma from the Armenian deli, sitting out on the patio amidst the impenetrable maze of lawn furniture, when Susan Certaine's crisp penetrating tones break through the muted roar of freeway traffic and sporadic birdsong: "Mr. Laxner? Are you there?"

Marsha, enthroned in wicker and browsing through a collectibles catalogue, gives him a quizzical look, expecting perhaps a delivery boy or a package from the UPS—Marsha, his Marsha, in her pastel shorts and oversized top, the quintessential innocent, so easily pleased. He loves her in that moment, loves her so fiercely he almost wants to call the whole thing off, but Susan Certaine is there, undeniable, and her voice rings out a second time, drilling him with its adamancy: "Mr. Laxner?"

He rises then, ducking ceramic swans and wrought-iron planters, feeling like Judas.

The martial tap of heels on the flagstone walk, the slap of twin briefcases against rigorously conditioned thighs, and there they are, the professional organizer and her colleague the psychologist, hovering over a bewildered Marsha like customs inspectors. There's a moment of silence, Marsha looking from Julian to the intruders and back again, before he realizes that it's up to him to make the introductions. "Marsha," he begins, and he seems to be having trouble finding his voice, "Marsha, this is Ms. Certaine. And her colleague, Dr. Doris Hauskopf—she's a specialist in aggregation disorders. They run a service for people like us . . . you remember a few weeks ago, when we—" but Marsha's look wraps fingers around his throat and he can't go on.

Blanching, pale to the roots of her hair, Marsha leaps up from the chair and throws a wild hunted look round her. "No," she gasps, "no," and for a moment Julian thinks she's going to bolt, but the psychologist, a compact woman with a hairdo even more severe than Susan Certaine's, steps forward to take charge of the situation. "Poor Marsha," she clucks, spreading her arms to embrace her, "poor, poor Marsha."

The trees bend under the weight of the carved birdhouses from Heidelberg and Zurich, a breeze comes up to play among the Taiwanese wind chimes that fringe the eaves in an unbroken line, and the house—the jam-packed house in which they haven't been able to prepare a meal or even find a frying pan in over two years—seems to rise up off its foundation and settle back again. Suddenly Marsha is sobbing, clutching Dr. Hauskopf's squared-up shoulders and sobbing like a child. "I know I've been wrong," she wails, "I know it, but I just can't, I can't—"

"Hush now, Marsha, hush," the doctor croons, and Susan Certaine gives Julian a fierce, tight-lipped look of triumph, "that's what we're here for. Don't you worry about a thing."

The next morning, at the stroke of seven, Julian is awakened from uneasy dreams by the deep-throated rumble of heavy machinery. In the first startled moment of waking, he thinks it's the noise of the garbage truck and feels a sudden stab of regret for having failed to put out the cans and reduce his load by its weekly fraction, but gradually he becomes aware that the sound is localized, static, stalled at the curb out front of the house. Throwing off the drift of counterpanes, quilts and granny-square afghans beneath which he and his wife lie entombed each night, he struggles through the pre-

cious litter of the floor to the bedroom window. Outside, drawn up
to the curb in a sleek dark glittering line, their engines snarling, are
three eighteen-wheel moving vans painted in metal-flake black and
emblazoned with the Certaine logo. And somewhere, deep in the
bowels of the house, the doorbell has begun to ring. Insistently.

Marsha isn't there to answer it. Marsha isn't struggling up bewildered from the morass of bedclothes to wonder who could be
ringing at this hour. She isn't in the bathroom trying to locate her
toothbrush among the mustache cups and fin-de-siècle Viennese
soap dishes or in the kitchen wondering which of the coffee drippers/
steamers/percolators to use. She isn't in the house at all, and the
magnitude of that fact hits him now, hard, like fear or hunger.

No, Marsha is twenty-seven miles away, in the Susan Certaine
Residential Treatment Center in Simi Valley, separated from him
for the first time in their sixteen years of marriage. It was Dr.
Hauskopf's idea. She felt it would be better this way, less traumatic
for everyone concerned. After the initial twilit embrace of the preceding evening, the doctor and Susan Certaine had led Marsha out
front, away from the house and Julian—her "twin crutches," as the
doctor put it—and conducted an impromptu three-hour therapy session on the lawn. Julian preoccupied himself with his lunar maps
and some calculations he'd been wanting to make relating to the
total area of the Mare Fecunditatis in the Southeast quadrant, but
he couldn't help glancing out the window now and again. The three
women were camped on the grass, sitting in a circle with their legs
folded under them, yoga style, while Marsha's tiki torches blazed
over their heads like a forest afire.

Weirdly lit, they dipped their torsos toward one another and
their hands flashed white against the shadows while Marsha's me-
nagerie of lawn ornaments clustered round them in silent witness.
There was something vaguely disquieting about the scene, and it
made Julian feel like an interloper, already bereft in some deep
essential way, and he had to turn away from it. He put down his
pencil and made himself a drink. He flicked on the TV. Paced. Finally, at quarter to ten, he heard them coming in the front door.
Marsha was subdued, her eyes downcast, and it was clear that she'd

been crying. They allowed her one suitcase. No cosmetics, two changes of clothing, underwear, a nightgown. Nothing else. Not a thing. Julian embraced his wife on the front steps while Susan Certaine and Dr. Hauskopf looked on impatiently, and then they were gone.

But now the doorbell is ringing and Julian is shrugging into his pants and looking for his shoes even as Susan Certaine's whiplash cry reverberates in the stairwell and stings him to action. "Mr. Laxner! Open up! Open up!"

It takes him sixty seconds. He would have liked to comb his hair, brush his teeth, reacquaint himself with the parameters of human life on the planet, but there it is, sixty seconds, and he's still buttoning his shirt as he throws back the door to admit her. "I thought . . . I thought you said eight," he gasps.

Susan Certaine stands rigid on the doorstep, flanked by two men in black jumpsuits with the Certaine logo stitched in gold over their left breast pockets. The men are big-headed, bulky, with great slabs of muscle ladled over their shoulders and upper arms. Behind them, massed like a football team coming to the aid of a fallen comrade, are the uncountable others, all in Certaine black. "I did," she breathes, stepping past him without a glance. "We like to keep our clients on their toes. Mike!" she cries, "Fernando!" and the two men spring past Julian and into the ranked gloom of the house. "Clear paths here"—pointing toward the back room—"and here"— and then to the kitchen.

The door stands open. Beyond it, the front lawn is a turmoil of purposefully moving bodies, of ramps, ladders, forklifts, flattened boxes in bundles six feet high. Already, half a dozen workers— they're women, Julian sees now, women cut in the Certaine mold, with their hair shorn or pinned rigidly back—have begun constructing the cardboard containers that will take the measure of his and Marsha's life together. And now others, five, six, seven of them, speaking in low tones and in a language he doesn't recognize, file past him with rolls of bar-code tape, while out on the front walk, just beyond the clutter of the porch, three men in mirror sunglasses set up a gauntlet of tables equipped with computers and electric-eye guns. Barefooted, unshaven, unshowered, his teeth unbrushed and his hair uncombed, Julian can only stand and gape—it's like an invasion. It *is* an invasion.

When he emerges from the shower ten minutes later, wrapped only in a towel, he finds a small hunched Asian woman squatting on her heels in front of the cabinets under the twin sinks, methodically affixing bar-code stickers to jars of petroleum jelly, rolls of toilet paper and cans of cleanser before stacking them neatly in a box at her side. "What do you think you're doing?" Julian demands. This is too much, outrageous, in his own bathroom no less, but the woman just grins out of a toothless mouth, gives him the thumbs-up sign and says, "A-OK, Number One Charlie!"

His heart is going, he can feel it, and he tries to stay calm, tries to remind himself that these people are only doing their job, doing what he could never do, liberating him, cleansing him, but before he can get his pants back on two more women materialize in the bedroom, poking through the drawers with their ubiquitous stickers. "Get out!" he roars, "out!" and he makes a rush at them, but it's as if he doesn't exist, as if he's already become an irrelevance in the face of the terrible weight of his possessions. Unconcerned, they silently hold their ground, heads bowed, hands flicking all the while over his handkerchiefs, underwear, socks, over Marsha's things, her jewelry, brassieres, her ashtray and lacquered-box collections and the glass case that houses her Thimbles of the World set.

"All right," Julian says, "all right. We'll just see about this, we'll just see," and he dresses right there in front of them, boldly, angrily, hands trembling on button and zipper, before slamming out into the hallway in search of Susan Certaine.

The only problem is, he can't find her. The house, almost impossible to navigate in the best of times, is like the hold of a sinking ship. All is chaos. A dark mutter of voices rises up to engulf him, shouts, curses, dust hanging in the air, the floorboards crying out, and things, objects of all shapes and sizes, sailing past him in bizarre array. Susan Certaine is not in the kitchen, not on the lawn, not in the garage or the pool area or the guest wing. Finally, in frustration, he stops a worker with a Chinese vase slung over one shoulder and asks if he's seen her. The man has a hard face, smoldering eyes, a mustache so thick it eliminates his mouth. "And who might you be?" he growls.

"The owner." Julian feels lightheaded. He could swear he's never seen the vase before.

"Owner of what?"

"What do you mean, owner of what? All this"—gesturing at the chaotic tumble of carpets, lamps, furniture and bric-a-brac—"the house. The, the—"

"You want *Ms.* Certaine," the man says, cutting him off, "I'd advise you best look upstairs, in the den," and then he's gone, shouldering his load out the door.

The den. But that's Julian's sanctuary, the only room in the house where you can draw a breath, find a book on the shelves, a chair to sit in—his desk is there, his telescopes, his charts. There's no need for any organizing in his den. What is she thinking? He takes the stairs two at a time, dodging Certaine workers laden with artifacts, and bursts through the door to find Susan Certaine seated at his desk and the room already half-stripped.

"But, but what are you doing?" he cries, snatching at his Velbon tripod as one of the big men in black fends him off with an unconscious elbow. "This room doesn't need anything, this room is off-limits, this is mine—"

"Mine," Susan Certaine mimics, leaping suddenly to her feet. "Did you hear that, Fernando? Mike?" The two men pause, grinning wickedly, and the wizened Asian woman, at work now in here, gives a short sharp laugh of derision. Susan Certaine crosses the room in two strides, thrusting her jaw at Julian, forcing him back a step. "Listen to yourself—'mine, mine, mine.' Don't you see what you're saying? Marsha's only half the problem, as in any codependent relationship. What did you think, that you could solve all your problems by depriving her of *her* things, making *her* suffer, while all your precious little star charts and musty books and whatnot remain untouched? Is that it?"

He can feel the eyes of the big men on him. Across the room, at the bookcase, the Asian woman applies stickers to his first edition of Percival Lowell's *Mars and Its Canals,* the astrolabe that once belonged to Captain Joshua Slocum, the Starview scope his mother gave him when he turned twelve. "No, but, but—"

"Would that be fair, Mr. Laxner? Would that be equitable? Would it?" She doesn't wait for an answer, turning instead to pose the question to her henchmen. "You think it's fair, Mike? Fernando?"

"No gain without pain," Mike says.

"Amen," Fernando chimes in.

"Listen," Julian blurts, and he's upset now, as upset as he's ever been, "I don't care what you say, I'm the boss here and I say the stuff stays, just as it is. You—now put down that tripod."

No one moves. Mike looks to Fernando, Fernando looks to Susan Certaine. After a moment, she lays a hand on Julian's arm. "You're not the boss here, Julian," she says, the voice sunk low in her throat, "not anymore. If you have any doubts, just read the contract." She attempts a smile, though smiles are clearly not her forte. "The question is, do you want to get organized or not? You're paying me a thousand dollars a day, which breaks down to roughly two dollars a minute. You want to stand here and shoot the breeze at two dollars a minute, or do you want action?"

Julian hangs his head. She's right, he knows it. "I'm sorry," he says finally. "It's just that I can't . . . I mean I want to do something, anything—"

"You want to do something? You really want to help?"

Mike and Fernando are gone, already heading down the stairs with their burdens, and the Asian woman, her hands in constant motion, has turned to his science-fiction collection. He shrugs. "Yes, sure. What can I do?"

She glances at her watch, squares her shoulders, fixes him with her dark unreadable gaze. "You can take me to breakfast."

Susan Certaine orders wheat toast, dry, and coffee, black. Though he's starving, though he feels cored out from the back of his throat to the last constricted loop of his intestines, he follows suit. He's always liked a big breakfast, eggs over easy, three strips of bacon, toast, waffles, coffee, orange juice, yogurt with fruit, and never more so than when he's under stress or feels something coming on, but with Susan Certaine sitting stiffly across from him, her lips pursed in distaste, disapproval, ascetic renunciation of all and everything he stands for, he just doesn't have the heart to order. Besides which, he's on unfamiliar ground here. The corner coffee shop, where he and Marsha have breakfasted nearly every day for the past three years, wasn't good enough for her. She had to drive halfway across the Valley to a place *she* knew, though for the life of him he can't see a whole lot of difference between the two places —same menu, same coffee, even the waitresses look the same. But they're not. And the fact of it throws him off balance.

"You know, I've been thinking, Mr. Laxner," Susan Certaine says, speaking into the void left by the disappearance of the waitress, "you really should come over to us. For the rest of the week, I mean."

Come over? Julian watches her, wondering what in god's name she's talking about, his stomach sinking over the thought of his Heinleins and Asimovs in the hands of strangers, let alone his texts and first editions and all his equipment—if they so much as scratch a lens, he'll, he'll . . . but his thoughts stop right there. Susan Certaine, locked in the grip of her black rigidity, is giving him a look he hasn't seen before. The liminal smile, the coy arch of the eyebrows. She's a young woman, younger than Marsha, far younger, and the apprehension hits him with a jolt. Here he is, sharing the most intimate meal of the day with a woman he barely knows, a young woman. He feels a wave of surrender wash over him.

"How can I persuade you?"

"I'm sorry," he murmurs, fumbling with his cup, "but I don't think I'm following you. Persuade me of what?"

"The Co-Dependent Hostel. For the spouses. The spoilers. For men like you, Mr. Laxner, who give their wives material things instead of babies, instead of love."

"But I resent that. Marsha's physically incapable of bearing children—and I *do* love her, very much so."

"Whatever." She waves her hand in dismissal. "But don't get

the impression that it's a men's club or anything—you'd be surprised how many women are the enablers in these relationships. You're going to need a place to stay until Sunday anyway."

"You mean you want me to, to move out? Of my own house?"

She lays a hand on his. "Don't you think it would be fairer to Marsha? She moved out, didn't she? And by the way, Dr. Hauskopf tells me she passed a very restful night. Very restful." A sigh. A glance out the window. "Well, what do you say?"

Julian pictures a big gray featureless building lost in a vacancy of smog, men in robes and pajamas staring dully at newspapers, the intercom crackling. "But my things—"

"Things are what we're disburdening you of, Mr. Laxner. Things are crushing you, stealing your space, polluting your soul. That's what you hired me for, remember?" She pushes her cup aside and leans forward, and the old look is back, truculent, disdainful. He finds himself gazing into the shimmering nullity of her eyes. "We'll take care of all that," she says, her voice pitched low again, subtle and entrancing, "right on down to your toothbrush, hemorrhoid cream and carpet slippers." As if by legerdemain, a contract has appeared between the creamer and the twin plates of dry unadulterated toast. "Just sign here, Mr. Laxner, right at the bottom."

Julian hesitates, patting down his pockets for his reading glasses. The original contract, the one that spelled out the responsibilities of Certaine Enterprises with respect to his things—and his and Marsha's obligations to Certaine Enterprises—had run to 327 pages, a document he barely had time to skim before signing, and now this. Without his reading glasses he can barely make out the letterhead. "But how much is it, per day, I mean? Marsha's, uh, treatment was four hundred a day, correct? This wouldn't be anywhere in that ballpark, would it?"

"Think of it as a vacation, Mr. Laxner. You're going away on a little trip, that's all. And on Sunday, when you get home, you'll have your space back. Permanently." She looks into his eyes. "Can you put a price on that?"

The Susan Certaine Co-Dependent Hostel is located off a shady street in Sherman Oaks, on the grounds of a defunct private boys' school, and it costs about twice as much as a good hotel in midtown Manhattan. Julian had protested—it was Marsha, Marsha was the problem, she was the one who needed treatment, not him—but Susan Certaine, over two slices of dry wheat toast, had worn him down. He'd given her control over his life, and she was exercising it. That's what he'd paid for, that's what he'd wanted. He asked only to go home and pack a small suitcase, an overnight bag, anything, but she refused him even that—and refused him the use of his own car on top of it. "Withdrawal has got to be total," she says, easing up to the curb out front of the sprawling complex of earth-toned buildings even as a black-clad attendant hustles up to the car to pull open the door, "for *both* partners. I'm sure you'll be very happy here, Mr. Laxner."

"You're not coming in?" he says, a flutter of panic seizing him as he shoots a look from her to the doorman and back again.

The black Mercedes hums beneath them. A bird folds its wings and dips across the lawn. "Oh, no, no, not at all. You're on your own here, Mr. Laxner, I'm afraid—but in the best of hands, I assure you. No, my job is to go back to that black hole of a house and make it livable, to catalogue your things, organize. *Organize*, Mr. Laxner, that's my middle name."

Ten minutes later Julian finds himself sitting on the rock-hard upper bunk in the room he is to share with a lugubrious man named Fred, contemplating the appointments. The place is certainly Essene, but then, he supposes that's the idea. Aside from the bunk bed, the room contains two built-in chests of drawers, two mirrors, two desks and two identical posters revealing an eye-level view of the Bonneville Salt Flats. The communal bathroom/shower is down the checked linoleum hallway to the right. Fred, a big pouchy sack of a man who owns a BMW dealership in Encino, stares gloomily out the window and says only, "Kind of reminds you of college, doesn't it?"

In the evening, there's a meal in the cafeteria—instant mashed potatoes with gravy, some sort of overcooked unidentifiable meatlike substance, Jell-O—and Julian is surprised at the number of his fellow sufferers, slump-shouldered men and women, some of them quite young, who shuffle in and out of the big room like souls in purgatory. After dinner, there's a private get-acquainted chat with Dr. Heiko Hauskopf, Dr. Doris's husband, and then an informational film about acquisitive disorders, followed by a showing of *The Snake Pit* in the auditorium. Fred, as it turns out, is a belcher, tooth grinder and nocturnal mutterer of the first degree, and Julian spends the night awake, staring into the dark corner above him and imagining tiny solar systems there, hanging in the abyss, other worlds radiant with being.

Next morning, after a breakfast of desiccated eggs and corrosive coffee, he goes AWOL. Strides out the door without a glance, calls a taxi from the phone booth on the corner and checks into the nearest motel. From there he attempts to call Marsha, though both Susan Certaine and Dr. Doris had felt it would be better not to "establish contact" during therapy. He can't get through. She's unavailable, indisposed, undergoing counseling, having her nails done, and who is this calling, please?

For two days Julian holes up in his motel room like an escaped convict, feeling dangerous, feeling like a lowlife, a malingerer, a bum, letting the stubble sprout on his face, reveling in the funk of his unwashed clothes. He could walk up the street and buy himself a change of underwear and socks at least—he's still got his credit cards, after all—but something in him resists. Lying there in the sedative glow of the TV, surrounded by the detritus of the local fast-food outlets, belching softly to himself and pulling meditatively at the pint of bourbon balanced on his chest, he begins to see the point of the exercise. He misses Marsha desperately, misses his home, his bed, his things. But this is the Certaine way—to know deprivation, to know the hollowness of the manufactured image and the slow death of the unquenchable tube, to purify oneself through renunciation. These are his thirty days and thirty nights, this is his trial, his penance. He lies there, prostrate, and when the hour of his class at the community college rolls round he gives no account of himself, not even a phone call.

On the third night, the telephone rings. Absorbed in a dramedy about a group of young musician/actor/models struggling to make ends meet in a rented beach house in Malibu, and well into his second pint of bourbon, he stupidly answers it. "Mr. Laxner?" Susan Certaine's hard flat voice drives at him through the wires.

"But, how—?" he gasps, before she cuts him off.

"Don't ask questions, just listen. You understand, of course, that as per the terms of your agreement, you owe Certaine Enterprises for six days' room and board at the Co-Dependent Hostel whether you make use of the facilities or not—"

He understands.

"Good," she snaps. "Fine. Now that that little matter has been resolved, let me tell you that your wife is responding beautifully to treatment and that she, unlike you, Mr. Laxner, is making the most of her stay in a nonacquisitive environment—and by the way, I should caution you against trying to contact her again; it could be terribly detrimental, traumatic, a real setback—"

Whipped, humbled, pried out of his cranny with a sure sharp stick, Julian can only murmur an apology.

There's a pause on the other end of the line—Julian can hear the hiss of gathering breath, the harsh whistle of the air rushing past Susan Certaine's fleshless lips, down her ascetic throat and into the repository of her disciplined lungs. "The good news," she says finally, drawing it out, "is that you're clean. Clean, Mr. Laxner. As pure as a babe sprung from the womb."

Julian is having difficulty putting it all together. His own breathing is quick and shallow. He rubs at his stubble, sits up and sets the pint of bourbon aside. "You mean—?"

"I mean twelve-o'clock noon, Mr. Laxner, Sunday the twenty-seventh. Your place. You be there."

On Sunday morning, Julian is up at six. Eschewing the religious programming in favor of the newspaper, he pores methodically over each of the twenty-two sections—including the obituaries, the personals and the recondite details of the weather in Rio, Yakutsk and Rangoon—and manages to kill an hour and a half. His things have been washed—twice now, in the bathroom sink, with a bar of Ivory soap standing in for detergent—and before he slips into them he shaves with a disposable razor that gouges his face in half-a-dozen places and makes him yearn for the reliable purr and gentle embrace of his Braun Flex Control. He breakfasts on a stale cruller and coffee that tastes of bile while flicking through the channels. Then he shaves a second time and combs his hair. It is 9:05. The room stinks of stir-fry, pepperoni, garlic, the sad reek of his take-out life. He can wait no longer.

Unfortunately, the cab is forty-five minutes late, and it's nearly ten-thirty by the time they reach the freeway. On top of that, there's a delay—roadwork, they always wait till Sunday for roadwork—and the cab sits inert in an endless field of gleaming metal until finally the cabbie jerks savagely at the wheel and bolts forward, muttering to himself as he rockets along the shoulder and down the nearest off-ramp. Julian hangs on, feeling curiously detached as they weave in and out of traffic and the streets become increasingly familiar. And then the cab swings into his block and he's there. Home. His heart begins to pound in his chest.

He doesn't know what he's been expecting—banners, brass bands, Marsha embracing him joyously on the front steps of an immaculate house—but as he climbs out of the cab to survey his domain, he can't help feeling a tug of disappointment: the place looks pretty much the same, gray flanks, white trim, a thin sorry plume of bougainvillea clutching at the trellis over the door. But then it hits him: the lawn ornaments are gone. The tiki torches, the plaster pickaninnies and flag holders and all the rest of the outdoor claptrap have vanished as if into the maw of some brooding tropical storm, and for that he's thankful. Deeply thankful. He stands there a moment, amazed at the expanse of the lawn, plain simple grass, each blade a revelation—he never dreamed he had this much grass. The place looks the way it did when they bought it, wondering naively if it would be too big for just the two of them.

He saunters up the walk like a prospective buyer, admiring the house, truly admiring it, for the first time in years. How crisp it looks, how spare and uncluttered! She's a genius, he's thinking, she really is, as he mounts the front steps fingering his keys and humming, actually humming. But then, standing there in the quickening sun, he glances through the window and sees that the porch is empty—swept clean, not a thing left behind—and the tune goes sour in his throat. That's a surprise. A real surprise. He would have thought she'd leave something—the wicker set, the planters, a lamp or two—but even the curtains are gone. In fact, he realizes with a shock, none of the windows seem to have curtains—or blinds, either. What is she thinking? Is she crazy?

Cursing under his breath, he jabs the key in the lock and twists, but nothing happens. He jerks it back out, angry now, impatient, and examines the flat shining indented surface: no, it's the right key, the same key he's been using for sixteen years. Once again. Nothing. It won't even turn. The truth, ugly, frightening, has begun to dawn on him, even as he swings round on his heels and finds himself staring into the black unblinking gaze of Susan Certaine.

"You, you changed the locks," he accuses, and his hands are trembling.

Susan Certaine merely stands there, the briefcase at her feet, two mammoth softbound books clutched under her arms, books the size of unabridged dictionaries. She's in black, as usual, a no-nonsense business suit growing out of sensible heels, her cheeks brushed ever so faintly with blusher. "A little early, aren't we?" she says.

"You changed the locks."

She waits a beat, unhurried, in control. "What did you expect? We really can't have people interfering with our cataloguing, can we? You'd be surprised how desperate some people get, Mr. Laxner. And when you ran out on your therapy . . . well, we just couldn't take the chance." A thin pinched smile. "Not to worry: I've got your new keys right here—two sets, one for you and one for Marsha."

Her heels click on the pavement, three businesslike strides, and she's standing right beside him on the steps, crowding him. "Here, will you take these, please?" she says, dumping the books in his arms and digging into her briefcase for the keys.

The books are like dumbbells, scrap iron, so heavy he can feel

the pull in his shoulders. "God, they're heavy," Julian mutters.
"What are they?"

She fits the key in the lock and pauses, her face inches from
his. "Your life, Mr. Laxner. The biography of your things. Did you
know that you owned five hundred and fifty-two wire hangers, sixty-
seven wooden ones and one hundred and sixty-nine plastic? Over
two hundred flowerpots? Six hundred doilies? Potholders, Mr. Laxner. You logged in over one hundred twenty—can you imagine that?
Can you imagine anyone needing a hundred and twenty potholders?
Excess, Mr. Laxner," and he watches her lip curl. "Filthy excess."

The key takes, the tumblers turn, the door swings open. "Here
you are, Mr. Laxner, *organization*," she cries, throwing her arms out.
"Welcome to your new life."

Staggering under the burden of his catalogues, Julian moves
across the barren porch and into the house, and here he has a second
shock: the place is empty. Denuded. There's nothing left, not even
a chair to sit in. Bewildered, he turns to her, but she's already moving past him, whirling round the room, her arms spread wide. He's
begun to sweat. The scent of Sen-Sen hangs heavy in the air. "But,
but there's nothing here," he stammers, bending down to set the
catalogues on the stripped floorboards. "I thought . . . well, I thought
you'd pare it down, organize things so we could live here more com-
fortably, adjust, I mean—"

"Halfway measures, Mr. Laxner?" she says, skating up to him
on the newly waxed floors. "Are halfway measures going to save a
man—and woman—who own three hundred and nine bookends,
forty-seven rocking chairs, over two thousand plates, cups and sau-
cers? This is tabula rasa, Mr. Laxner, square one. Did you know you
owned a hundred and thirty-seven dead penlight batteries? Do you
really need a hundred and thirty-seven dead penlight batteries, Mr.
Laxner? Do you?"

"No, but"—backing off now, distraught, his den, his den—"but
we need the basics, at least. Furniture. A TV. My, my textbooks. My
scopes."

The light through the unshaded windows is harsh, unforgiving.
Every corner is left naked to scrutiny, every board, every nail. "All

taken care of, Mr. Laxner, no problem." Susan Certaine stands there in the glare of the window, hands on her hips. "Each couple is allowed to reclaim one item per day from the warehouse—anything you like—for a period of sixty days. Depending on how you exercise your options, that could be as many as sixty items. Most couples request a bed first, and to accommodate them, we consider a bed one item—mattress, box spring, headboard and all."

Julián is stunned. "Sixty items? You're joking."

"I never joke, Mr. Laxner. Never."

"And what about the rest—the furniture, the stereo, our clothes?"

"Read your contract, Mr. Laxner."

He can feel himself slipping. "I don't want to read the contract, damn it. I asked you a question."

"Page two hundred and seventy-eight, paragraph two. I quote: 'After expiration of the sixty-day grace period, all items to be sold at auction, the proceeds going to Certaine Enterprises, Inc., for charitable distribution, charities to be chosen at the sole discretion of the above-named corporation.'" Her eyes are on him, severe, hateful, bright with triumph. This is what it's all about, this—cutting people down to size, squashing them. "You'd be surprised how many couples never recall a thing, not a single item."

"No," Julian says, stalking across the room, "no, I won't stand for it. I won't. I'll sue."

She shrugs. "I won't even bother to remind you to listen to yourself. You're like the brat on the playground—you don't like the way the game goes, you take your bat and ball and go home, right? Go ahead, sue. You'll find it won't be so easy. You signed the contract, Mr. Laxner. Both of you."

There's a movement in the open doorway. Shadow and light. Marsha. Marsha and Dr. Hauskopf, frozen there on the doorstep, watching. "Julian," Marsha cries, and then she's in his arms, clinging to him as if he were the last thing in the world, the only thing left her.

Dr. Doris and Susan Certaine exchange a look. "Be happy,"

Susan Certaine says after a moment. "Think of that couple in Ethiopia." And then they're gone.

Julian doesn't know how long he stands there, in the middle of that barren room in the silence of that big empty house, holding Marsha, holding his wife, but when he shuts his eyes he sees only the sterile deeps of space, the remotest regions beyond even the reach of light. And he knows this: it is cold out there, inhospitable, alien. There's nothing there, nothing contained in nothing. Nothing at all.

WITHOUT A HERO

IN THE END, through luck and perseverance and an unwavering commitment to the spirit of glasnost, she did finally manage to get what she wanted. It was amazing. With two weeks to go on her six-month visa, she fell head-over-heels in love, got swept up in a whirl-wind romance and found herself married—and to an American, no less. His name was Yusef Ozizmir, he was a naturalized citizen from a small town outside of Ankara, and he was production manager for a prosthetics firm based in Culver City. She called me late one night to give me the news and gloat a bit over her honeymoon in Las Vegas and her new apartment in Manhattan Beach that featured three bedrooms, vast closets and a sweet clean smell of the sea. Her voice was just as I'd remembered it: tiny, heavily accented and with the throaty arrhythmic scratch of sensuality that had awakened me in every fiber when I first heard it—the way she said "wodka" still aroused me even after all that had happened.

"I'm happy for you, Irina," I said.

"Oh," she gasped in her tiny voice that was made tinier by the uncertain connection, "that is very kind of you; I am very grateful. Yusef has made me very happy too, yes? He has given me a ring of twenty-four karats gold and a Lincoln automobile."

There was a pause. I glanced across my apartment at the sag-ging bookshelves, the TV tuned to a dim romantic comedy from the black-and-white era, the darkened window beyond. Her voice be-came tinier still, contracting till it was barely audible, a hesitant little squeak of passion. "You know . . . I miss you, Casey," she breathed. "I will always miss you too much."

"Listen, Irina, I have to go . . ." I was trying to think of an excuse—the kitchen was on fire, my mother had been stricken with ptomaine and rushed to the hospital, my knives needed sharpening —but she cut me off.

"Yes, Casey, I know. You have to go. You must go. Always you go."

"Listen," I began, and then I caught myself. "See you," I said.

For a moment there was nothing. I listened to the cracks and pops of static. Finally her voice came back at me, the smallest voice in the world: "Yes," she said. "See you."

When I first saw her—when I laid eyes on her for the first time, that is—it was by prearrangement. She was in the baggage-claim area of the Tom Bradley International Terminal at LAX, and I was there to pick her up. I was late—a failing of mine, I admit it—and anxious on several counts: about meeting her, missing her, about sleeping arrangements and dinner and a hundred other things, ranging from my total deficiency in Russian to my passing acquaintance with the greats of Russian literature and the fear that she would offer to buy my jeans with a fistful of rubles. I was jogging through the corridors, dodging bleary-eyed Sikhs, hearty Brits and circumspect salesmen from Japan and Korea, the big names—Solzhenitsyn, Chekhov, Dostoevsky and Tolstoy—running through my head like an incantation, when I spotted her.

There was no mistaking her. I had Rob Peterman's description to go by—twenty-eight, blond, with a figure right out of the Bolshoi and a face that could kill—but I didn't need it. She was the center of a vortex of activity, a cigarette in one hand, a plastic cup of vodka in the other, her things scattered about her in cyclonic disarray— newspapers, luggage, makeup, paper towels and tissues, a sweater, several purses, half-a-dozen stuffed animals and a Dodgers cap oc-cupying the two rows of seats behind her. She was engaged in an animated discussion of perestroika, Lithuanian independence, the threat of nuclear war and the relative merits of the Jaguar XJS as opposed to the Mercedes 560 SEC with three well-lubricated busi-

nessmen in rumpled suits. The cigarette—"A Gauloise, of course;
what else is there?"—described an arc in the air, the hopelessly out-
of-date go-go boots did a mazurka on the carpet, the fringe of the
baby-blue patent-leather jacket trembled and shook. I didn't know
what to do. I was sweating from my dash through the airport and I
must have had that crazed, trapped-in-a-burning-barn look in my
eyes.

"And do you know what I give you for that Mercedes?" she
demanded of the shortest and most rumpled of the businessmen.
"Eh?"

No response. All three men just stared at her, their mouths
slightly agape, as if she'd just touched down from the far reaches of
space.

"*Nichevo.*" A little laugh escaped her. "This is what means
'nothing' in Russia. *Nichevo.*"

I edged into her line of sight and made an extenuating gesture,
describing a little circle of apology and lament with my hands and
shirtsleeve arms. "Irina?" I asked.

She looked at me then, stopped dead in the middle of her next
phrase and focused her milky blue—and ever so slightly exophthal-
mic—eyes on me. And then she smiled, allowing me my first take
of her slim, sharp-toothed grin, and I felt a rush of warmth as the
blood shot through me—a Russian smile, I thought, my first Russian
smile. "Casey," she said, and there was no interrogatory lift to it, no
doubt. "Casey." And then she turned away from her three interloc-
utors, dismissing them as if they'd never existed, and fell into my
arms.

There was no shame in wanting things, and Irina wanted plenty.
"Where I come from," she would say in her tiny halting breathy
voice, "we do not have."

She revealed this to me for the first time in the car on the way
back from the airport. Her eyes were shining, the Dodgers cap (a
gift from one of the businessmen) rode the crown of her head like
a victory wreath, and she gaily sang out the names and citations of

the cars we passed on the freeway: "Corvette! Z-car! BMW 750!" I tried to keep my eyes on the road, but couldn't help stealing a glance at her from time to time.

Rob Peterman had been generous in his description, I could see that now. In the rush of excitement at the airport I saw only the exotic Irina, Rob Peterman's ideal made flesh, but as I began to study her I saw that she was no beauty—interesting, certainly, and pretty to a degree, but a far cry from the hyperborean goddess I'd been led to expect. But isn't that the way it always is?

"Is that not I. Magnin?" she cried as we pulled off the freeway. And then she turned to me and gave me that smile again, purring, cooing. "Oh, Casey, this is so—how do I say it?—so very much exciting to me."

There was the bulge of her eyes, too much forehead, the drawn mouth and sharp little teeth, but she fit her jeans as if they'd been tailored for her, and there was her hair, and her smile too. To a man three months divorced, as I then was, she looked good—better than good: I forgot the ideal and tumbled into the actual. "I'll take you there tomorrow," I said, "and you can run wild through the store." She was beaming at me, worshiping me with her eyes. "Tonight," I said, letting my voice trail off a bit so as not to betray my eagerness, "tonight I thought we'd just have a quiet dinner—I mean, that is, if you're not too tired—"

Two weeks earlier Rob Peterman had called me from George-town, where he was one of the principal buttresses of the International Relations Department at the university. He'd just come back from a six-week lecture tour of Russia and he had some good news for me—better, even: he'd brought back a little gift for me.

I'd known Rob since college. We were fraternity brothers, and we'd had some wild times. We'd kept in touch ever since. "Gift?"

"Let me put it to you this way, Case," he said. "There are a lot of university students in Moscow, thousands upon thousands of them, and a high percentage of them are young women from the provinces who'll do anything to stay in the big city. Or to travel, for that matter."

He had my attention, I had to admit it.

"You'd be surprised how many of them tend to gather round the Intourist bars and hotels, and how polished and intelligent they are, not to mention beautiful—you know, the Ukrainian princess, the Georgian fleshpot, the exotic long-limbed Slav . . ."

"Yes? And so?"

"Her name's Irina, Case," he said, "and she'll be in L.A. next week, TWA flight number eight nine five, arriving from Paris, where she connects from Moscow. Irina Sudeikina. I, uh, met her while I was over there, and she needs attachments." He lowered his voice. "If Sarah found out about her she'd take me to the vet and have me fixed, know what I mean?"

"What does she look like?"

"Who, Irina?" And then he gave me his generous description, which ran to twelve paragraphs and fanned the flames of my anticipation until I was a fireball of need, greed, hope and lust.

"Okay," I said finally, "okay, I hear you. What flight did you say she was on?"

And so there we were, in the car, driving up Pico to my apartment, my question about dinner, with all its loaded implications, hanging in the air between us. I'd pulled out the sofa bed in the back bedroom, stuck a pole lamp in the corner, tidied up a bit. She hadn't said anything about a hotel, and I hadn't asked. I glanced at the road ahead, and then back at her. "You're tired, aren't you?" I said.

"Do you not live in Beverly Hills, Casey?" she asked.

"Century City," I said. "It borders on Beverly Hills."

"In a mansion?"

"An apartment. It's nice. Plenty of room."

She shifted the Dodgers cap so that the brim fell over the crown of her sunstruck hair. "Oh, I have slept on the aeroplane," she said, turning her smile up a notch. "I am not tired. I am not tired at all."

As it turned out, Irina was to be my houseguest for the next two months. She settled into the back room like a Bedouin settling into a desert outpost, and within a week her things were everywhere, ubiquitous, from the stuffed panda perched atop the TV to the sweat

socks beneath the kitchen table and the Harlequin romances sprout-
ing up from the carpet like toadstools. She took a free, communistic
approach to my things as well, thinking nothing of scattering my
classic Coltrane albums across the couch or breezing down to the
Beverly Center on my eight-hundred-dollar Bianchi all-terrain bike,
without reference to lock or chain (where it was promptly stolen),
not to mention using the telephone as if it had been provided by
the state for the convenience of apartment dwellers and their guests.
Slovenly, indolent, nearly inert, she was the end product of three
generations of the workers' paradise, that vast dark crumbling empire in which ambition and initiative counted for nothing. Do I
sound bitter? I am bitter. But I didn't know all this back then, and
if I had known, I wouldn't have cared. All I knew was Irina's smile
and her hair and the proximity of her flesh; all I knew was that she
was in the bedroom, unpacking and dressing for dinner.

I took her to a sushi place on Wilshire, thinking to impress her
with my savoir-faire and internationalism, but she surprised me not
only in being an adept at *ebi*, *unagi* and *katsuo*, but by ordering in
flawless Japanese to boot. She was wearing a low-cut minidress made
of some shiny brittle material, she'd drawn her hair back severely
and knotted it up over her head in a big puffy bun, and she'd put
some effort into her makeup. The sushi chef was all over her, chattering away in Japanese, fashioning whimsical creations of radish and
carrot for her, rolling out his rare stock of *fugu*, the Japanese blow-
fish. I'd been a regular at the restaurant for two years at least, and
he'd never looked at me twice. "Uh, Irina," I said, as the chef
slouched reluctantly off to make a scallop roll for the couple beside
me, "where did you learn your Japanese? I mean, I'm impressed."

She paused, a sliver of Norwegian salmon tucked neatly between her lips, patted her mouth and gasped, "Oh, this is nothing.
I have spent six months in Japan in 1986."

I was surprised. "They—the government, I mean, the Russian
government—they let you travel then?"

She gave me a wink. "I am at that time a student of languages
at Moscow State University, Casey . . . am I not then to learn these
languages by visiting the countries in which they are spoken?" She

turned back to her plate, plucked a morsel from some creation the chef had set before us. "Besides," she said, speaking to the plate in her tiny voice, "there is a man I know in Moscow and he is able to arrange things—even difficult things."

I had a hundred questions for her—about life behind the iron curtain, about Japan, about her girlhood and college and the mysterious benefactor in Moscow—but I focused instead on my sake and a slippery bit of *maguro* that kept eluding my chopsticks, and thought only of getting in the car and driving home with her.

I was a little tense on the way back—the first-date jitters, the sort of thing every male goes through from adolescence to the grave: will she or won't she?—and I couldn't think of much to say. It didn't really matter. Irina was oblivious, lit with sake and three big pint-and-a-half bottles of Asahi, waving her cigarette, crossing and uncrossing her legs and rolling the exotic Anglo-Saxon and Latinate phrases over her tongue with real relish. How nice it was here in America, she thought, how sympathetic, and what a nice car I had, but wouldn't I prefer a sportier model? I made a lot of money, didn't I?—she could tell because I was so generous—and wasn't it nice to have Japanese food, something you could find in one place only in Moscow, and then only if you were an apparatchik?

At home we had an after-dinner drink in the living room— Grand Marnier, twenty-six dollars the fifth; she filled the snifter to the top—while Coltrane serenaded us with "All or Nothing at All." We talked about little things, inconsequential things, and she became progressively more animated as the level fell in her glass. And then, without a word of explanation—hello, goodbye, good night and thank you for dinner, nothing—she stood, refilled her glass and disappeared into the bedroom.

I was devastated. So this is it, I thought bitterly, this is my passionate Russian experience—a hundred and twenty bucks for sushi, half a bottle of Grand Marnier and a rush-hour schlep to the airport and back. I sat there, a little sick in the stomach, and listened to the sad expiring click of the turntable as the record ended and the machine shut itself down.

With all she'd had to drink, with the time change and the long flight from Moscow, I figured she'd probably hit the bed in a cold faint, but I was wrong. Just as I was about to give it up, heave myself out of the chair and tumble into my own comfortless bed, she appeared in the doorway. "Casey," she murmured, her voice rich and low, and in the muted light I could see that she was wearing something silky and diaphanous—a teddy, a Russian teddy. "Casey," she crooned, "I cannot seem to sleep."

It was about a week later that she first asked me if I knew Akhmatova. I did know her, but not personally. She was dimmer to me even than Pushkin or Lermontov, a fading memory out of a drowsy classroom

"We studied her in college," I said lamely. "After she died—in the sixties, right? It was a survey course in Russian literature. In translation, I mean."

Irina was sitting cross-legged on the couch in a litter of newspapers and magazines. She was wearing only a T-shirt and a pair of panties, and I'd just watched in fascination as she applied a glistening coat of neon-pink polish to her toenails. She looked up at me a moment and narrowed her pale-blue eyes. Then she closed them and began to recite:

> "FROM THE YEAR NINETEEN-FORTY
> AS FROM A HIGH TOWER I LEAN,
> ONCE MORE BIDDING GOODBYE
> TO WHAT I LONG AGO FORSOOK,
> AS THOUGH I HAVE CROSSED MYSELF
> AND AM GOING DOWN UNDER DARK
> VAULTS.

"It is from Akhmatova's great work, 'Poem Without A Hero.' Is it not sad and beautiful?"

I looked at her toenails shimmering in the light of the morning; I looked at her bare legs, her face, her eyes. We'd been out every night—I'd taken her to Chinatown, Disneyland, the Music Center and Malibu pier—and the glow of it was on me. "Yes," I said.

"This is a great work about dying for love, Casey, about a poet who kills himself because his lover will not have him." She shut her eyes again. " 'For one moment of peace I would give the peace of the tomb.' " She let the moment hang, mesmeric, motes of dust floating in a shaft of light through the window, the bird of paradise gilded with sun, the traffic quiet on the street. And then she was looking at me, soft and shrewd at once. "Tell me, Casey, where does one find such a hero today? Where does one find a man who will die for love?"

The next day was the day she took my bike to the Beverly Center and we had our first falling-out.

I'd come home late from work—there was a problem with the new person we'd hired, the usual semiliteracy and incompetence—and the place was a mess. No: actually, "mess" didn't do it justice. The apartment looked as if a troop of baboons had been locked inside it for a week. Every record I owned was out of its jacket and collecting dust; my books were scattered throughout the living room, spread open flat like crippled things; there were clothes and sheets and pillows wadded about, and every horizontal surface was inundated with a farrago of take-out food and crumpled wrappers: Colonel Sanders, Chow Foo Luck, McDonald's, Arby's, Taco Bell. She was on the phone in the back room—long-distance to Russia—and she hadn't changed out of the T-shirt she'd been wearing the previous morning. She said something in Russian, and then I heard her say, "Yes, and my American boyfriend he is so very wealthy—"

"Irina?"

"I must go now. *Do svidaniya.*"

I stepped into the bedroom and she flew across the room to fling herself into my arms, already sobbing, sobbing in midair. I was disconcerted. "What's the matter?" I said, clutching her hopelessly. I had a sudden intimation that she was leaving me, that she was going on to visit Chicago and New Orleans and New York, and I felt a sinkhole of loss open up inside me. "Are you—is everything all right?"

Her breath was hot on my throat. She began to kiss me there, over and over, till I took hold of her shoulders and forced her to look me in the eye. "Irina, tell me: what is it?"

"Oh, Casey," she gasped, and her voice was so diminished I could barely hear her. "I have been so stupid. Even in Russia we must lock up our things, I know, but I have never dreamed that here, where you have so much—"

And so I discovered that my eight-hundred-dollar bicycle was no more, just as I was to learn that she'd sheared the blades off the Cuisinart attempting to dice a whole pineapple and that half my records had gouges in them and that my new white Ci Siamo jacket was stained with lipstick or cranberry juice or what might have been blood for all I knew.

I lost my sense of humor, my forbearance, my graciousness, my cool. We had a scene. Accusations flew. I didn't care about her, she shrieked; things meant more to me than she did. "Things!" I snorted. "And who spends half her time at Robinson's and Saks and the May Company? Who calls Russia as if God Himself would come down from heaven and pay the bills? Who hasn't offered to pay a penny of anything, not even once?"

Her hair hung wild in her face. Strands of it adhered to the sudden moisture that glistened on her cheekbones. "You do not care for me," she said in her tiniest voice. "I am only for you a momentary pleasure."

I had nothing more to say. I stood there fuming as she fussed round the room, drawing on her jeans and boots, shrugging into the baby-blue patent-leather jacket and tamping out a cigarette in an abandoned coffee mug. She gave me a look—a look of contempt, anger, sorrow—and then she snatched up her purse and slammed out the door.

I didn't sleep well that night. I kept listening for her key in the lock, kept picturing her shouldering her way through the punks and beggars on the boulevard and wondering if she had friends to go to. She had some money, I knew that, but she hoarded it like a capitalist, and though she knew all the brand names, she bought nothing.

I saw the absurd go-go boots, the fringed jacket, the keen sexy spring in her walk that belied her phlegmatic Russian nature, and half-a-dozen times I got up to look for her and then thought better of it. In the morning, when I got up for work, the apartment was desolate.

I called home sporadically throughout the day, but there was no answer. I was angry, hurt, sick with worry. Finally, around four, she picked up the phone. "It is Irina," she said, her voice tired and small.

"It's me, Casey."

No response.

"Irina? Are you all right?"

A pause. "I am very well, thank you."

I wanted to ask where she'd spent the night, wanted to know and possess her and make demands, but I faltered in the presence of that quavering whispery voice. "Irina, listen, about last night . . . I just want to say I'm sorry."

"That is no problem," she said. And then, after a pause, "I leave you fifty dollars, Casey, on the table in the kitchen."

"What do you mean?"

"I am going now, Casey. I know when I am not wanted."

"No, no—I didn't mean . . . I mean I was mad, I was angry, that was all. You're wanted. You are." I was pleading with her and even as I pleaded I could hear that I'd subconsciously picked up something of her diction, clipping my phrases in a too-formal way, a Russian way. "Listen, just wait there a minute, will you? I'm on my way home from work. I'll take you wherever you want to go— you want to go to the airport? The bus? Whatever you want."

Nothing.

"Irina?"

The smallest voice: "I will wait."

I took her out to Harry's that night for Italian food, and she was radiant, beaming, almost giddy—she couldn't stop grinning at me, and everything I said was the funniest thing she'd ever heard. She cut her veal into neat little strips, chattered at the waiter in a breathy fluid Italian, tossed off one glass of Chianti after another, all the while pecking kisses at me and entwining her fingers with mine as if we were sixteen-year-olds at the mall. I didn't mind. This was our reconciliation, and the smoke of sensuality hung over the table.

She leaned toward me over dessert—mille foglie with a cappuccino and Grand Marnier—and gave me the full benefit of her swollen eyes. The lights were low. Her voice was a whisper. I expected her to say, "Do you not want to take me home to bed now?" but she surprised me. With a randy look, she cleared her throat and said, "Casey, I have been wondering"—pause—"do you think I should put my money in CD or mutual fund?"

I couldn't have been more stunned if she'd asked me who played third base for the Dodgers. "What?"

"The Magellan has performed best, has it not?" she whispered, and the talk of money seemed to make her voice sultrier still. "But then the founder is retiring, is this not so?"

A sudden anger came over me. Was she hustling me, was that it? She had money to invest and yet accepted her room and meals and all the rest from me as if it were her divine right? I stared down into my cappuccino and muttered, "Hell, I don't know. What are you asking me for?"

She patted my hand and then said in her fading slip of a voice, "Perhaps this is not the time." Her mouth made a little moue of contrition. And then, almost immediately, she brightened again, "It is early yet, Casey," she said, quaffing her Grand Marnier and rising. "Do you not want to take me to the Odessa?"

The Odessa was a club in the Fairfax district where Russian émigrés of all ages would gather to sit at long cafeteria-style tables and listen to schmaltzy singers and third-rate comedians. They drank water glasses of warm Coke and vodka—the Coke in the left hand, vodka in the right, alternating swigs—and they sang along with and got up from the table and careened round the room to the frenetic Tatar strains of the orchestra. We stayed past closing, danced till we were soaked in sweat and drank enough vodka to fuel a 747. In the course of the evening we toasted Gorbachev, Misha Baryshnikov, the girls of Tbilisi, Leningrad and Murmansk, and drank the health of everyone in the room, individually, at least three times. Irina passed out in the car on the way home, and the night ended after she vomited gloriously in the potted ficus and I helped her to bed as if she were an invalid.

I felt queasy myself the next morning and called in sick at the office. When I finally got out of bed, around noon, Irina's door was still closed. I was brewing coffee when she slumped through the kitchen door and fell into a chair. She was wearing a rumpled housecoat and she looked as if she'd been buried and dug up again.

"Me too," I said, and I put both hands to my temples.

She said nothing, but accepted the coffee I poured for her. After a moment she pointed out the window to where one of my neighbors was letting her dog nose about in the shrubs that rimmed our little patch of lawn. "Do you see that dog, Casey?" she asked.

I nodded.

"It is a very lucky dog."

"Lucky?"

"Yes," she said, slow and lethargic, drawing it out. "It is a dog that has never tasted wodka."

I laughed, but my eyes felt as if they were being sucked into my head and the coffee set my insides churning.

And then she took me by surprise again. Outside, the dog had disappeared, jerked rudely away at the end of a leash. The coffee machine dripped coffee. Someone gunned an engine two blocks away. "Casey," she said, utterly composed, utterly serious, and she looked deep into my eyes. "Do you not want to marry me?"

The second blowup came at the end of the month, when the phone bill arrived. Four hundred twenty-seven dollars and sixty-two cents. I recognized a few calls—my lawyer's number, Rob Peterman's, a drunken cri de coeur I'd made to an old flame (now married) in Santa Barbara. But the rest were long-distance overseas—to Moscow, Novgorod, London, Paris, Milan. I was outraged. I was in shock. Why should I be responsible for her bills? I did not want to marry her, as I'd explained to her the morning after the Odessa. I told her I'd just been divorced and was leery of new attachments, which was true. I told her I still had feelings for my wife, which was also true (of course, those feelings were exclusively antipathetic, but I didn't mention that). Irina had only stared at me, and then she got up from the kitchen table and went into her room, shutting the door firmly behind her.

But now, now she was out somewhere—no doubt looking at popcorn makers or water-purifying systems at some department store—the house was in a shambles, I hadn't even loosened my tie yet and the phone bill was sending shock waves through me. I'd just poured a drink when I heard her key in the door; she came in beaming, oblivious, in a rustle of shopping bags and cheap trinkets, and I was all over her. "Don't you know what this means?" I shouted. "Don't you know that the telephone isn't free in this society, that somebody has to pay for it? That *I* have to pay for it?"

She gave me a hard cold look. Her eyes narrowed; her chin trembled. "I will pay it," she said, "if that is how you feel."

"How I feel?" I shouted. "How I feel? Everybody pays their way in life, that's how I feel. That's the way society works, like it or not. Maybe it's different in the workers' paradise, I don't know, but over here you play by the rules."

She had nothing to say to that—she just held me with her contemptuous look, as if I were the one being unreasonable, and in that moment she reminded me of Julie, my ex-wife, as if she were in league with her, as if she were her double, and I felt bitter and disgusted to the core. I dropped the bill on the coffee table and stalked out the door.

When I got home from work the next day, the phone bill was still there, but there were five pristine one-hundred-dollar bills laid out beside it like a poker hand. Irina was in the kitchen. I didn't know what to say to her. Suddenly I felt ashamed of myself.

I drifted into the room and draped my sportcoat over the back of one of the chairs and went to the refrigerator for a glass of orange juice. "Hello, Casey," she said, glancing up from her magazine. It was one of those women's magazines, thick as a phone book.

"Hi," I said. And then, after an interval during which the level of the orange juice mounted in the glass and I gazed numbly out the window on a blur of green, I turned to her. "Irina," I murmured, and my voice seemed to be caught in my throat, "I want to say thanks for the phone bill—the money, I mean."

She looked up at me and shrugged. "It is nothing," she said. "I have a job now."

"A job?"

And there was her smile, the sharp little teeth. "*Da*," she said. "I have met a man at the Odessa when I go for tea last Thursday? Do you remember I told you? His name is Zhenya and he has offered me a job."

"Great," I said. "Terrific. We should celebrate." I lifted my glass as if it contained Perrier-Jouët. "What kind of work?"

She looked down at her magazine and then back up again, holding my eyes. "Escort service."

I thought I hadn't heard her right. "What? What are you saying?"

"It is an escort service, Casey. Zhenya says the men who come here for important business—in the movies, banking, real estate—they will like me. He says I am very beautiful."

I was stunned. I felt as if I'd had the wind knocked out of me. "You can't be serious?" My voice was pitched high, a yelp. "Irina, this is"—I couldn't find the words—"this is not right, it's not legitimate. It's, it's prostitution, don't you know that?"

She was studying me, her shrewd eyes, the little nugget of her face. She sighed, closed the magazine and rose from her seat. "It is not a problem," she said finally. "If I do not like them I will not sleep with them."

And what about me? I wanted to say. *What about Disneyland and Zuma Beach and all the rest of it?* Instead I turned on her. "You're crazy," I spat. "Nuts. Don't you know what you're getting into?"

Her eyes hadn't left mine, not for a second. She was a foot away from me. I could smell her perfume—French, four hundred dollars the ounce. She shrugged and then stretched her arms so that

her breasts rose tight against her chest. "What am I to do," she said
in her smallest voice, so languid and sad. "I have nothing, and you
will not marry me."

That was the end for us, and we both knew it.

I took her out to dinner that night, but it was a requiem, an
interment. She stared off into vacancy. Neither of us had much to
say. When we got home I saw her face illuminated for an instant as
she bent to switch on the lamp, and I felt something stir in me, but
I killed it. We went to our separate rooms and to our separate beds.

In the morning, I sat over a cup of lukewarm coffee and
watched her pack. She looked sweet and sad, and she moved as if
she were fighting an invisible current, her hair streaming, imaginary
fish hanging in the rafters. I didn't know if the escort-service business was a bluff or not, didn't know how naive—or how calculating—she was, but I felt that a burden had been lifted from my
shoulders. Now that it was over, I began to see her in a different
light, a softer light, and a sliver of guilt began to stab at me. "Look,
Irina," I said as she struggled to force her suitcase shut, "I'm sorry.
I really am."

She threw her hair back with a jerk of her chin, shrugged into
the baby-blue patent-leather jacket.

"Irina, look at me—"

She wouldn't look. She leaned over to snap the latches on her
suitcase.

"This is no poem, Irina," I said. "This is life."

She swung round so suddenly I flinched. "I am the one, Casey,"
she said, and her eyes leapt at me. "I am the one who can die for
love."

All the bitterness came back to me in that instant, all the hurt
and guilt. Zhenya, Japan, the mysterious benefactor in Moscow, Rob
Peterman and how many others? This was free enterprise, this was
trade and barter and buying and selling—and where was the love
in that? Worse yet: where was the love in me?

I was hard, a rock, granite. "Then die for it," I said.

The phrase hung between us like a curtain. A car moved up

the street. I could hear the steady drip-drip-drip of the kitchen tap.
And then she bowed her head, as if accepting a blow, and bent for
her suitcases. I was paralyzed. I was dead. I watched her struggle
with her things, watched her fight the door, and then, as the sudden
light gave way to darkness, I watched the door swing shut.

RESPECT

WHEN SANTO R. STEPPED into my little office in Partinico last fall, I barely recognized him. He'd been a corpulent boy, one of the few in this dry-as-bones country, and a very heavyset young man. I remembered his parents—peasants, and poor as church mice—and how I'd treated him for the usual childhood ailments—rubella, chicken pox, mumps—and how even then the gentlest pressure of my fingers would leave marks on the distended flesh of his upper arms and legs. But if he'd been heavy then, now, at the age of twenty-nine, he was like a pregnant mule, so big around the middle he hardly fit through the door. He was breathing hard, half-choked on the dust of the streets, and he was wet through to the skin with sweat. "Doctor," he wheezed, sinking a thumb into the morass of his left pectoral, just above the heart, "it hurts here." An insuck of breath, a dab at the brow, a wince. I watched his bloated pale hand sink to cradle the great tub of his abdomen. "And here," he whispered.

Behind him, through the open door, the waiting room full of shopkeepers, widows and hypochondriacs looked on in awe as I motioned Crocifissa, my nurse, to pull the door closed and leave us. My patients might have been impressed—here was a man of respect, who in the company of his two endomorphic bodyguards had waddled up the stairs and through the waiting room without waiting for anyone or anything—but for my part, I was only alarmed at the state he was in. The physician and his patient, after all, have a bond that goes far deeper than the world of getting and keeping, of violence and honor and all the mess that goes with them—and from the patient's point of view, self-importance can take you only so far when you come face to face with the man who inserts the rectal thermometer.

"Don R.," I said, getting up from the desk and simultaneously fitting the stethoscope to my ears, "I can see that you're suffering --but have no fear, you've come to the right man. Now, let's have a look. . . ."

Well, I examined him, and he was as complete and utter a physical wreck as any man under seventy who has ever set foot in my office. The chest pain, extending below the breastbone and down the left arm to the wrist and little finger, was symptomatic of angina, a sign of premature atherosclerosis; his liver and spleen were enlarged; he suffered from hypertension and ulcers; and if he didn't yet have a full-blown case of emphysema, he was well on his way to developing it. At least, this was my preliminary diagnosis—we would know more when the test results came back from the lab.

Crocifissa returned to inform me that Signora Malatesta seemed to be having some sort of attack in the waiting room, and as the door swung shut behind her, I could see one of Santo's bodyguards bent over the old woman, gently patting her on the back. "*Momento,*" I called out, and turned to Santo with my gravest expression. "You are a very unwell man, Don R.," I told him, "and I can't help but suspect that your style of living has been a contributing factor. You do smoke, do you not?"

A grunt. The blocky fingers patted down the breast pocket of his jacket and he produced an engraved cigarette case. He offered me a Lucky Strike with a gallant sweep of his arm and, when I refused, lit one up for himself. For a long moment he sat meditating over my question with a lungful of tobacco smoke. Finally, he shrugged his shoulders. "Two or three packs a day," he rasped, and appended a little cough.

"And alcohol?"

"What is this, Doctor, the confessional?" he growled, fixing me with a pair of dangerous black eyes. But then he subsided, shrugging again. "A liter of Chianti or Valpolicella with my meals—at breakfast,

lunch, evening snack and dinner—and maybe two or three *fiaschi*
of brandy a day to keep my throat open."

"Coffee?"

"A pot or two in the morning. And in the evening, when I can't
sleep. And that's another problem, Doctor—these pills that Bernardi
gave me for sleeping? Well, they have no effect on me, nothing, I
might as well be swallowing little blue capsules of cat piss. I toss, I
turn. My stomach is on fire. And this at four and five in the
morning."

"I see, yes," I said, and I pulled at the little Vandyke I've worn
for nearly forty years now to inspire confidence in my patients. "And
do you—how shall I put it? Do you exercise regularly?"

Santo looked away. His swollen features seemed to close in on
themselves and in that moment he was the pudgy boy again, ready
to burst into tears at some real or imagined slight. When he spoke,
his voice had sunk to a whisper. "You mean with the women then,
eh?" And before I could answer he went on, his voice so reduced I
could barely hear him: "I—I just don't seem to feel the urge anymore. And not only when it comes to my wife, as you might expect
after ten years of marriage, but with the young girls too."

Somehow, we had steered ourselves into dangerous conversa-
tional waters, and I saw that these waters foamed with naked shoals
and rocky reefs. "No, no," I said, and I almost gasped out the words,
"I meant physical exercise, jogging, bicycling, a regular twenty-
minute walk, perhaps?"

"Ha!" he spat. "Exercise!" And he rose ponderously from the
chair, his face as engorged and lopsided as a tomato left out to rot
in the sun. "That's all I do is exercise. My whole frigging life is
exercise, morning to night and back to morning again. I can't sleep,
I can't eat, I can't ball the girls in the brothel and my cigarettes taste
like shit. And do you know why? Do you?"

Suddenly his voice had risen to a roar and the door popped
open so that I could see the burnished faces of the two bodyguards
as they clutched at their waistbands for the heavy pistols they wore
there. "Bastiano!" he bellowed. "Bastiano Frigging C., that's why.

That's my problem. Not the cigarettes, not the booze, not the heart or the liver or the guts, but that bony pussy-licking son of a bitch Bastiano!"

A week later, in the middle of a consultation with Signora Trombetta over her hot flashes and crying spells, the door to my office burst open and there, looking like death in a dishpan, stood Bastiano C. I hadn't seen him in over a year, since I'd last treated him for intestinal worms, and, as with Santo R., I was stunned by his visible deterioration. Even as a boy he'd been thin, the sullen elder child of the village schoolmaster, all legs and arms, like a spider, but now it was as if the flesh had been painted on his bones. At five feet, nine inches tall, he must have weighed less than a hundred pounds. His two bodyguards, expressionless men nearly as emaciated as he, flanked him like slats in a fence. He gave a slight jerk of his neck, barely perceptible, and the widow Trombetta, though she was in her sixties and suffering from arthritis in every joint, scurried out the door as if she'd been set afire.

"Don C.," I said, peering at him through the upper portion of my bifocals, "how good to see you. And how may I help you?"

He said nothing, merely stood there in the doorway looking as if a breeze would blow him away if it weren't for the pistols, shivs and cartridges that anchored him to the floor. Another minute gesture, so conservative of energy, the merest flick of the neck, and the two henchmen melted away into the waiting room, the door closing softly behind them.

I cleared my throat. "And what seems to be the matter?" I asked in my most mellifluous, comforting tones, the tones I used on the recalcitrant child, the boy who doesn't like the look of the needle or the girl who won't stick out her tongue for the depressor.

Nothing.

The silence was unlike him. I'd always known him as a choleric personality, quick to speak his mind, exchange insults, fly into a rage—both in the early days of our acquaintance, when he was a spoiled boy living at home with his parents, and afterward, when he began to make his mark on the world, first as a *campiere* on the

Buschetta estate and later as a man of respect. He wasn't one to hold anything back.

I rearranged the things on my desk, took off my glasses and wiped them with my handkerchief. Bastiano C. was twenty-six or twenty-seven years old, somewhere in that range, and his medical history had been unremarkable as far as I could recall. Oh, there had been the usual doses of clap, the knife and gun wounds, but nothing that could begin to explain the physical shambles I now saw before me. I listened to the clock in the square toll the hour—it was 4:00 P.M. and hotter than even Dante could have imagined— and then I tried one last time. "So, Don C., you're not feeling well. Would you like to tell me about it?"

The man's face was sour, the gift of early handsomeness pressed from it like grappa from the dregs. He scratched his rear casually, then took a seat as if he were stuffed with feathers, and leaned forward. "Pepto-Bismol," he said in the moist high-pitched tones that made it seem as if he were sucking his words like lozenges. "I live Pepto-Bismol. I breathe it, drink it by the quart, it runs through my veins. I even shit pink."

"Ah, it's your stomach, then," I said, rising now, the stethoscope dangling from my neck, but he gestured for me to remain seated. He wasn't yet ready to reveal himself, to become intimate with my diagnostic ways.

"I am telling you, Doctor," he said, "I do not eat, drink, smoke; my taste is gone and my pleasure in things is as dead as the black cat we nailed over Miraglia Sciacca's door. I take two bites of pasta with a little butter and grated Romano and it's like they stabbed me in my guts." He looked miserably at the floor and worked the bones of his left wrist till they clicked like dice thrown against a wall. "And do you know why?" he demanded finally.

I didn't know, but I certainly had a suspicion.

"Santo R.," he said, slowing down to inject some real venom into his voice. "The fat-ass bastard."

That night, over a mutton chop and a bowl of bean soup, I consulted my housekeeper about the situation. Santuzza is an ignorant woman, crammed from her toes to her scalp with the superstitious claptrap that afflicts the Sicilian peasantry like a congenital defect (I once caught her rubbing fox fat on her misshapen feet and saying a Salve Regina backwards in a low moaning singsong voice), but she has an uncanny and all-encompassing knowledge of the spats, feuds and sex scandals not only of Partinico but of the entire Palermo province. The minute I leave for the office, the telephone receiver becomes glued to the side of her head—she cooks with it in place, sweeps, does the wash and changes the sheets, and all the while the pertinacious voice of the telephone buzzes in her ear. All day long it's gossip, gossip, gossip.

"They had a falling-out," Santuzza said, putting a loaf in front of me and refilling my glass from the carafe on the sideboard. "They were both asked to be a go-between in the dispute of Gaspare Pantaleo and Miraglia Sciacca."

"Ah," I murmured, breaking off a crust and wiping it thoughtfully round the rim of my plate, "I should have known."

As Santuzza told it, the disaffection between Pantaleo and Sciacca, tenant farmers on the C. and R. estates, respectively, arose over a question of snails. It had been a dry year following hard on the heels of the driest year anyone could remember, and the snails hadn't appeared in any numbers during the previous fall. But recently we'd had a freak rain, and Gaspare Pantaleo, a poor man who has to do everything in his power to make ends meet, went out to gather snails for a stew to feed his children. He knew a particular spot, high on the riverbank where there was a tumble of stones dumped to prevent erosion, and though it was on private property, the land belonged neither to the C. nor R. family holdings. Miraglia Sciacca discovered him there. Apparently Sciacca knew of this spot also, a good damp protected place where the snails clumped together in bunches in the cracks between the rocks, and he too had gone out to collect snails for a stew. His children—there were eight of them, and each with an identical cast in the right eye—were hungry too, always hungry. Like Pantaleo, he lived close to the bone, hunting snails, frogs, elvers and songbirds, gathering borage and wild

asparagus and whatnot to stretch his larder. Well, they had words
over the snails, one thing led to another, and when Miraglia Sciacca
came to he was lying in the mud with maybe a thousand snails
crushed into his groin.

Two days later he marched up to the Pantaleo household with
an antiquated carbine and shot the first two dogs he saw. Gaspare
Pantaleo's brother Filippo retaliated by poisoning the Sciacca family's pig, and then Rosario Bontalde, Miraglia Sciacca's uncle by marriage, sent a fifteen-pound wheel of cheese to the Pantaleos as an
apparent peace offering. But the cheese was hexed—remember, this
is Santuzza talking—and within the week Girolama Pantaleo, Gaspare's eldest daughter and one of the true and astonishing beauties
of the province, lost all her hair. Personally, I suspected ringworm
or perhaps a dietary deficiency, but I didn't want to distract Santuzza, so I ate my soup and said nothing.

Things apparently came to a head when Gaspare Pantaleo
stormed up the road to the Sciacca place to demand that the hex
be lifted—the cheese they'd disposed of, but in such cases the hex,
Santuzza assured me, lingers in all who've eaten of it. At the time,
Miraglia Sciacca was out in the yard, not five paces from the public
street, splitting olive wood so he could stack it against the fence for
the coming winter. "You're a fraud and a pederast," Gaspare Pantaleo accused in a voice the neighbors could hear half a mile away,
"and I demand that you take the hex off that cheese."

Miraglia's only response was a crude epithet.

"All right then, you son of a bitch, I'll thrash it out of you,"
Gaspare roared, and he set his hand down on the fence post to hoist
himself over, and that was when Miraglia Sciacca, without so much
as a hitch in his stroke, brought the ax down and took Gaspare
Pantaleo's right hand off at the wrist. That was bad enough, but it
wasn't the worst of it. What really inflamed the entire Pantaleo clan,
what drove them to escalate matters by calling in Don Bastiano C.
as mediator, was that the Sciaccas wouldn't return the hand. As
Santuzza had it from Rosa Giardini, an intimate of the Sciaccas,
Miraglia kept the hand preserved in a jar on the mantelpiece, taking

it down at the slightest excuse to show off to his guests and boast
of his prowess.

Three weeks passed and the sun held steady in the sky, though
by now we should have been well into the rains, and I heard nothing
of the feuding parties. I saw Santo R. one evening as I was sitting
in the cafe, but we didn't speak—he was out in the street, along
with his two elephantine bodyguards, bending painfully to inspect
the underside of his car for explosives before lumbering into the
driver's seat, firing up the ignition and roaring away in a cyclone of
leaves and whirling trash. It was ironic to think that snails had been
the cause of all this misunderstanding and a further burden to the
precarious health of the two men of respect, Don Santo R. and Don
Bastiano C., because now you couldn't find snails for love or money.
Not a trattoria, cafe or street vendor offered them for sale, and the
unseasonable sun burned like a cinder in the sky.

It was a festering hot day toward the end of November, no rain
in sight and the sirocco tearing relentlessly at the withered branches
of the trees, when Santo R. next showed up at my office. Business
was slow—the season of croup and bronchitis, head colds and flu
depended upon the rains as much as the snails did—and I was gazing out the window at a pair of buzzards spiraling over the slaugh-
terhouse when he announced himself with a delicate little cough.
"Don R.," I said, rising to greet him with a smile, but the smile must
have frozen on my face—I was shocked at the sight of him. If he'd
looked bad a month ago, bloated and pale and on the verge of collapse, now he was so swollen I could think of nothing so much as a
sausage ready to burst its skin on the grill.

"Doctor," he rasped, and his face was like chalk beside the
ruddy beef of the bodyguard who supported him, "I don't feel so
good." Through the open door I could see Crocifissa making the
sign of the cross. The second bodyguard was nowhere to be seen.

Alarmed, I hurried out from behind the desk and helped the
remaining henchman settle Don R. in the chair. Don R.'s fingers
were so puffed up as to be featureless, and I saw that he'd removed
the laces of his shoes to ease the swelling of his feet—this was no

mere obesity, but a sign that something was desperately wrong. Generalized edema, difficulty breathing, cardiac arrhythmia—the man was a walking time bomb. "Don R.," I said, bending forward to listen to the fitful thump and wheeze of his heart, "you've been taking your medication, haven't you?" I'd prescribed nitroglycerine for the angina, a diuretic and Aldomet for hypertension, and strictly warned him against salt, alcohol, tobacco and saturated fats.

Santo's eyes were closed. He opened them with a grunt of command, made eye contact with the bodyguard and ordered him from the room. When the door had closed, he let out a deep, world-weary sigh. "A good man, Francesco," he said. "He's about all I have left. I had to send my wife and kids away till this blows over, and Guido, my other man, well"—he lifted his hand and let it drop like a guillotine—"no one lives forever."

"Listen to me, Don R.," I said, stern now, my patience at an end, "you haven't been taking your medication, have you?"

No reaction. I might as well have been addressing a stump, a post in the ground.

"And the alcohol, the cigarettes, the pastries and all the rest?"

A shrug of the shoulders. "I'm tired, Doctor," he said.

"Tired?" I was outraged. "I should think you'd be tired. Your system's depleted. You're a mess. You're taking your life in your hands just to mount a flight of stairs. But you didn't come here for lectures, and I'm not going to give you one—no, I'm going to lift up that telephone receiver on the desk and call the hospital. You're checking in this afternoon."

The eyes, which had fallen shut, blinked open again. "No, Doctor," he rasped, and his words came in a slow steady procession, "you're not going to touch that telephone. Do you know how long I'd last in a hospital? Were you born yesterday? Bastiano'd have me strung up like a side of beef before the night was out."

"But your blood pressure is through the roof, you, you—"

"Fuck blood pressure."

There was a silence. The sirocco, so late for the season, rattled the panes of the window. The overhead fan creaked on its bearings. After a moment he spoke, and his voice was thick with emotion.

"Doctor," he began, "Doctor, you've known me all my life—I'm not thirty yet and I feel like I'm a hundred. Do you know what it takes to be a man of respect in this country, do you?" His voice broke. "All the beatings, the muggings, the threats and kidnappings, cutting off the heads of the dogs and horses, nailing the cats to the walls . . . I tell you, Doctor, I tell you: it takes a toll on a man."

He was about to go on when a noise from the outer room froze him—it was nothing, barely audible above the wind, the least gurgle in the throat, but it was enough. With a swiftness that astonished me, he was up from the chair, the pistol clenched in his hand. I heard Crocifissa suddenly, a truncated cry, and then the door flew open and there stood Bastiano C., one hand clutching a gleaming silver snub-nosed revolver, the other pinned to his gut.

This was the longest moment of my life. It seemed to play out over the course of an hour, but in reality, the whole thing took no more than a minute or two. Behind Bastiano, I could make out the sad collapsed form of Santo's bodyguard, stretched out like a sea lion on the beach, a wire garrote sunk into the fleshy folds of his throat. Beneath him, barely visible, lay the expiring sticklike shadow of Bastiano's remaining bodyguard—Bastiano too, as it turned out, had lost one to the exigencies of war. Crocifissa, wide-eyed and with a fist clamped to her mouth, sat at her desk in shock.

And Bastiano—he stood there in the doorway nearly doubled over with abdominal pain, more wasted even than he'd been three weeks earlier, if that was possible. The pistol was leveled on Santo, who stood rigid at the back of the room, heaving for breath like a cart horse going up the side of Mount Etna. Santo's pistol, a thing the size of a small cannon, was aimed unflinchingly at his antagonist. "Son of a whore," Bastiano breathed in his wet slurping tones. There was no flesh to his face, none at all, and his eyes were glittering specks sunk like screws in his head.

"*Puttana!*" Santo spat, and he changed color twice—from parchment white to royal *pomodoro*—with the rush of blood surging through his congested arteries.

"Now I am going to kill you," Bastiano whispered, even as he clutched with his left hand at the place where his ulcers had eaten through the lining of his stomach and the surrounding vessels that were quietly filling his body cavity with blood.

"In a pig's eye," Santo growled, and it was the last thing he ever said, because in that moment, even as he wrapped his bloated finger round the trigger and attempted to squeeze, his poor congested fat-clogged heart gave out and he died before my eyes of a massive coronary.

I went to him, of course, my own heart pounding as if it would burst, but even as I bent over him I was distracted by a noise from Bastiano—a delicate little sigh that might have come from a schoolgirl surprised by love—and I glanced up in confusion to see his eyes fall shut as he pitched face-forward onto the linoleum. Though I tried with all my power, I couldn't revive him, and he died that night in a heavily guarded room at the Ospedale Regionale.

I don't know what it was, and I don't like to speculate, being a man of science, but the rains came three days later. Santuzza claimed it was a question of propitiating the gods, of bloodletting, of settling otherworldly accounts, but the hidebound and ignorant will have their say. At any rate, a good portion of the district turned out for the funerals, held on the same day and at the same cemetery, while the rain drove down as if heaven and earth had been reversed. Don Bastiano C.'s family and retainers were careful not to mingle with Don Santo R.'s, and the occasion was somber and without incident. The snails turned out, though, great snaking slippery chains of them, mounting the tombstones in their legions and fearlessly sailing the high seas of the greening grass. The village priest intoned the immortal words, the widows wept, the children huddled beneath their umbrellas and we buried both men, if not with pomp and circumstance, then at least with a great deal of respect.

ACTS OF GOD

HE'D BEEN MARRIED BEFORE, and now he was married again. The last wife, Dixie, had taken the house, the car, the dog, the blender and his collection of Glenn Miller and Tommy Dorsey records. The wife before that, Margot, had been his first, and he'd known her since he'd worn shoulder pads and spikes and she cried out his name from the sidelines, her big chocolate eyes wide with excitement and the black bobbed hair cutting a Spanish fringe across her brow; she'd taken the first house, the children and his self-respect. Muriel was different. She was a force upon the earth, an act of God, demanding, unshakable, born a queen, an empress, born to dictate and command. She took everything that was left.

And there wasn't a whole lot of that. Willis was seventy-five years old—seventy-six, come October—he had some money in CDs and an undeveloped lot or two, he owned a pair of classic 1972 Ford Fairlanes—"classic" being a code word for junk—and he was so weak in the hips he had to work on his feet for fear he wouldn't be able to get up again once he sat down. And work he did. He was a builder, a master builder, and he'd been in the trade for sixty years, working with the pride and compulsion his mother had instilled in him in a bygone era. No retirement villages for him, no putting greens or clubhouses. If you're not working you might as well be dead, that's how he saw it. And it wasn't as if he had a choice—Muriel would never let him retire, or rest even. She worked him like a mule and he bowed his head and did what was expected of him.

For her part, Muriel had been married four times, counting the present arrangement. She'd pretty well forgotten the middle two husbands—tired men, tired under the eyes, in the blood, in bed—but the first had been a saint. Handsome, a saxophone player with wavy dark hair and a perfect little Ronald Colman mustache—and rich, too. His father owned a whole constellation of rental properties and a resort in the Catskills, with a lake and a casino and quaint little bungalows that looked as if they'd been lifted off their foundations in the English countryside and transported, lock, stock and barrel, to Gaudinet Lake. The shoulders on that man, Lester Gaudinet . . . she didn't know why she'd ever divorced him. Of course, she had Willis now, and he was all right—if she kept after him. Still, as she sat through the long afternoons with a bottle of Petite-Sirah, clipping things from the newspaper, baking roasts and hams and pies enough for an army though she wouldn't eat two bites herself and Willis, even with his appetite, couldn't begin to make a dent in them, she couldn't help pining, just a bit, for Lester Gaudinet and the lilting breathy rhapsody of his saxophone, and she couldn't help feeling that at sixty-eight, life had begun to pass her by.

It was a close brooding morning in late September, and Willis was up at six, as usual, washing last night's dishes, sweeping up, sneaking a half-eaten leg of lamb coated with a greenish fluorescent fuzz into the trash. He fetched the newspaper from the front lawn and was about to sit down over a cup of coffee and a slice of toast when he discovered that they were out of Vita-Health Oat Bran Nutri-Nugget bread. Each morning for her breakfast, which Willis prepared with care and trepidation before hurrying off to the job site, Muriel had two slices, lightly toasted and dry, of Vita-Health Oat Bran Nutri-Nugget bread with a two-minute, twenty-seven-second egg, six ounces of fresh-squeezed Florida orange juice and three thimble-sized cups of espresso. If she was difficult in the evening, when all he wanted was to collapse in front of the TV with a tall scotch and water, she was impossible in the morning, crawling out of the blood-red cave of her insomniac's sleep like a lioness poked with a stick, and he'd long since learned the survival value of presenting her with the placebo of a flawless breakfast. Willis squinted in vain into the cavernous depths of the breadbox and understood that he had a full-blown crisis on his hands.

A sunless dawn was breaking beyond the windows and it filled the kitchen with a sick hopeless light. For a moment Willis stood there at the counter, gaping round him as if he didn't recognize the place, and then he got hold of himself and fastened on the thought of the twenty-four-hour Quick-Stop on the corner. Would they have it? Not a chance, he decided, mentally browsing the bright but niggardly shelves—beer they had, yes, cigarettes, pornographic magazines, candy, videotape, gum—but who needed bread? He could already picture the six stale loaves of Wonder bread stiffening in their wrappers, but he fished his Mets cap out of the closet, stepped out the front door and crossed the dewy lawn to the car, figuring he had nothing to lose.

Outside, as he stood fumbling with the keys at the door of Muriel's car—they called it Muriel's car because she'd insisted on buying the thing though she'd been raised in the city and had never been behind the wheel of a car in her life—he was struck by something in the air. What was it? There was a raw smell of the ocean, much stronger than usual, and the atmosphere seemed to brood over him, heavy, damp, the pull and tug of a thousand tiny fingers. And the birds—where were the birds? There was no sound except for the rattle of a truck out on the highway . . . but then he really didn't have time to dawdle and smell the breeze and linger over the little mysteries of life like some loopy-eyed kid on his way to school, and he ducked into the car, fired up the mufflerless engine with a roar and shriek that set every dog in the neighborhood howling—and there was noise now, noise to spare—and rumbled up the road for the Quick-Stop.

The man behind the counter gave a violent start when Willis stepped through the door but relaxed almost immediately—the store had been robbed once or twice a week for as long as Willis could remember, and he supposed they had a right to be nervous. He shuffled up to the counter, patting his pockets unconsciously to locate his wallet, keys and checkbook, and said, "Bread?," making a question of it. The clerk was small, slight, dark-skinned, and he peered up at Willis in mute incomprehension, as if he'd been speaking another language, which in fact he had: Willis didn't know what the man was—Pakistani, Puerto Rican or Pathan—but it was apparent that English was not his first language. *"Pan?"* Willis tried, tossing out a nugget of the Spanish he'd picked up in Texas during the war. The man stared at him out of deep-set eyes. He must have been twenty-one—he'd have to be to work here—but to Willis, from the perspective of his accumulating years, the man was a boy, absurdly young, twelve, ten years old, a baby. The boy/man raised a languid arm and pointed, and Willis moved off in the direction indicated. Pasta, kitty litter, nachos . . . and there it was, sure enough—bread, sandwiched between the suntan oil and disposable diapers. A sad little collection of hot-dog buns, pita bread, tortillas and a single fortified nut loaf greeted him: there was no Vita-Health Oat Bran Nutri-Nugget bread. What did he expect, miracles?

When he shuffled back into the kitchen, running late now, the fortified nut loaf tucked like a football under his arm, he had a shock: Muriel was up. There were telltale traces of her on the counter, at the door of the refrigerator and on the base of the coffeemaker. He saw where yesterday's grounds had been flung at the trash can and dribbled down the wall behind it, saw where she'd set her cup down on the stove and where she'd torn through the cabinet in search of her pills and artificial sweetener; in the same moment the muted rumble of the TV came to him from the next room. He was fumbling with the espresso machine, hurrying, the framers due at seven-thirty and the plumber at eight, when she appeared in the doorway.

Muriel's face composed itself around the point of her Scotch-Irish nose and the tight little pout of her stingy lips. She was short and busty, and the tips of her toes peeked out from beneath the hem of her nightgown. "Where the hell have you been?" she demanded.

He turned to the stove. A jolt of pain shot through his hips—there was weather coming, he could feel it. "We were out of bread, sweetie," he said, presenting the side of his face to her as he spooned the eggs from their shells. "I had to go down to the Quick-Stop."

This seemed to placate her, and she subsided into the living room and huddled over her coffee mug in front of the TV screen. Willis could see the TV from the kitchen, where he popped the toast, brewed the espresso and squeezed the oranges. A chirpy woman with a broad blond face and hair that might have been spun sugar was chirping something about weight loss and a new brand of cracker made from seaweed. Willis arranged Muriel's things on a tray and brought them in to her.

She gave him a hard look as he set the tray down on the coffee table, but then she smiled and grabbed his arm to pull his face down, peck him a kiss and tell him how much he spoiled her. "Got to go, sweetie," he murmured, already backing away, already thinking of the car, the road, the house by the ocean that was rising before his eyes like a dream made concrete.

"You'll be home for lunch?"

"Yes, sweetie," he murmured, and then he made a fatal miscalculation: he lingered there before the glowing ball of the TV. The weatherman, in a silly suit and bow tie and mugging like a shill, had replaced the chirping confection of a woman, and Willis lingered— he'd smelled the weather on the air and felt it in his hips, and he was briefly curious. After all, he was going to be out in it all day long.

It was at that moment that Muriel's cry rose up out of the depths of the couch as from the ringside seats at a boxing match— harsh, querulous, the voice of disbelief and betrayal. "And what do you call *this*?" she boomed, nullifying the weatherman, his maps and pointers and satellite photos, the TV itself.

"What, sweetie?" Willis managed, his voice a small scuttling thing receding into its hole. The windows were gray. The weatherman blathered about wind velocity and temperature readings.

"This, this *toast.*"

"They didn't have your bread, sweetie, and Waldbaum's won't be open for another hour yet—"

"You son of a bitch." Suddenly she was on her feet, red-faced and panting for breath. "Didn't I tell you I wanted to go shopping last night? Didn't I tell you I needed things?"

They'd been together for two years now, and Willis knew there was no reasoning with her, not at this hour, not before she'd had her eggs and toast, not before she'd been sedated by the parade of game shows and soap operas that marched relentlessly through her mornings. All he could do was slump his shoulders penitently and edge toward the door.

But she anticipated him, darting furiously at him and crying, "That's right, leave me, go on off to work and leave me here, you son of a bitch!" She was in a mood, she could do anything, he knew it, and he shrank away from her as she changed course suddenly, jerked back from him and snatched up the breakfast tray in an explosion of crockery, cutlery and searing black liquid. "Toast!" she shrieked, "you call this toast!?" And then, as he watched in horror, the tray itself sailed across the room like a heat-seeking missile, sure and swift, dodging the lamp and coasting over the crest of the couch to discover its inevitable target in the grinning, winking, pointer-wielding image of the weatherman.

Later, after Willis had gone off to work and Muriel had had a chance to calm herself and reflect on the annihilation of the TV and the espresso stains on the rug, she felt ashamed and repentant. She'd let her nerves get the better of her and she was wrong, she'd be the first to admit it. And not only that, but who had she hurt but herself—it was like murdering her only friend, cutting herself off from the world like a nun in a convent—worse: at least a nun had her prayers. The repairman—in her grief and confusion she very nearly dialed 911, and she was so distraught when she finally got through to him that he was there before a paramedic would even have got his jacket on—the repairman told her it was hopeless. The picture tube was shot and the best thing to do was just go out to Caldor and buy herself a new set, and then he named half-a-dozen Japanese brands and she lost control all over again. She'd be god-damned and roasted three times over in hell before she'd ever buy anything from a Jap after what they did to her brother in the war and what was he, the repairman, an American or what? Didn't he know how they laughed at us, the Japs? He hit his van on the run and didn't look back.

It was 10:00 A.M. Willis was at work, the weather was rotten and she was missing "Hollywood Squares" and couldn't even salve her hurt with the consolation of shopping—not till Willis came home, anyway. God, he was such a baby, she thought as she sat there at the kitchen table over a black and bitter cup of espresso. He'd been a real mess when she'd met him—the last wife had squeezed him like a dishrag and hung him out to dry. His clothes were filthy, he was drunk from morning till night, he'd been fired from his last three jobs and the car he was driving was like a coffin on wheels. She'd made a project of him. She'd rescued him, given him a home and clean underwear and hankies, and if he thanked her a hundred times a day it wouldn't be enough. If she kept the reins tight, it was because she had to. Let him go—even for an hour—and he'd come home three days later stinking of gin and vomit.

The house was silent as a tomb. She gazed out the window; the clouds hung low and roiled over the roof, strung out like sausage, like entrails, black with blood and bile. There was a storm watch on, she'd heard that much on the "Morning" show, and again she felt a tug of regret over the TV. She wanted to get up that minute and turn on the news channel, but the news channel was no more—not for her, at any rate. There was the radio—and she experienced a sudden sharp stab of nostalgia for her girlhood and the nights when the whole family would crowd around the big Emerson console and listen to one program after another—but these days she never listened; it just gave her a headache. And with Willis around, who needed another headache?

She thought of the newspaper then and pushed herself up from the table to poke through the living room for it—if there was anything serious, a hurricane or something, they'd have a story on the front page. She was thinking about that, fixating on the newspaper, and she forgot all about the TV, so that when she stepped through the door, the sight of it gave her a shock. She'd swept up the broken glass, feeling chastened and heartbroken, but now the shattered screen accused her all over again. Guiltily, she shuffled through the heap of papers and magazines stuffed under the coffee table, then

poked through the bedroom and finally went outside to comb the
front lawn. No newspaper. Of all days, Willis must have taken it to
work with him. And suddenly, standing there on the hushed and
gray lawn in her housecoat and slippers, she was furious again. The
son of a bitch. He never thought of her, never. Now she had the
whole drizzling black miserable day ahead of her—TV-less, friend-
less, joyless—and she didn't even have the consolation of the
newspaper.

While she was standing there out front of the house, poking
halfheartedly under the bushes and noticing how shabby a job the
gardener had done—and he'd hear from her, by god he would—a
big brown UPS van glided into the driveway with a gentle sigh
of the brakes. The driver was a young man, handsome, broad-
shouldered, and for a minute she had a vision of Lester Gaudinet
as he was all those many years ago. Lester Gaudinet. And where was
he now? God knew if he was even alive still . . . but how she'd like
to see him, wouldn't that be something?

"Mrs. Willis Blythe?" The man had crossed the lawn and he
stood at her elbow now, a parcel tucked under his arm.

"Yes," she said, and the wind came up and took her hair out of
its bun.

The man held out a clipboard to her, pages flapping. "Sign
here," he said, handing her a pen, and she saw a list of names and
signatures and the big red X he'd scrawled beside the space for her
name.

She took the clipboard from him and smiled up into his sea-
green eyes, into Lester's eyes, and she couldn't help trying to hold
on to the moment. "Rotten day," she said.

He looked tense, anxious, looked as if he were about to lunge
out of the blocks and disappear down a cinder track. "Hurricane
weather," he said. "Supposed to miss us except for some rain later
on—that's what the radio says, anyway."

She held the clipboard in her hand still and she bent forward
to sign the form, but then a thought occurred to her and she straightened up again. "Hurricanes," she said with a little snort of contempt.
"And I suppose it's called Bill or Fred or something like that—not

like in the old days, when they had the sense to name them after women. It's a shame, isn't it?"

The UPS man was shuffling his feet on the spongy carpet of the lawn. "Yeah," he said, "sure—but would you sign, please, ma'am? I've got—"

She held up her hand to forestall him. God, he was handsome—the image of Lester. Of course, Lester had the mustache and he was taller and his eyes were prettier, brighter somehow . . . "I know, I know—you've got a million deliveries to make." She gave him a bright steady look. "It's women that're like hurricanes, they used to understand that"—was she flirting with him? Yes, of course she was—"but now it's Hurricane Tom, Dick or Harry. It just makes you sick, doesn't it?"

"Yeah," he said, "I know, but—"

"Okay, okay already, I'm signing." She inscribed his delivery sheet for him in the neat geometric script she'd mastered in parochial school in another age and then turned her coquette's smile on him—why not, was she so old it was impossible? Not in this world, not with the things that went on on TV these days. She touched his arm and held it a moment as he handed her the package. "Thank you," she murmured. "You're so handsome, do you know that?"

And then he stood there like an oaf, like a schoolboy, and he actually blushed. "Yes, yes," he stammered, "I mean no, I mean thank you," and then he was darting across the lawn with his clipboard flapping and the wind took her hair again. "Have a nice day!" she called, but he didn't hear her.

Inside, she examined the package briefly—*The Frinstell Corporation,* the label read—and then she went into the sewing room to fetch her scissors. The Frinstell Corporation, she thought, running it over in her mind, and what was this all about? She was forever clipping things out of magazines and sending away for them—once-in-a-lifetime offers and that sort of thing—but Frinstell didn't ring a bell. It took her a moment, the scissors gleaming dully in the crepuscular light of the kitchen, and then she had the tape slit up the seam and she was digging through the welter of tissue paper stuffed inside. And there—oh yes, of course—there was her genuine

U.S.-Weather-Service-Approved Home Weather Center mounted on a genuine polished-walnut veneer plaque—thermometer, barometer and humidity gauge all in one—with a lifetime guarantee.

It was a pretty sort of thing, she thought, holding it up to admire it. Polished brass, good bold figures and hash marks you didn't need binoculars to read, made in the U.S. of A. It would look nice up on the wall over the fireplace—or maybe in the dining room; the walnut would match the color of the dining set, wouldn't it? She was on her way into the dining room, the genuine Home Weather Center in hand, when she noticed that the barometer needle was stuck all the way down in the left-hand corner. Pinned. She shook it, patted the glass lens. Nothing. It was stuck fast.

Suddenly she couldn't help herself—she could feel the rage coming up on her, a rage as inevitable and relentless as the smashing of the sea on the rocks—and how many pills had she swallowed and how many doctors, not to mention husbands, had tried to quell it? The Frinstell Corporation. Cheats and con artists, that's what they were. You couldn't get anything anymore that wasn't a piece of junk and no wonder America was the laughingstock of the world. Not ten seconds out of the box and it was garbage already. She was seething. It was all she could do to keep from smashing it against the wall, stamping it underfoot—dope addicts, hopheads, the factories were full of them—but then she remembered the TV and she held on till the first hot wave of fury passed over her.

All right, she would be rational about it, she would. It had a lifetime guarantee, didn't it? But what a joke, she thought bitterly, and again she had to restrain herself from flinging the thing into the wall—a glass of wine, that's what she needed. Yes. To calm her. And then she'd wrap the thing up in the box and send it right back to the bastards—they'd see how fast their own shit came sailing back to them, they'd see whether they could put anything over on her . . . she'd have Willis down at the post office the minute he came in the door. And she'd be damned if she'd pay postage on it either. *Return to Sender*, that's how she'd mark it. *Damaged in Transit, Take Your Garbage and*—

But then she glanced up at the clock. It was quarter to twelve

already and he'd be home any minute now. Suddenly all the rage
she'd generated over the Frinstell Corporation was gone, extinguished as quickly as it had arisen, and she felt a wild rush of affection for her man, her husband, for Willis—the poor guy, out there
in all kinds of weather, working like a man half his age, providing
for her and protecting her . . . and she'd been hard on him at
breakfast, she had. What he needed was a nice lunch, she decided,
a nice hot lunch. She set the Home Weather Center back in the
box as gently as if she were lowering a baby into its crib, and then
she wrapped the package up again, retaped the seams, and went to
the cupboard. She poured herself a glass of wine from the jug and
then fastened on a can of split-pea-and-ham soup—she'd heat that
for Willis, and she'd make him a nice egg salad on toast. . . .

Toast. But they were out of bread, weren't they? There was
nothing but that sawdust-and-nut crap he'd tried to pawn off on her
for breakfast. She thought about that for a moment and a black cloud
seemed to rise up before her. And then, before she knew it, the fury
of the morning swept over her again, the tragedy of the TV and the
cheat of the Home Weather Center doubling it and redoubling it,
and by the time she heard Willis's key turn in the lock, she was
smoldering like Vesuvius.

If she was testy in the morning, if she lashed into him for no
reason and jumped down his throat at the slightest provocation, by
lunchtime she was inevitably transformed, so that an all-embracing
cloud of maternal sweetness wrapped him up as he stepped through
the door, and then ushered him out again, half an hour later, with
a series of tender lingering hugs, squeezes and back pats. That was
the usual scenario, but today was different. Willis sensed it even
before he shambled down the hallway to discover her in the kitchen
fussing over a can of soup and a box of saltines. He saw that she
was still in her nightdress and housecoat, a bad sign, and he recognized the stunned, hurt, put-upon look in her eyes. He just stood
there at the kitchen door and waited.

"Willis, oh, Willis," she sighed—or no, moaned, bleated, wailed
as if all the trials of Job had been visited on her in the five hours

since he'd seen her last. He knew the tone and knew it was trouble—anything could have set her off, from a stopped-up drain to the war in Bosnia or teary memories of her first husband, the saint. "Honey," she cried, crossing the room to catch him up in an embrace so fierce it nearly ruptured his kidneys, "you've got to help me out—just a little favor, a tiny little one." Her voice hardened almost imperceptibly as she clung to him and swayed back and forth in a kind of dance of grief: "Everything is just so, so *rotten*."

He was seventy-five years old and he'd been working since the day he climbed out of the cradle. Most men his age were dead. He was tired. His hips felt as if an army of mad acupuncturists had been driving hot needles into them. All he wanted was to sit down.

"Honey, here," she said, cooing now, nothing but concern, and she led him awkwardly to the table, still half-clinging to him. "Sit down and eat; poor man, you're probably starved. And exhausted, too. Is it raining out there?"

It was a question that didn't require an answer, a variant on her luncheon monologue, a diversion to distract him from the true subject at hand, the crisis, whatever it was—the shattered TV screen, was that it?—the crisis which required his immediate attention and expertise. And no, it wasn't raining, not yet, but it was blowing like holy hell out there and his morning had been an unmitigated disaster, a total waste of time. The framers hadn't showed—or the damn plumber, either—and he'd spent the whole morning in the skeleton of the house, which was already behind schedule, watching the wind whip the waves to a froth and batter the seawall as if it were made of cardboard instead of concrete. He'd called the sons of bitches five or six times from the pay phone out front of the bank, but they weren't answering. Pups, that's what they were, afraid of a little weather. He glanced up and the soup appeared on the table before him, along with a platter of sardines, six neat squares of cheddar, saltines, and a glass of apple juice. Muriel hovered over him.

He took a sip of the juice, fingered his spoon and set it down again. Why forestall the inevitable? "What's the trouble, sweetie?" he asked.

"I know you're not going to like this, but you're going to have to go to the post office for me."

"The post office?" He didn't want to go to the post office—he wanted to get back to the torn earth and wooden vertebrae of the rising house, to the mounds of rubble and refuse and the hot sudden smell of roofing tar. He thought of the doctor and his wife who'd hired him, a young couple in their forties, building their dream house by the sea. He'd promised them fifty-five hundred square feet with balconies, sundeck and wraparound view in six months' time— and here two months had gone by already and the damn frame wasn't even up yet. And Muriel wanted him to go to the post office.

"It's the Home Weather Center," she said. "It's got to go back. And I mean today, immediately, right now." Her voice threatened to ignite. "I won't have it here in the house another minute . . . if those bastards think they can—"

She was working herself up, her ire directed for the moment at the Home Weather Center, whatever that was, and the unnamed bastards, whoever they were, but he knew that if he didn't watch himself, if he didn't look sharp, the full weight of her outrage would shift to him with the sudden killing swiftness of an avalanche. He heard himself saying, "I'll take care of it, sweetie, don't you worry."

But when he glanced up to gauge her reaction, he found he was talking to himself: she'd left the room. Now what? There were sounds from the dining room—a fierce rending of tape and an impatient rustle of tissue paper, followed by the sharp tattoo of her approaching footsteps—and before he could lift the spoon to his lips she was back with a cardboard box the size of an ottoman. She swept across the room and dropped it on the table with a percussive thump that jarred the soup bowl and sent the juice swirling round the rim of the glass. Outside, the wind howled at the windows.

"Just look at this, will you?" she was saying, her elbows leaping as she tore the package open and extracted a long slim wooden plaque with three gleaming gauges affixed to it. He had a moment of enlightenment: the weather center. "Did you ever see such junk in your life?"

It looked all right to him. He wanted soup, he wanted sleep, he wanted the doctor's house to rise up out of the dunes and bravely confront the sea, perfect in every detail. "What's wrong with it, sweetie?"

"What's wrong with it?" Her voice jumped an octave. "Are you blind? Look at this"—a blunt chewed fingernail stabbed at the middle gauge—"that's what wrong. Junk. Nothing but junk."

He frowned over the thing while his soup got cold and then he fished his glasses out of his shirt pocket and studied it. The barometer needle was pinned all the way down at twenty-eight inches—he'd never seen anything like it. He lifted the plaque from the table and shook it. He inverted it. He tapped the glass. Nothing.

Muriel was seething. She went off into a tirade about con men, cheats, the Japanese and what they'd done to her brother, not to mention the American economy, and all he could do to calm her was agree with everything she said and croon "sweetie" over and over again till his soup turned gelid and he pushed himself up from the table, tucked the package under his arm, and headed out the door for the post office.

The wind was up, whipping the treetops like rags, and the smell of the ocean was stronger now, rank and enveloping, as if the bottom of the sea had turned over and littered the shore with its dead. A trash can skittered down the street and a shopping bag shot across the lawn to cling briefly to his ankles. As he settled into the car, the package beside him, the wind jerked the door out of his hand and he began to realize that there would be no more work today. At this rate he'd be lucky if what they'd put up so far was still there in the morning. No wonder the framers hadn't showed: this was a real blow.

He dodged trash-can lids and branches that glided magically across the road, the car pulling him along to the post office as faithfully as an old horse. The streets were deserted. He encountered exactly three other cars, all with their lights on and all going like hell. By the time he got to the traffic light outside the post office and sat there for an eternity watching the stoplight heave on its wires, it was so dark it might have been dusk. Maybe it was a hurricane after all, he thought, maybe that was it. He would have turned on the radio, but the damn thing had never worked to begin with, and then, two months ago, some jerk had smashed out the window on the driver's side and made off with it.

Sitting there watching the stoplight leap and sway over the deserted pavement, he felt a sudden sense of foreboding, a quick hot jolt of fear that made him gun the engine impatiently and inch forward into the intersection. He was thinking he'd better get home and see to the windows, see to Muriel—he'd been caught in a hurricane in Corpus Christi once and they'd been without lights or water for six days. He remembered an old woman sitting in the middle of a flooded street with a bloody strip of somebody's parlor curtains knotted round her head. That was an image. And he and his buddies with two cases of tequila they'd fished out of the wreckage of a liquor store. He'd better get home. He'd better.

But then the light changed and he figured he was here already and might as well take care of business—there'd be hell to pay at home if he didn't, hurricane or no—and he pulled into the lot, parked the car and reached for the package. Five minutes, that's all it would take. Then he'd be home.

As he came up the walk—and it was blowing now, Jesus, dirt or sand or something in his eyes—he saw the postmaster and a bearded guy with a ponytail scurrying around with a sheet of plywood big enough to seal off a shopping mall. The postmaster had a hammer in his hand and he was shouting something to the other one, but then a gust took hold of the plywood and sent them both sprawling into the bushes. Willis hunched himself and snatched at the Mets cap, but it was too late: it shot from his head and sailed up over the trees like a clay pigeon. Hurrying now, he fought his way through the heavy double doors and into the post office.

There was no one at the counter, no one waiting in line, no one in the building at all as far as he could see. The lights were all up full and the polished floor ran on down the corridor as usual, but the place was eerily silent. Outside, the sky raged at the plate-glass windows, a wild spatter of rain driving before it now. Willis hit the handbell, just to be sure no one was back there in the sorting room or on the toilet or something, and then he turned to go. Muriel would have to understand, that was all: they were closed down. There was a hurricane coming. He'd done all he could.

He'd just pulled back the inner door when the big plate-glass window in the lobby gave way with a pop like a champagne cork, followed by the splash of shattering glass. *Leave the damn package,* his brain told him, *drop it and get on home and lock yourself up in the basement with Muriel and the cat and a case of pork and beans,* but his legs failed him. He just stood there as a window shattered somewhere in the back and the lights faltered and then blew. "Hey, you, old man!" a voice was shouting, and there was the postmaster, right beside him, his face drawn and white, hair disheveled. The bearded man was with him and their eyes were jumping with excitement. In the next moment they had Willis by the arms, wind screaming in his ears; a flurry of white envelopes lifted suddenly into the air, and he was moving, moving fast, down a hallway and into the darkness and the quiet.

He could smell the postmaster and the other one, could smell the wet and the fear on them. Their breath came in quick greedy pants. Outside, way in the distance, he could hear the muted keening of the wind.

"Anybody got a match?" It was the postmaster's voice, a voice he knew from the roped-off line and the window and the gleaming tiled expanse of the lobby.

"Here," came another voice and a match flared to reveal the pockmarked face of the bearded man and a cement-block storage room of some kind, mailbags, cardboard boxes, heaps of paper.

The postmaster fumbled through a cabinet behind him and came up with a flashlight, one of those big boxy jobs with a lighthouse beam at one end and a little red emergency light at the other. He played it round the room, then set the flashlight down on a carton and cut the beam. The room glowed with an eerie reddish light. "Holy shit," he said, "did you see the way that window blew? You didn't get cut, did you, Bob?"

Bob answered in the negative.

"Man, we were lucky." The postmaster was a big bearish man in his fifties who'd worn a beard for years but now had the pasty stubbly look of a man newly acquainted with a razor. He paused. The wind screamed in the distance. "God, I wonder if Becky's okay—she was supposed to take Jimmy to the dentist, to the orthodontist, I mean—"

Bob said nothing, but then both of them turned to Willis, as if they'd just realized he was there.

"You okay?" the postmaster asked him.

"I'm all right," Willis said. He was, wasn't he? But what about the car? What about Muriel? "But listen, I've got to get home—"

The postmaster let out a little bark of a laugh. "Home? Don't you get it? That's Hurricane Leroy out there—you'll be lucky if you got a home left to go to—and whatever possessed you to come out in this mess? I mean, don't you listen to the TV? Christ," he said, as if that summed it all up.

There was a silence, and then, with a sigh, Bob eased himself back into a cradle of folded cardboard boxes. "Well," he said, and the faint red light glinted off the face of the pint bottle he extracted from his shirt, "we might as well enjoy ourselves—looks like we're going to be here a while."

Willis must have dozed. They'd passed the bottle and he'd got a good deep burning taste of whiskey—a taste Muriel denied him; she was worse than the Schick Center when it came to that, though she sipped wine all day herself—and then Bob had begun to drone on in a stopped-up, back-of-the-throat sort of voice, complaining about his marriage, his bad back, his sister on welfare and the way the cat sprayed the bedposts and the legs of the kitchen table, and Willis had found it increasingly difficult to focus on the glowing red beacon of the light. He was slouched over in a folding chair the postmaster had dragged in from one of the offices, and when awareness gripped him, Bob was enumerating the tragic flaws of the auto-insurance industry, his face ghastly in the hellish light. For a moment Willis didn't know where he was, but then he heard the wind in the distance and it all came back to him.

"With only two accidents, Bob? I can't believe it," the post-master said.

"Hell," Bob countered, "I'll show you the damn bill."

Willis tried to get up but his hips wouldn't allow it. "Muriel," he said.

The two faces turned to him then, the bearded one and the one that should have been bearded, and they looked strange and menacing in that unnatural light. "You all right, old-timer?" the post-master asked.

Willis felt like Rip Van Winkle, like Methuselah; he felt tired and hopeless, felt as if everything he'd known and done in his life had been wasted. "I've got to"—he caught himself; he'd been about to say *I've got to go home,* but they'd probably try to stop him and he didn't want any arguments. "I've got to take a leak," he said.

The postmaster studied him a moment. "It's still blowing out there," he said, "but the radio says the worst of it's past." Willis heard the faint whisper of the radio then—one of those little transistors the kids all wear; it was tucked into the postmaster's breast pocket. "Give it another hour," the postmaster said, "and we'll make sure you get home all right. And your car's okay, if that's what's worrying you. Nothing worse than maybe a branch on the roof."

Willis said nothing.

"Down the hall and to your left," the postmaster said.

It took him a moment to fight the inertia of his hips, and then he was emerging from the shadows of the storage room and into the somber gray twilight of the hallway. Nuggets of glass crunched and skittered underfoot and everything was wet. It was raining hard outside and there was that rank smell in the air still, but the wind seemed to have tapered off. He found the toilet and he kept on going.

The lobby was a mess of wet clinging paper and leaves, but the doors swung open without a hitch, and in the next moment Willis was out on the front steps and the rain was driving down with a vengeance on his bare bald head. He reached automatically for the Mets cap, but then he remembered it was gone, and he hunched his shoulders and started off across the parking lot. He moved cautiously, wary of the slick green welter of leaves and windblown debris underfoot, and he was wet through by the time he reached the car. A single crippled branch was draped over the windshield, but there was no damage; he swept it to the ground and ducked into the driver's seat.

His mind wasn't working well at this point—perhaps it was the shock of the storm or the effects of the whiskey and his nap in the folding chair. The keys. He fumbled twice through his pants and jacket before he finally found them, and then he flooded the engine and had to hold his foot to the floor while the starter whined and the rain smeared the windshield. Finally he got the thing going with a roar and jerked it into gear; it was then that he discovered the tree blocking the exit. And now what? The specter of Muriel rose before him, pale and trembling, and then he glanced up to see the postmaster and Bob planted on the steps and gawking at him as if he'd just dropped down from another planet. What the hell, he thought, and he gave them a jaunty wave, revved the engine and shot up over the curb and into the street.

But here the world was truly transformed. It was as if a big hand had swept the street, slapping down trees and telephone poles, obliterating windows, stripping shingles from the roofs. The road that led out to the highway was impassable, churning with shit-brown water and one of those little Japanese cars awash in it, overturned on its roof. Willis tried Meridian Street and then Seaboard, but both were blocked. An oak tree that must have been five hundred years old had taken the veranda out of the house where Joe Diggs had lived before he passed on, and there were live wires thrashing the shattered shaft of a telephone pole out front. Even through the tattoo of the rain on the roof Willis could hear the sirens, a continuous, drawn-out wail of grief.

He was worried now—this was as bad as Corpus Christi, worse—and his hands trembled on the wheel when he turned into his own street and found the entrance buried in rubble and vegetation. The house on the corner—the Needlemans'—was untouched, but across the street, on his side, the Stovers' place had lost its roof. And the street itself, the placid tree-lined street that had attracted Muriel in the first place, was unrecognizable, a double row of maples laid down flat like a deck of cards. Willis backed out of the street, water running up to his hubcaps, and made a left on Susan and then another left on Massapequa, trying to make it around the block and come up on the house from the far side.

He was in luck. Neither street seemed to have suffered much damage, and he was able to make his way round a fallen telephone pole at the entrance to Massapequa by climbing up over the curb as he'd done at the post office. And then he was turning into Laurel, his own street, dodging refuse and swinging wide to avoid the clogged storm drain at the corner. People were out on their lawns now, assessing the damage—he saw Mrs. Tilden or Tillotson or whatever her name was trying to brace up a cypress that clung to her front porch like a wet mustache. It was almost comical, that little woman and that big limp tree, and he began to relax—everything was going to be okay, it was, there was hardly any damage on this end—and there was the fat guy—what was his name?—holding his head and dancing round the carcass of his crushed Cadillac. Yes, he said aloud, everything's going to be all right, and he repeated it to himself, making a little prayer of it.

He was more afraid of Muriel now than of the storm—he could hear her already: how could he leave her in the middle of a hurricane? Where had he been? Was that liquor on his breath? The damage he could take care of—he was a builder, wasn't he? It was just a matter of materials, that was all—bricks, lumber, drywall, shingles. And glass. The glaziers would be busy, that was for sure. As he eased past a lawn mower standing forlornly in the middle of the street and crept round the big sweeping curve that gave him his first view of the house, he was expecting the worst—shutters gone, a hole in the roof, the elm lying atop the garage like a crippled beast—but the reality made his heart seize.

There was nothing there. Nothing. Where the house had stood not two hours ago, the elm towering over it, the two-car garage in back with his tools and workbench and all the rest, there was now a vacant lot. The yard had been swept clean but for the torn and crenellated foundation, filled with rubble like some ancient ruin.

Panic seized him, shock, and he hit the brake instinctively, sending the car into a fishtail that carried him across the street and slammed him into the curb with a jolt.

Trembling, he pried his fingers from the wheel. There was a throb of pain above his right eye where he'd hit the rearview mirror. His hands were shaking. But no, he thought, looking up again, it couldn't be. He was on the wrong street, that was it—he'd got turned around and fetched up in front of somebody else's place. It took him a moment, but then he swung the door open and stepped tentatively into the litter of the street, and there was the number on the curb to refute him, there the mailbox with his name stenciled across it in neat white letters, untouched, the red flag still standing tall. And that was the Novaks' place next door, no doubt about it, a sick lime green with pink trim. . . .

Then he thought of Muriel. Muriel. She was, she was . . . he couldn't form the thought, and he staggered across the lawn like a drunk to stand gaping into that terrible hole in the ground. "Muriel," he bleated, "Muriel!" and the rain drove down at him.

He stood there a long while, head bowed, feeling as old as the stones themselves, as old as the gashed earth and the dead gray sky. And then, the car still rumbling and stuttering behind him, he had the very first intimation of a thought that sparked and swelled till it glowed like a torch in his brain: *Dewar's and water.* He saw himself as he was when Muriel first found him, wedded to the leatherette stool at the Dew Drop Inn, and his lips formed the words involuntarily: "Make mine a Dewar's and water." The house was gone, but he'd lost houses before—mainly to wives, which were a sort of natural disaster anyway; that he could live with—and he'd lost wives, too, but never like this.

It hit him then, a wave of grief that started in his hips and crested in his throat: Muriel. He saw her vividly, the lunchtime Muriel who rubbed his shoulders and fussed over him, making those little crackers with anchovy paste and avocado . . . he saw her turning down the sheets on the bed at night, saw her frowning over a crossword puzzle, the glasses perched on the end of her nose—little things, homey things. With a pang he remembered the way she'd kid him over the TV programs or a football game and how she'd dance round the kitchen with a bottle of wine and a beef brisket studded with cloves of garlic . . . and now it was over. He was seventy-five—seventy-six, come October—and he stared into that pit and felt the icy breath of eternity on his face.

His jacket was wet through and his arms hung limp at his sides by the time he turned away and limped back over the sodden lawn, a soldier returning from the wars. He dragged himself across the street to the car, and all he could think of was Ted Casselman, down at the Dew Drop—he would know what to do—and he actually had the door open, one foot poised on the rocker panel, when he glanced up for a final bewildered look, and a movement on the Novaks' porch caught his eye. All at once the storm door swung back with a dull flash of light and there she was, Muriel, rescued from oblivion. She was in her housecoat still and it was bedraggled and wet, and her long white hair hung tangled round her shoulders so that she was like some old woman of the woods in a children's tale. Anna Novak hovered behind her, a tragic look pressed into the immobile Slavic folds of her eyes. Muriel just stood there, gazing across the street to where he hovered at the door of the car, half a beat from release.

The wind came up then and rattled the branches of the trees that were still standing. Someone was calling a dog up the street: "Hermie, Hermie! Here, baby!" The rain slackened. "Willis!" Muriel suddenly cried, "Willis!" and the spell was broken. She was coming down the steps, grand and invincible, her arms spread wide.

What could he do? He dropped his foot to the pavement, ignoring the pain that shot through his hip, and opened his arms to receive her.

BACK IN THE
EOCENE

Abscissa, ordinate, isosceles, Carboniferous, Mesozoic, holothurian: the terms come to him in a rush of disinterred syllables, a forgotten language conjured by the sudden sharp smell of chalk dust and blackboards. It happens every time. All he has to do is glance at the bicycle rack out front or the flag snapping crisply atop the gleaming aluminum pole, and the memories begin to wash over him, a typhoon of faces and places and names, Ilona Sharrow and Richie Davidson, Manifest Destiny, Heddy Grieves, the Sea of Tranquillity and the three longest rivers in Russia. He takes his daughter's hand and shuffles toward the glowing auditorium, already choked up.

Inside, it's worse. There, under the pale yellow gaze of the overhead lights, recognition cuts at him like a knife. It's invested in the feel of the hard steel frames and cushionless planks of the seats, in the crackling PA system and the sad array of frosted cupcakes and chocolate-chip cookies presided over by a puffy matron from the PTA. And the smells—Pine Sol, floor wax, festering underarms and erupting feet, a faint lingering whiff of meat loaf and wax beans. *Wax beans:* he hasn't had a wax bean, hasn't inserted a wax bean in his mouth, in what—twenty years? The thought overwhelms him and he stands there awkwardly a moment, just inside the door, and then there's a tug at his hand and his daughter slips away, flitting through the crowd like a bird to chase after her friends. He finds a seat in back.

The big stark institutional clock shows five minutes of eight. Settling into the unforgiving grip of the chair, he concentrates on the faces of his fellow parents, vaguely familiar from previous incarnations, as they trudge up and down the aisles like automatons. Voices buzz round him in an expectant drone. High heels click on the linoleum. Chairs scrape. He's dreaming a scene from another auditorium an ice age ago, detention hall, the soporific text, shouts from beyond the windows and a sharp sweet taste of spring on the air, when Officer Rudman steps up to the microphone.

A hush falls over the auditorium, the gale of chatter dropping off to a breeze, a stir in the rafters, nothing. His daughter, ten years old and beautiful, her feet too big and her shoulders slumped, strides up the aisle and drops into the chair beside him as if her legs have been shot out from under her. "Dad," she whispers, "that's Officer Rudman."

He nods. Who else would it be, up there in his spit and polish, his close-cropped hair and custom-fit uniform? Who else, with his sunny smile and weight lifter's torso? Who else but Officer Rudman, coordinator of the school's antidrug program and heartthrob of all the fifth-grade girls?

A woman with frosted hair and remodeled hips ducks in late and settles noiselessly into the chair in front of him. "Good evening," Officer Rudman says, "I'm Officer Rudman." Someone coughs. Feedback hisses through the speakers.

In the next moment they're rising clumsily in a cacophony of rustling, stamping and nose blowing, as Officer Rudman leads them in the Pledge of Allegiance. Hands over hearts, a murmur of half-remembered words. He's conscious of his daughter's voice beside him, and of his own, and he shifts his eyes to steal a glimpse of her. Her face is serene, shining, hopeful, a recapitulation and refinement of her mother's, and suddenly it's too much for him and he has to look down at his feet: ". . . with liberty and justice for all." More coughing. The seats creak. They sit.

Officer Rudman gives the crowd a good long look, and then he begins. "Drugs are dangerous," he says, "we all know that," and he pauses while the principal, a thick-ankled woman with feathered hair and a dogged expression, translates in her halting Spanish: "Las drogas son peligrosas." The man sits there in back, his daughter at his side, tasting wax beans, rushing with weltschmerz and nostalgia.

Eocene: designating or of the earliest epoch of the Tertiary Period in the Cenozoic Era, during which mammals became the dominant animals.

Je romps; tu romps; il rompt; nous rompons; vous rompez; ils rompent.

They didn't have drugs when he was in elementary school, didn't have crack and crank, didn't have ice and heroin and AIDS to go with it. Not in elementary school. Not in the fifties. They didn't even have pot.

Mary Jane, that's what they called it in the high school health films, but no one ever called it that. Not on this planet, anyway. It was pot, pure and simple, and he smoked it, like anyone else. He's remembering his first joint, age seventeen, a walkup on Broome Street, holes in the walls, bottles, rats, padlocks on the doors, one puff and you're hooked, when Officer Rudman beckons a skinny dark-haired kid to the microphone. Big adult hands choke the neck of the stand and the mike drops a foot. Stretching till his ankles rise up out of his high-tops, the kid clutches at the microphone and recites his pledge to stay off drugs in a piping timbreless voice. "My name is Steven Taylor and I have good feelings of self-esteem about myself," he says, his superamplified breathing whistling through the interstices, "and I pledge never to take drugs or to put anything bad in my body. If somebody asks me if I want drugs I will just say no, turn my back, change the subject, walk away or just say no."

Brain-washing, that's what Linda called it when he phoned to break their date for tonight. Easy for her to say, but then she didn't have a daughter, didn't know, couldn't imagine what it was like to feel the net expand beneath you, high out over that chasm of crashing rock. *What good did it do you?* she said. *Or me?* She had a point. Hash, kif, LSD, cocaine, heroin. He'd heard all the warnings, watched all the movies, but how could you take anyone's word for it? Was it possible, even? He'd sat through driver's ed, sobering statistics, scare films and all, and then taken his mother's Ford out on the highway and burned the tires off it. Scotch, gin, whiskey, Boone's Farm, Night Train, Colt 45, Seconal, Tuinal, Quaalude. He'd heard all the warnings, yes, but when the time came he stuck

the needle in his arm and drew back the plunger to watch the clear
solution flush with his own smoldering blood. You remember to take
your vitamins today?

"My name is Lucy Fadel and I pledge never to abuse drugs,
alcohol or tobacco because I like myself and the world and my school
and I can get high from just life."

"My name is Roberto Campos and I don't want to die from
drugs. Peer pressure is what makes kids use drugs and I will just say
no, I will walk away and I will change the subject."

"Voy a decir no—"

Officer Rudman adjusts the microphone, clasps his hands in
front of him. The parents lean forward. He holds their eyes. "You've
all just heard the fifth graders' pledges," he says, "and these kids
mean it. I'm proud of them. Let's have a big hand for these kids."

And there it is, thunderous, all those parents in their suits and
sportcoats and skirts, wearing sober, earnest, angry looks, pounding
their hands together in relief, as if that could do it, as if the force
of their acclamation could drive the gangs from the streets or nullify
that infinitely seductive question to which "no" is never the answer.
He claps along with them, not daring to glance down at his daughter,
picturing the first boy, the skinny dark one, up against the wall with
the handcuffs on him, dead in the street, wasting away in some
charity ward. And the girl, mother of four, twice divorced, strung
out on martinis and diet pills and wielding the Jeep Cherokee like
a weapon. That's what it came down to: that's what the warnings
meant. *Agon, agape, Ulysses S. Grant, parthenogenesis, the* Monitor
and the Merrimac, *yond Cassius has a lean and hungry look.* His
daughter takes his hand. "Now there's a movie," she whispers.

What happened to finger painting, hearts for Valentine's Day
and bunnies for Easter? Fifth grade, for christ's sake. Where was
Treasure Island, Little Women, Lassie, Come Home? What had happened? Who was responsible? Where did it go wrong?

He's on the verge of raising his hand and demanding an answer
of Officer Rudman, the nostalgia gone sour in his throat now, but
the lights dim and the film begins. A flicker of movement on the
screen, bars, a jail cell. He watches a junkie writhe and scream, a

demonic sunken-eyed man beating his head against a wall, someone, somewhere, lights flashing, police, handcuffs, more screams. Smoke a joint and you're hooked: how they'd laughed over that one, he and Tony Gaetti, and laughed again to realize it was true, cooking the dope in a bottle cap, stealing disposable syringes, getting off in the rest room on the train and feeling they'd snowed the world. Things were different then. That was a long time ago.

Cro-Magnon, Neanderthal, Homo erectus: his daughter's hand is crushing him, prim and cool, lying across his palm like a demolished building, a cement truck, glacial moraine. Up on the screen, the junkies are gone, replaced by a sunny school yard and a clone of Officer Rudman, statistics now, grim but hopeful. Inspiring music, smiling faces, kids who Just Say No.

When it's over, he feels dazed, the lights flashing back on to transfix him like some animal startled along a darkened highway. All he wants is to be out of here, no more questions, no more tricks of memory, no more Officer Rudman or the vapid stares of his fellow parents. "Honey," he whispers, bringing his face down close to his daughter's, "we've got to go." Officer Rudman's chin is cocked back, his arms folded across his chest. "Any questions?" he asks.

"But Dad, the cake sale."

The cake sale.

"We'll have to miss it this time," he whispers, and suddenly he's on his feet, slumping his shoulders in the way people do when they duck out of meetings early or come late to the concert or theater, a gesture of submission and apology. His daughter hangs back—she wants to stay, wants cake, wants to see her friends—but he tugs at her hand and then they're fighting their way through the gauntlet of concerned parents at the door and out into the night. "Dad!" she cries, tugging back at him, and only then does he realize he's hurting her, clutching her hand like a lifeline in a swirl of darkening waters.

"I mean, have a cow, why don't you?" she says, and he drops her hand.

"Sorry. I wasn't thinking."

The flag is motionless, hanging limp now against the pole. He gazes up at the stars fixed in their tracks, cold and distant, and then the gravel crunches underfoot and they're in the parking lot. "I just wanted a piece of cake," his daughter says.

In the car, on the way home to her mother's house, she stares moodily out the window to let him feel the weight of her disappointment, but she can't sustain it. Before long she's chattering away about Officer Rudman and Officer Torres, who sometimes helps with the program, telling him how nice they are and how corrupt the world is. "We have gangs here," she says, "did you know that? Right here in our neighborhood."

He gazes out on half-million-dollar homes. Stone and stucco, mailboxes out front, basketball hoops over garage doors. The streets are deserted. He sees no gangs. "Here?"

"Uh-huh. Chrissie Mueller saw two guys in Raiders hats at the 7-Eleven the other day—"

"Maybe they were buying Ho-Ho's, maybe they just wanted a piece of cake."

"Come on, Dad," she says, but her tone tells him all is forgiven.

Her mother's house is lighted like an arena, porch light, security lights, even the windows poking bright gleaming holes in the fabric of the night. He leans over to kiss his daughter good night, the car vibrating beneath him.

"Dad?"

"Yes?"

"I just wanted to, you know, ask you: did you ever use drugs? Or Mom?"

The question catches him by surprise. He looks beyond her, looks at that glowing bright house a moment, curtains open wide, the wash of light on the lawn. *Abstersion, epopt, Eleusinian, the shortest distance between two points is a straight line.*

"No," he says finally. "No."

CARNAL KNOWLEDGE

I'D NEVER REALLY THOUGHT MUCH about meat. It was there in
the supermarket in a plastic wrapper; it came between slices of bread
with mayo and mustard and a dill pickle on the side; it sputtered
and smoked on the grill till somebody flipped it over, and then it
appeared on the plate, between the baked potato and the julienne
carrots, neatly cross-hatched and floating in a puddle of red juice.
Beef, mutton, pork, venison, dripping burgers and greasy ribs—it
was all the same to me, food, the body's fuel, something to savor a
moment on the tongue before the digestive system went to work on
it. Which is not to say I was totally unconscious of the deeper implications. Every once in a while I'd eat at home, a quartered
chicken, a package of Shake 'n Bake, Stove Top stuffing and frozen
peas, and as I hacked away at the stippled yellow skin and pink flesh
of the sanitized bird I'd wonder at the darkish bits of organ clinging
to the ribs—what was that, liver? kidney?—but in the end it didn't
make me any less fond of Kentucky Fried or Chicken McNuggets.
I saw those ads in the magazines, too, the ones that showed the veal
calves penned up in their own waste, their limbs atrophied and their
veins so pumped full of antibiotics they couldn't control their bowels,
but when I took a date to Anna Maria's, I could never resist the veal
scallopini.

And then I met Alena Jorgensen.

It was a year ago, two weeks before Thanksgiving—I remember
the date because it was my birthday, my thirtieth, and I'd called in
sick and gone to the beach to warm my face, read a book and feel
a little sorry for myself. The Santa Anas were blowing and it was

clear all the way to Catalina, but there was an edge to the air, a
scent of winter hanging over Utah, and as far as I could see in either
direction I had the beach pretty much to myself. I found a sheltered
spot in a tumble of boulders, spread a blanket and settled down to
attack the pastrami on rye I'd brought along for nourishment. Then
I turned to my book—a comfortingly apocalyptic tract about the
demise of the planet—and let the sun warm me as I read about the
denuding of the rain forest, the poisoning of the atmosphere and
the swift silent eradication of species. Gulls coasted by overhead. I
saw the distant glint of jetliners.

I must have dozed, my head thrown back, the book spread open
in my lap, because the next thing I remember, a strange dog was
hovering over me and the sun had dipped behind the rocks. The
dog was big, wild-haired, with one staring blue eye, and it just looked
at me, ears slightly cocked, as if it expected a Milk-Bone or something. I was startled—not that I don't like dogs, but here was this
woolly thing poking its snout in my face—and I guess I must have
made some sort of defensive gesture, because the dog staggered
back a step and froze. Even in the confusion of the moment I could
see that there was something wrong with this dog, an unsteadiness,
a gimp, a wobble to its legs. I felt a mixture of pity and revulsion—
had it been hit by a car, was that it?—when all at once I became
aware of a wetness on the breast of my windbreaker, and an unmistakable odor rose to my nostrils: I'd been pissed on.

Pissed on. As I lay there unsuspecting, enjoying the sun, the
beach, the solitude, this stupid beast had lifted its leg and used me
as a pissoir—and now it was poised there on the edge of the blanket
as if it expected a reward. A sudden rage seized me. I came up off
the blanket with a curse, and it was only then that a dim apprehension seemed to seep into the dog's other eye, the brown one, and it
lurched back and fell on its face, just out of reach. And then it
lurched and fell again, bobbing and weaving across the sand like a
seal out of water. I was on my feet now, murderous, glad to see that
the thing was hobbled—it would simplify the task of running it down
and beating it to death.

"Alf!" a voice called, and as the dog floundered in the sand, I

turned and saw Alena Jorgensen poised on the boulder behind me.
I don't want to make too much of the moment, don't want to my-
thologize it or clutter the scene with allusions to Aphrodite rising
from the waves or accepting the golden apple from Paris, but she
was a pretty impressive sight. Bare-legged, fluid, as tall and uncom-
promising as her Nordic ancestors and dressed in a Gore-Tex bikini
and hooded sweatshirt unzipped to the waist, she blew me away, in
any event. Piss-spattered and stupefied, I could only gape up at her.

"You bad boy," she said, scolding, "you get out of there." She
glanced from the dog to me and back again. "Oh, you bad boy, what
have you done?" she demanded, and I was ready to admit to anything, but it was the dog she was addressing, and the dog flopped
over in the sand as if it had been shot. Alena skipped lightly down
from the rock, and in the next moment, before I could protest, she
was rubbing at the stain on my windbreaker with the wadded-up
hem of her sweatshirt.

I tried to stop her—"It's all right," I said, "it's nothing," as if
dogs routinely pissed on my wardrobe—but she wouldn't hear of it.

"No," she said, rubbing, her hair flying in my face, the naked
skin of her thigh pressed unconsciously to my own, "no, this is terrible, I'm so embarrassed—Alf, you bad boy—I'll clean it for you,
I will, it's the least—oh, look at that, it's stained right through to
your T-shirt—"

I could smell her, the mousse she used in her hair, a lilac soap
or perfume, the salt-sweet odor of her sweat—she'd been jogging,
that was it. I murmured something about taking it to the cleaner's
myself.

She stopped rubbing and straightened up. She was my height,
maybe even a fraction taller, and her eyes were ever so slightly mis-
matched, like the dog's: a deep earnest blue in the right iris, shading
to sea-green and turquoise in the left. We were so close we might
have been dancing. "Tell you what," she said, and her face lit with
a smile, "since you're so nice about the whole thing, and most people
wouldn't be, even if they knew what poor Alf has been through, why
don't you let me wash it for you—and the T-shirt too?"

I was a little disconcerted at this point—I was the one who'd been pissed on, after all—but my anger was gone. I felt weightless, adrift, like a piece of fluff floating on the breeze. "Listen," I said, and for the moment I couldn't look her in the eye, "I don't want to put you to any trouble. . . ."

"I'm ten minutes up the beach, and I've got a washer and dryer. Come on, it's no trouble at all. Or do you have plans? I mean, I could just pay for the cleaner's if you want. . . ."

I was between relationships—the person I'd been seeing off and on for the past year wouldn't even return my calls—and my plans consisted of taking in a solitary late-afternoon movie as a birthday treat, then heading over to my mother's for dinner and the cake with the candles. My Aunt Irene would be there, and so would my grandmother. They would exclaim over how big I was and how handsome and then they would begin to contrast my present self with my previous, more diminutive incarnations, and finally work themselves up to a spate of reminiscence that would continue unabated till my mother drove them home. And then, if I was lucky, I'd go out to a singles bar and make the acquaintance of a divorced computer programmer in her mid-thirties with three kids and bad breath.

I shrugged. "Plans? No, not really. I mean, nothing in particular."

Alena was housesitting a one-room bungalow that rose stump-like from the sand, no more than fifty feet from the tide line. There were trees in the yard behind it and the place was sandwiched between glass fortresses with crenellated decks, whipping flags and great hulking concrete pylons. Sitting on the couch inside, you could feel the dull reverberation of each wave hitting the shore, a slow steady pulse that forever defined the place for me. Alena gave me a faded UC Davis sweatshirt that nearly fit, sprayed a stain remover on my T-shirt and windbreaker, and in a single fluid motion flipped down the lid of the washer and extracted two beers from the refrigerator beside it.

There was an awkward moment as she settled into the chair

opposite me and we concentrated on our beers. I didn't know what to say. I was disoriented, giddy, still struggling to grasp what had happened. Fifteen minutes earlier I'd been dozing on the beach, alone on my birthday and feeling sorry for myself, and now I was ensconced in a cozy beach house, in the presence of Alena Jorgensen and her naked spill of leg, drinking a beer. "So what do you do?" she said, setting her beer down on the coffee table.

I was grateful for the question, too grateful maybe. I described to her at length how dull my job was, nearly ten years with the same agency, writing ad copy, my brain gone numb with disuse. I was somewhere in the middle of a blow-by-blow account of our current campaign for a Ghanian vodka distilled from calabash husks when she said, "I know what you mean," and told me she'd dropped out of veterinary school herself. "After I saw what they did to the animals. I mean, can you see neutering a dog just for our convenience, just because it's easier for us if they don't have a sex life?" Her voice grew hot. "It's the same old story, species fascism at its worst."

Alf was lying at my feet, grunting softly and looking up mournfully out of his staring blue eye, as blameless a creature as ever lived. I made a small noise of agreement and then focused on Alf. "And your dog," I said, "he's arthritic? Or is it hip dysplasia or what?" I was pleased with myself for the question—aside from "tapeworm," "hip dysplasia" was the only veterinary term I could dredge up from the memory bank, and I could see that Alf's problems ran deeper than worms.

Alena looked angry suddenly. "Don't I wish," she said. She paused to draw a bitter breath. "There's nothing wrong with Alf that wasn't inflicted on him. They tortured him, maimed him, mutilated him."

"Tortured him?" I echoed, feeling the indignation rise in me— this beautiful girl, this innocent beast. "Who?"

Alena leaned forward and there was real hate in her eyes. She mentioned a prominent shoe company—spat out the name, actually. It was an ordinary name, a familiar one, and it hung in the air between us, suddenly sinister. Alf had been part of an experiment to market booties for dogs—suede, cordovan, patent leather, the works. The dogs were made to pace a treadmill in their booties, to assess wear; Alf was part of the control group.

"Control group?" I could feel the hackles rising on the back of my neck.

"They used eighty-grit sandpaper on the treads, to accelerate the process." Alena shot a glance out the window to where the surf pounded the shore; she bit her lip. "Alf was one of the dogs without booties."

I was stunned. I wanted to get up and comfort her, but I might as well have been grafted to the chair. "I don't believe it," I said. "How could anybody—"

"Believe it," she said. She studied me a moment, then set down her beer and crossed the room to dig through a cardboard box in the corner. If I was moved by the emotion she'd called up, I was moved even more by the sight of her bending over the box in her Gore-Tex bikini; I clung to the edge of the chair as if it were a plunging roller coaster. A moment later she dropped a dozen file folders in my lap. The uppermost bore the name of the shoe company, and it was crammed with news clippings, several pages of a diary relating to plant operations and workers' shifts at the Grand Rapids facility and a floor plan of the laboratories. The folders beneath it were inscribed with the names of cosmetics firms, biomedical research centers, furriers, tanners, meatpackers. Alena perched on the edge of the coffee table and watched as I shuffled through them.

"You know the Draize test?"

I gave her a blank look.

"They inject chemicals into rabbits' eyes to see how much it'll take before they go blind. The rabbits are in cages, thousands of them, and they take a needle and jab it into their eyes—and you know why, you know in the name of what great humanitarian cause this is going on, even as we speak?"

I didn't know. The surf pounded at my feet. I glanced at Alf and then back into her angry eyes.

"Mascara, that's what. Mascara. They torture countless thousands of rabbits so women can look like sluts."

I thought the characterization a bit harsh, but when I studied her pale lashes and tight lipstickless mouth, I saw that she meant it. At any rate, the notion set her off, and she launched into a two-hour lecture, gesturing with her flawless hands, quoting figures, digging through her files for the odd photo of legless mice or morphine-addicted gerbils. She told me how she'd rescued Alf herself, raiding the laboratory with six other members of the Animal Liberation Front, the militant group in honor of which Alf had been named. At first, she'd been content to write letters and carry placards, but now, with the lives of so many animals at stake, she'd turned to more direct action: harassment, vandalism, sabotage. She described how she'd spiked trees with Earth-First!-ers in Oregon, cut miles of barbed-wire fence on cattle ranches in Nevada, destroyed records in biomedical research labs up and down the coast and insinuated herself between the hunters and the bighorn sheep in the mountains of Arizona. I could only nod and exclaim, smile ruefully and whistle in a low "holy cow!" sort of way. Finally, she paused to level her unsettling eyes on me. "You know what Isaac Bashevis Singer said?"

We were on our third beer. The sun was gone. I didn't have a clue.

Alena leaned forward. "'Every day is Auschwitz for the animals.'"

I looked down into the amber aperture of my beer bottle and nodded my head sadly. The dryer had stopped an hour and a half ago. I wondered if she'd go out to dinner with me, and what she could eat if she did. "Uh, I was wondering," I said, "if . . . if you might want to go out for something to eat—"

Alf chose that moment to heave himself up from the floor and urinate on the wall behind me. My dinner proposal hung in the balance as Alena shot up off the edge of the table to scold him and then gently usher him out the door. "Poor Alf," she sighed, turning back to me with a shrug. "But listen, I'm sorry if I talked your head off—I didn't mean to, but it's rare to find somebody on your own wavelength."

She smiled. *On your own wavelength:* the words illuminated me, excited me, sent up a tremor I could feel all the way down in the deepest nodes of my reproductive tract. "So how about dinner?" I persisted. Restaurants were running through my head—would it have to be veggie? Could there be even a whiff of grilled flesh on the air? Curdled goat's milk and tabbouleh, tofu, lentil soup, sprouts: *Every day is Auschwitz for the animals.* "No place with meat, of course."

She just looked at me.

"I mean, I don't eat meat myself," I lied, "or actually, not anymore"—since the pastrami sandwich, that is—"but I don't really know any place that . . ." I trailed off lamely.

"I'm a Vegan," she said.

After two hours of blind bunnies, butchered calves and mutilated pups, I couldn't resist the joke. "I'm from Venus myself."

She laughed, but I could see she didn't find it all that funny. Vegans didn't eat meat or fish, she explained, or milk or cheese or eggs, and they didn't wear wool or leather—or fur, of course.

"Of course," I said. We were both standing there, hovering over the coffee table. I was beginning to feel a little foolish.

"Why don't we just eat here," she said.

The deep throb of the ocean seemed to settle in my bones as we lay there in bed that night, Alena and I, and I learned all about the fluency of her limbs and the sweetness of her vegetable tongue. Alf sprawled on the floor beneath us, wheezing and groaning in his sleep, and I blessed him for his incontinence and his doggy stupidity. Something was happening to me—I could feel it in the way the boards shifted under me, feel it with each beat of the surf—and I was ready to go along with it. In the morning, I called in sick again.

Alena was watching me from bed as I dialed the office and described how the flu had migrated from my head to my gut and beyond, and there was a look in her eye that told me I would spend the rest of the day right there beside her, peeling grapes and dropping them one by one between her parted and expectant lips. I was wrong. Half an hour later, after a breakfast of brewer's yeast and what appeared to be some sort of bark marinated in yogurt, I found myself marching up and down the sidewalk in front of a fur emporium in Beverly Hills, waving a placard that read HOW DOES IT FEEL TO WEAR A CORPSE? in letters that dripped like blood.

It was a shock. I'd seen protest marches on TV, antiwar rallies and civil-rights demonstrations and all that, but I'd never warmed my heels on the pavement or chanted slogans or felt the naked stick in my hand. There were maybe forty of us in all, mostly women, and we waved our placards at passing cars and blocked traffic on the sidewalk. One woman had smeared her face and hands with cold cream steeped in red dye, and Alena had found a ratty mink stole somewhere—the kind that features whole animals sewed together, snout to tail, their miniature limbs dangling—and she'd taken a can of crimson spray paint to their muzzles so that they looked freshly killed. She brandished this grisly banner on a stick high above her head, whooping like a savage and chanting, "Fur is death, fur is death," over and over again till it became a mantra for the crowd. The day was unseasonably warm, the Jaguars glinted in the sun and the palms nodded in the breeze, and no one, but for a single tight-lipped salesman glowering from behind the store's immaculate windows, paid the slightest bit of attention to us.

I marched out there on the street, feeling exposed and conspicuous, but marching nonetheless—for Alena's sake and for the sake of the foxes and martens and all the rest, and for my own sake too: with each step I took I could feel my consciousness expanding like a balloon, the breath of saintliness seeping steadily into me. Up to this point I'd worn suede and leather like anybody else, ankle boots and Air Jordans, a bombardier jacket I'd had since high school. If I'd drawn the line with fur, it was only because I'd never had any use for it. If I lived in the Yukon—and sometimes, drowsing through a meeting at work, I found myself fantasizing about it—I would have worn fur, no compunction, no second thoughts.

But not anymore. Now I was a protestor, a placard waver, now I was fighting for the right of every last weasel and lynx to grow old and die gracefully, now I was Alena Jorgensen's lover and a force to be reckoned with. Of course, my feet hurt and I was running sweat and praying that no one from work would drive by and see me there on the sidewalk with my crazy cohorts and denunciatory sign.

We marched for hours, back and forth, till I thought we'd wear a groove in the pavement. We chanted and jeered and nobody so much as looked at us twice. We could have been Hare Krishnas, bums, antiabortionists or lepers, what did it matter? To the rest of the world, to the uninitiated masses to whose sorry number I'd belonged just twenty-four hours earlier, we were invisible. I was hungry, tired, discouraged. Alena was ignoring me. Even the woman in red-face was slowing down, her chant a hoarse whisper that was sucked up and obliterated in the roar of traffic. And then, as the afternoon faded toward rush hour, a wizened silvery old woman who might have been an aging star or a star's mother or even the first dimly remembered wife of a studio exec got out of a long white car at the curb and strode fearlessly toward us. Despite the heat—it must have been eighty degrees at this point—she was wearing an ankle-length silver fox coat, a bristling shouldery wafting mass of peltry that must have decimated every burrow on the tundra. It was the moment we'd been waiting for.

A cry went up, shrill and ululating, and we converged on the lone old woman like a Cheyenne war party scouring the plains. The man beside me went down on all fours and howled like a dog, Alena slashed the air with her limp mink and the blood sang in my ears. "Murderer!" I screamed, getting into it. "Torturer! Nazi!" The strings in my neck were tight. I didn't know what I was saying. The crowd gibbered. The placards danced. I was so close to the old woman I could smell her—her perfume, a whiff of mothballs from the coat—and it intoxicated me, maddened me, and I stepped in front of her and blocked her path with all the seething militant bulk of my one hundred eighty-five pounds of sinew and muscle.

I never saw the chauffeur. Alena told me afterward that he was a former kickboxing champion who'd been banned from the sport for excessive brutality. The first blow seemed to drop down from above, a shell lobbed from deep within enemy territory; the others came at me like a windmill churning in a storm. Someone screamed.

I remember focusing on the flawless rigid pleats of the chauffeur's trousers, and then things got a bit hazy.

I woke to the dull thump of the surf slamming at the shore and the touch of Alena's lips on my own. I felt as if I'd been broken on the wheel, dismantled and put back together again. "Lie still," she said, and her tongue moved against my swollen cheek. Stricken, I could only drag my head across the pillow and gaze into the depths of her parti-colored eyes. "You're one of us now," she whispered.

Next morning I didn't even bother to call in sick.

By the end of the week I'd recovered enough to crave meat, for which I felt deeply ashamed, and to wear out a pair of vinyl huaraches on the picket line. Together, and with various coalitions of antivivisectionists, militant Vegans and cat lovers, Alena and I tramped a hundred miles of sidewalk, spray-painted inflammatory slogans across the windows of supermarkets and burger stands, denounced tanners, farriers, poulterers and sausage makers, and somehow found time to break up a cockfight in Pacoima. It was exhilarating, heady, dangerous. If I'd been disconnected in the past, I was plugged in now. I felt righteous—for the first time in my life I had a cause—and I had Alena, Alena above all. She fascinated me, fixated me, made me feel like a tomcat leaping in and out of second-story windows, oblivious to the free-fall and the picket fence below. There was her beauty, of course, a triumph of evolution and the happy interchange of genes going all the way back to the cavemen, but it was more than that—it was her commitment to animals, to the righting of wrongs, to morality that made her irresistible. Was it love? The term is something I've always had difficulty with, but I suppose it was. Sure it was. Love, pure and simple. I had it, it had me.

"You know what?" Alena said one night as she stood over the miniature stove, searing tofu in oil and garlic. We'd spent the afternoon demonstrating out front of a tortilla factory that used rendered animal fat as a congealing agent, after which we'd been chased three blocks by an overweight assistant manager at Von's who objected to

Alena's spray-painting MEAT IS DEATH over the specials in the front window. I was giddy with the adolescent joy of it. I sank into the couch with a beer and watched Alf limp across the floor to fling himself down and lick at a suspicious spot on the floor. The surf boomed like thunder.

"What?" I said.

"Thanksgiving's coming."

I let it ride a moment, wondering if I should invite Alena to my mother's for the big basted bird stuffed with canned oysters and buttered bread crumbs, and then realized it probably wouldn't be such a great idea. I said nothing.

She glanced over her shoulder. "The animals don't have a whole lot to be thankful for, that's for sure. It's just an excuse for the meat industry to butcher a couple million turkeys, is all it is." She paused; hot safflower oil popped in the pan. "I think it's time for a little road trip," she said. "Can we take your car?"

"Sure, but where are we going?"

She gave me her Gioconda smile. "To liberate some turkeys."

In the morning I called my boss to tell him I had pancreatic cancer and wouldn't be in for a while, then we threw some things in the car, helped Alf scrabble into the back seat, and headed up Route 5 for the San Joaquin Valley. We drove for three hours through a fog so dense the windows might as well have been packed with cotton. Alena was secretive, but I could see she was excited. I knew only that we were on our way to rendezvous with a certain "Rolfe," a longtime friend of hers and a big name in the world of ecotage and animal rights, after which we would commit some desperate and illegal act, for which the turkeys would be eternally grateful.

There was a truck stalled in front of the sign for our exit at Calpurnia Springs, and I had to brake hard and jerk the wheel around twice to keep the tires on the pavement. Alena came up out of her seat and Alf slammed into the armrest like a sack of meal, but we made it. A few minutes later we were gliding through the ghostly vacancy of the town itself, lights drifting past in a nimbus of fog, glowing pink, yellow and white, and then there was only the blacktop road and the pale void that engulfed it. We'd gone ten miles or so when Alena instructed me to slow down and began to study the right-hand shoulder with a keen, unwavering eye.

The earth breathed in and out. I squinted hard into the soft drifting glow of the headlights. "There, there!" she cried and I swung the wheel to the right, and suddenly we were lurching along a pitted dirt road that rose up from the blacktop like a goat path worn into the side of a mountain. Five minutes later Alf sat up in the back seat and began to whine, and then a crude unpainted shack began to detach itself from the vagueness around us.

Rolfe met us on the porch. He was tall and leathery, in his fifties, I guessed, with a shock of hair and rutted features that brought Samuel Beckett to mind. He was wearing gumboots and jeans and a faded lumberjack shirt that looked as if it had been washed a hundred times. Alf took a quick pee against the side of the house, then fumbled up the steps to roll over and fawn at his feet.

"Rolfe!" Alena called, and there was too much animation in her voice, too much familiarity, for my taste. She took the steps in a bound and threw herself in his arms. I watched them kiss, and it wasn't a fatherly-daughterly sort of kiss, not at all. It was a kiss with some meaning behind it, and I didn't like it. Rolfe, I thought: What kind of name is that?

"Rolfe," Alena gasped, still a little breathless from bouncing up the steps like a cheerleader, "I'd like you to meet Jim."

This was my signal. I ascended the porch steps and held out my hand. Rolfe gave me a look out of the hooded depths of his eyes and then took my hand in a hard callused grip, the grip of the wood splitter, the fence mender, the liberator of hothouse turkeys and laboratory mice. "A pleasure," he said, and his voice rasped like sandpaper.

There was a fire going inside, and Alena and I sat before it and warmed our hands while Alf whined and sniffed and Rolfe served Red Zinger tea in Japanese cups the size of thimbles. Alena hadn't stopped chattering since we stepped through the door, and Rolfe came right back at her in his woodsy rasp, the two of them exchanging names and news and gossip as if they were talking in code. I studied the reproductions of teal and widgeon that hung from the peeling walls, noted the case of Heinz vegetarian beans in the corner and the half-gallon of Jack Daniel's on the mantel. Finally, after the third cup of tea, Alena settled back in her chair—a huge old Salvation Army sort of thing with a soiled antimacassar—and said, "So what's the plan?"

Rolfe gave me another look, a quick predatory darting of the eyes, as if he weren't sure I could be trusted, and then turned back to Alena. "Hedda Gabler's Range-Fed Turkey Ranch," he said. "And no, I don't find the name cute, not at all." He looked at me now, a long steady assay. "They grind up the heads for cat food, and the neck, the organs and the rest, that they wrap up in paper and stuff back in the body cavity like it was a war atrocity or something. Whatever did a turkey go and do to us to deserve a fate like that?"

The question was rhetorical, even if it seemed to have been aimed at me, and I made no response other than to compose my face in a look that wedded grief, outrage and resolve. I was thinking of all the turkeys I'd sent to their doom, of the plucked wishbones, the pope's noses and the crisp browned skin I used to relish as a kid. It brought a lump to my throat, and something more: I realized I was hungry.

"Ben Franklin wanted to make them our national symbol," Alena chimed in, "did you know that? But the meat eaters won out."

"Fifty thousand birds," Rolfe said, glancing at Alena and bringing his incendiary gaze back to rest on me. "I have information they're going to start slaughtering them tomorrow, for the fresh-not-frozen market."

"Yuppie poultry." Alena's voice was drenched in disgust.

For a moment, no one spoke. I became aware of the crackling of the fire. The fog pressed at the windows. It was getting dark.

"You can see the place from the highway," Rolfe said finally, "but the only access is through Calpurnia Springs. It's about twenty miles—twenty-two point three, to be exact."

Alena's eyes were bright. She was gazing on Rolfe as if he'd just dropped down from heaven. I felt something heave in my stomach.

"We strike tonight."

Rolfe insisted that we take my car—"Everybody around here knows my pickup, and I can't take any chances on a little operation like this"—but we did mask the plates, front and back, with an inch-thick smear of mud. We blackened our faces like commandos and collected our tools from the shed out back—tin snips, a crowbar and two five-gallon cans of gasoline. "Gasoline?" I said, trying the heft of the can. Rolfe gave me a craggy look. "To create a diversion," he said. Alf, for obvious reasons, stayed behind in the shack.

If the fog had been thick in daylight, it was impermeable now, the sky collapsed upon the earth. It took hold of the headlights and threw them back at me till my eyes began to water from the effort of keeping the car on the road. But for the ruts and bumps we might have been floating in space. Alena sat up front between Rolfe and me, curiously silent. Rolfe didn't have much to say either, save for the occasional grunted command: "Hang a right here"; "Hard left"; "Easy, easy." I thought about meat and jail and the heroic proportions to which I was about to swell in Alena's eyes and what I intended to do to her when we finally got to bed. It was 2:00 A.M. by the dashboard clock.

"Okay," Rolfe said, and his voice came at me so suddenly it startled me, "pull over here—and kill the lights."

We stepped out into the hush of night and eased the doors shut behind us. I couldn't see a thing, but I could hear the not-so-distant hiss of traffic on the highway, and another sound, too, muffled and indistinct, the gentle unconscious suspiration of thousands upon thousands of my fellow creatures. And I could smell them, a seething rancid odor of feces and feathers and naked scaly feet that crawled down my throat and burned my nostrils. "Whew," I said in a whisper, "I can smell them."

Rolfe and Alena were vague presences at my side. Rolfe flipped open the trunk and in the next moment I felt the heft of a crowbar and a pair of tin snips in my hand. "Listen, you, Jim," Rolfe whispered, taking me by the wrist in his iron grip and leading me half-a-dozen steps forward. "Feel this?"

I felt a grid of wire, which he promptly cut: *snip, snip, snip.*

"This is their enclosure—they're out there in the day, scratching around in the dirt. You get lost, you follow this wire. Now, you're going to take a section out of this side, Alena's got the west side and I've got the south. Once that's done I signal with the flashlight and we bust open the doors to the turkey houses—they're these big low white buildings, you'll see them when you get close—and flush the birds out. Don't worry about me or Alena. Just worry about getting as many birds out as you can."

I was worried. Worried about everything, from some half-crazed farmer with a shotgun or AK 47 or whatever they carried these days, to losing Alena in the fog, to the turkeys themselves: How big were they? Were they violent? They had claws and beaks, didn't they? And how were they going to feel about me bursting into their bedroom in the middle of the night?

"And when the gas cans go up, you hightail it back to the car, got it?"

I could hear the turkeys tossing in their sleep. A truck shifted gears out on the highway. "I think so," I whispered.

"And one more thing—be sure to leave the keys in the ignition."

This gave me pause. "But—"

"The getaway." Alena was so close I could feel her breath on my ear. "I mean, we don't want to be fumbling around for the keys when all hell is breaking loose out there, do we?"

I eased open the door and reinserted the keys in the ignition, even though the automatic buzzer warned me against it. "Okay," I murmured, but they were already gone, soaked up in the shadows and the mist. At this point my heart was hammering so loudly I could barely hear the rustling of the turkeys—this is crazy, I told myself, it's hurtful and wrong, not to mention illegal. Spray-painting slogans was one thing, but this was something else altogether. I thought of the turkey farmer asleep in his bed, an entrepreneur working to make America strong, a man with a wife and kids and a

mortgage . . . but then I thought of all those innocent turkeys con-
signed to death, and finally I thought of Alena, long-legged and lov-
ing, and the way she came to me out of the darkness of the bathroom
and the boom of the surf. I took the tin snips to the wire.

I must have been at it half an hour, forty-five minutes, gradually
working my way toward the big white sheds that had begun to
emerge from the gloom up ahead, when I saw Rolfe's flashlight
blinking off to my left. This was my signal to head to the nearest
shed, snap off the padlock with my crowbar, fling open the doors
and herd a bunch of cranky suspicious gobblers out into the night.
It was now or never. I looked twice round me and then broke for
the near shed in an awkward crouching gait. The turkeys must have
sensed that something was up—from behind the long white win-
dowless wall there arose a watchful gabbling, a soughing of feathers
that fanned up like a breeze in the treetops. *Hold on, you toms and
hens,* I thought, *freedom is at hand.* A jerk of the wrist, and the
padlock fell to the ground. Blood pounding in my ears, I took hold
of the sliding door and jerked it open with a great dull booming
reverberation—and suddenly, there they were, turkeys, thousands
upon thousands of them, cloaked in white feathers under a string of
dim yellow bulbs. The light glinted in their reptilian eyes. Somewhere a dog began to bark.

I steeled myself and sprang through the door with a shout,
whirling the crowbar over my head. "All right!" I boomed, and the
echo gave it back to me a hundred times over, "this is it! Turkeys,
on your feet!" Nothing. No response. But for the whisper of rustling
feathers and the alertly cocked heads, they might have been sculptures, throw pillows, they might as well have been dead and butchered and served up with yams and onions and all the trimmings.
The barking of the dog went up a notch. I thought I heard voices.

The turkeys crouched on the concrete floor, wave upon wave
of them, stupid and immovable; they perched in the rafters, on
shelves and platforms, huddled in wooden stalls. Desperate, I rushed
into the front rank of them, swinging my crowbar, stamping my feet
and howling like the wishbone plucker I once was. That did it. There
was a shriek from the nearest bird and the others took it up till an

unholy racket filled the place, and now they were moving, tumbling down from their perches, flapping their wings in a storm of dried excrement and pecked-over grain, pouring across the concrete floor till it vanished beneath them. Encouraged, I screamed again—"Yeeee-ha-ha-ha-ha!"—and beat at the aluminum walls with the crowbar as the turkeys shot through the doorway and out into the night.

It was then that the black mouth of the doorway erupted with light and the *ka-boom!* of the gas cans sent a tremor through the earth. *Run!* a voice screamed in my head, and the adrenaline kicked in and all of a sudden I was scrambling for the door in a hurricane of turkeys. They were everywhere, flapping their wings, gobbling and screeching, loosing their bowels in panic. Something hit the back of my legs and all at once I was down amongst them, on the floor, in the dirt and feathers and wet turkey shit. I was a roadbed, a turkey expressway. Their claws dug at my back, my shoulders, the crown of my head. Panicked now, choking on feathers and dust and worse, I fought to my feet as the big screeching birds launched themselves round me, and staggered out into the barnyard. "There! Who's that there?" a voice roared, and I was off and running.

What can I say? I vaulted turkeys, kicked them aside like so many footballs, slashed and tore at them as they sailed through the air. I ran till my lungs felt as if they were burning right through my chest, disoriented, bewildered, terrified of the shotgun blast I was sure would cut me down at any moment. Behind me the fire raged and lit the fog till it glowed blood-red and hellish. But where was the fence? And where the car?

I got control of my feet then and stood stock-still in a flurry of turkeys, squinting into the wall of fog. Was that it? Was that the car over there? At that moment I heard an engine start up somewhere behind me—a familiar engine with a familiar coughing gurgle in the throat of the carburetor—and then the lights blinked on briefly three hundred yards away. I heard the engine race and listened, helpless, as the car roared off in the opposite direction. I stood there a moment longer, forlorn and forsaken, and then I ran blindly off into the night, putting the fire and the shouts and the barking and the incessant mindless squawking of the turkeys as far behind me as I could.

When dawn finally broke, it was only just perceptibly, so thick was the fog. I'd made my way to a blacktop road—which road and where it led I didn't know—and sat crouched and shivering in a clump of weed just off the shoulder. Alena wouldn't desert me, I was sure of that—she loved me, as I loved her; needed me, as I needed her—and I was sure she'd be cruising along the back roads looking for me. My pride was wounded, of course, and if I never laid eyes on Rolfe again I felt I wouldn't be missing much, but at least I hadn't been drilled full of shot, savaged by farm dogs or pecked to death by irate turkeys. I was sore all over, my shin throbbed where I'd slammed into something substantial while vaulting through the night, there were feathers in my hair and my face and arms were a mosaic of cuts and scratches and long trailing fissures of dirt. I'd been sitting there for what seemed like hours, cursing Rolfe, developing suspicions about Alena and unflattering theories about environmentalists in general, when finally I heard the familiar slurp and roar of my Chevy Citation cutting through the mist ahead of me.

Rolfe was driving, his face impassive. I flung myself into the road like a tattered beggar, waving my arms over my head and giving vent to my joy, and he very nearly ran me down. Alena was out of the car before it stopped, wrapping me up in her arms, and then she was bundling me into the rear seat with Alf and we were on our way back to the hideaway. "What happened?" she cried, as if she couldn't have guessed. "Where were you? We waited as long as we could."

I was feeling sulky, betrayed, feeling as if I was owed a whole lot more than a perfunctory hug and a string of insipid questions. Still, as I told my tale I began to warm to it—they'd got away in the car with the heater going, and I'd stayed behind to fight the turkeys, the farmers and the elements, too, and if that wasn't heroic, I'd like to know what was. I looked into Alena's admiring eyes and pictured Rolfe's shack, a nip or two from the bottle of Jack Daniel's, maybe a peanut-butter-and-tofu sandwich and then the bed, with Alena in it. Rolfe said nothing.

Back at Rolfe's, I took a shower and scrubbed the turkey droppings from my pores, then helped myself to the bourbon. It was ten in the morning and the house was dark—if the world had ever been without fog, there was no sign of it here. When Rolfe stepped out on the porch to fetch an armload of firewood, I pulled Alena down into my lap. "Hey," she murmured, "I thought you were an invalid."

She was wearing a pair of too-tight jeans and an oversize sweater with nothing underneath it. I slipped my hand inside the sweater and found something to hold on to. "Invalid?" I said, nuzzling at her sleeve. "Hell, I'm a turkey liberator, an ecoguerrilla, a friend of the animals and the environment, too."

She laughed, but she pushed herself up and crossed the room to stare out the occluded window. "Listen, Jim," she said, "what we did last night was great, really great, but it's just the beginning." Alf looked up at her expectantly. I heard Rolfe fumbling around on the porch, the thump of wood on wood. She turned round to face me now. "What I mean is, Rolfe wants me to go up to Wyoming for a little bit, just outside of Yellowstone—"

Me? Rolfe wants me? There was no invitation in that, no plurality, no acknowledgment of all we'd done and meant to each other. "For what?" I said. "What do you mean?"

"There's this grizzly—a pair of them, actually—and they've been raiding places outside the park. One of them made off with the mayor's Doberman the other night and the people are up in arms. We—I mean Rolfe and me and some other people from the old Bolt Weevils in Minnesota?—we're going to go up there and make sure the Park Service—or the local yahoos—don't eliminate them. The bears, I mean."

My tone was corrosive. "You and Rolfe?"

"There's nothing between us, if that's what you're thinking. This has to do with animals, that's all."

"Like us?"

She shook her head slowly. "Not like us, no. We're the plague on this planet, don't you know that?"

Suddenly I was angry. Seething. Here I'd crouched in the bushes all night, covered in turkey crap, and now I was part of a plague. I was on my feet. "No, I don't know that."

She gave me a look that let me know it didn't matter, that she was already gone, that her agenda, at least for the moment, didn't include me and there was no use arguing about it. "Look," she said, her voice dropping as Rolfe slammed back through the door with a load of wood, "I'll see you in L.A. in a month or so, okay?" She gave me an apologetic smile. "Water the plants for me?"

An hour later I was on the road again. I'd helped Rolfe stack the wood beside the fireplace, allowed Alena to brush my lips with a goodbye kiss, and then stood there on the porch while Rolfe locked up, lifted Alf into the bed of his pickup and rumbled down the rutted dirt road with Alena at his side. I watched till their brake lights dissolved in the drifting gray mist, then fired up the Citation and lurched down the road behind them. *A month or so:* I felt hollow inside. I pictured her with Rolfe, eating yogurt and wheat germ, stopping at motels, wrestling grizzlies and spiking trees. The hollowness opened up, cored me out till I felt as if I'd been plucked and gutted and served up on a platter myself.

I found my way back through Calpurnia Springs without incident—there were no roadblocks, no flashing lights and grim-looking troopers searching trunks and back seats for a tallish thirty-year-old ecoterrorist with turkey tracks down his back—but after I turned onto the highway for Los Angeles, I had a shock. Ten miles up the road my nightmare materialized out of the gloom: red lights everywhere, signal flares and police cars lined up on the shoulder. I was on the very edge of panicking, a beat away from cutting across the meridian and giving them a run for it, when I saw the truck jackknifed up ahead. I slowed to forty, thirty, and then hit the brakes again. In a moment I was stalled in a line of cars and there was something all over the road, ghostly and white in the fog. At first I thought it must have been flung from the truck, rolls of toilet paper or crates of soap powder ruptured on the pavement. It was neither. As I inched closer, the tires creeping now, the pulse of the lights in

my face. I saw that the road was coated in feathers, turkey feathers.
A storm of them. A blizzard. And more: there was flesh there too,
slick and greasy, a red pulp ground into the surface of the road,
thrown up like slush from the tires of the car ahead of me, ground
beneath the massive wheels of the truck. Turkeys. Turkeys everywhere.

The car crept forward. I flicked on the windshield wipers, hit
the washer button, and for a moment a scrim of diluted blood ob-
scured the windows and the hollowness opened up inside of me till
I thought it would suck me inside out. Behind me, someone was
leaning on his horn. A trooper loomed up out of the gloom, waving
me on with the dead yellow eye of his flashlight. I thought of Alena
and felt sick. All there was between us had come to this, expectations
gone sour, a smear on the road. I wanted to get out and shoot myself,
turn myself in, close my eyes and wake up in jail, in a hair shirt, in
a straitjacket, anything. It went on. Time passed. Nothing moved.
And then, miraculously, a vision began to emerge from behind the
smeared glass and the gray belly of the fog, lights glowing golden in
the waste. I saw the sign, Gas/Food/Lodging, and my hand was on
the blinker.

It took me a moment, picturing the place, the generic tile, the
false cheer of the lights, the odor of charred flesh hanging heavy on
the air, Big Mac, three-piece dark meat, carne asada, cheeseburger.
The engine coughed. The lights glowed. I didn't think of Alena then,
didn't think of Rolfe or grizzlies or the doomed bleating flocks and
herds, or of the blind bunnies and cancerous mice—I thought only
of the cavern opening inside me and how to fill it. "Meat," and I
spoke the word aloud, talking to calm myself as if I'd awakened from
a bad dream, "it's only meat."

THE 100 FACES OF DEATH, VOLUME IV

HE KNEW HE'D REALLY SCREWED UP. Screwed up in a major and unforgiving way. You could see the perception solidifying in his eyes—eyes that seemed to swell out of his head like hard-cooked eggs extruded through the sockets, and the camera held steady. He was on a stage, faultlessly lit, and a banner proclaimed him RENALDO THE GREAT ESCAPE ARTIST. He was running sweat. Oozing it. His pores were huge, saturated, craters trenching his face like running sores. Suspended six feet above his head, held aloft by block and tackle, was a fused meteorite of junkyard metal the size of a truck engine, its lower surface bristling with the gleaming jagged teeth of a hundred kitchen knives annealed in the forges of Guadalajara. Renaldo's hands were cuffed to his ankles, and what looked like a tugboat anchor chain was wound round his body six or eight times and bolted to the concrete floor. His lovely assistant, a heavily made-up woman whose thighs ballooned from her lacy tutu like great coppery slabs of meat, looked as if her every tremor and waking nightmare had been distilled in the bitter secretions of that moment. This was definitely not part of the act.

"Watch this," Jamie said. "Watch this."

Janine tightened her grip on my hand. The room shrank in on us. The beer in my free hand had gone warm, and when I lifted it to my lips it tasted of yeast and aluminum. And what did I feel? I felt the way the lovely assistant looked, felt the cold charge of revulsion and exhilaration that had come over me when I'd seen my first porno movie at the age of fourteen, felt a hairy-knuckled hand slide up my throat and jerk at a little lever there.

When the video opened, over the credits, Renaldo was clench-
ing a straw between his teeth—a straw, a single straw, yellow and
stiff, the smallest part of a broom. He was leaning forward, working
the straw in the tiny aperture that controlled the release mechanism
of the handcuffs. But now, because he'd begun to appreciate that
this wasn't his day, and that the consequences of that fact were
irrevocable, his lips began to tremble and he lost his grip on the
straw. The lovely assistant gave the camera a wild strained look and
then made as if to dash forward and restore that essential wisp of
vegetation to the artist's mouth, but it was too late. With a thick
slushing sound, the sound of tires moving through wet snow, the
timer released the mechanism that restrained the iron monolith, and
Renaldo was no more.

Jamie said something like, "Dude really bought it," and then,
"Anybody ready for a beer?"

I sat through another ninety-nine permutations of the final moment, variously lit and passionately or indifferently performed,
watched the ski-masked bank robber pop his hostage's head like a
grape with the aid of a .44 Magnum and then pop his own, saw the
fire-eater immolate herself and the lumberjack make his final cut.
Jamie, who'd seen the video half-a-dozen times, couldn't stop laughing. Janine said nothing, but her grip on my hand was unyielding.
For my part, I remember going numb after the third or fourth death,
but I sat there all the same, though there were ninety-six to go.

But then, who was counting?

The following weekend, my Aunt Marion died. Or "passed on,"
as my mother put it, a delicate euphemistic phrase that conjured up
ethereal realms rather than the stark black-and-white image of damp
soil and burrowing insects. My mother was in New York, I was in
Los Angeles. And no, I wasn't flying in for the funeral. She cried
briefly, dryly, and then hung up.

I was twenty-five at the time, a graduate of an indifferent university, a young man who went to work and made money, sought
the company of young women and was perhaps too attached to the
friends of his youth, Jamie in particular. I listened to the silence a

moment, then phoned Janine and asked her to dinner. She was busy. What about tomorrow, then? I said. She planned to be busy then, too.

I hadn't laid eyes on my Aunt Marion in ten years. I remembered her as a sticklike woman in a wheelchair with an unsteady lip and a nose that overhung it like a cutbank, a nose that wasn't qualitatively different from my mother's and, in the fullness of generation, my own. Her death was the result of an accident—negligence, my mother insisted—and already, less than twenty-four hours after the fact, there was an attorney involved.

It seemed that Aunt Marion had been on an outing to the art museum with several other inmates of the nursing home where she'd been in residence since Nixon's presidency, and the attendant, in placing her at the head of the ramp out back of the museum dining hall, had failed to properly set the brake on the back wheels of her chair. Aunt Marion suffered from some progressive nervous disorder that had rendered her limbs useless—she was able to control her motorized chair only through the use of a joystick which she gripped between her teeth, and even then only at the best of times. Left alone at the summit of the ramp while the attendant went off to fetch another patient, Aunt Marion felt her chair begin to slip inexorably forward. The chair picked up speed, and one of the two witnesses to the accident claimed that she'd bent her face to the controls to arrest it, while the other insisted she'd done nothing at all to save herself, but had simply glided on down the ramp and into eternity with a tight little smile frozen to her face. In any case, there was blame to be assigned, very specific and undeniable blame, and a cause-and-effect reaction to explain Aunt Marion's removal from this sphere of being, and, in the end, it seemed to give my mother some measure of comfort.

Try as I might, though, I couldn't picture the face of Aunt Marion's death. My own blood was involved, my own nose. And yet it was all somehow remote, distant, and the death of Renaldo the Great stayed with me in a way Aunt Marion's could never have begun to. I don't know what I wound up doing that weekend, but in retrospect I picture the Coast Highway, an open convertible, Jamie, a series of bars with irradiated decks and patios, and women who were very much alive.

Janine passed into oblivion, as did Carmen, Eugenie and Katrinka, and Jamie went off to explore the wide bleeding world. He spent the next eight months dredging the dark corners of countries whose names changed in the interim, the sort of places where people died in the streets as regularly as flowers sprang through the soil and pigeons fouled the monuments to the generalissimo of the month. I worked. I turned over money. Somebody gave me a cat. It shat in a box under the sink and filled the house with a graveyard stink.

Jamie had been back two months before he called to invite me to a party in the vast necropolis of the San Fernando Valley. He'd found a job inculcating moral awareness in the minds of six- and seven-year-olds at the Thomas Jefferson Elementary School in Pacoima five days a week, reserving the weekends for puerile thrills. I didn't realize how much I'd missed him until I saw him standing there on the landing outside my apartment. He looked the same—rangy, bug-eyed, a plucked chicken dressed in surfer's clothes—but for his nose. It was inflamed, punished, a dollop of meat grafted to his face by some crazed body snatcher. "What's with the nose?" I said, dispensing with the preliminaries.

He hesitated, working up to a slow grin under the porch light. "Got in a fight in this bar," he said. "Some dude bit it off."

They'd sewed the tip of his nose back in place—or almost in place; it would forever be canted ever so slightly to the left—but that wasn't what excited him. He moved past me into the living room and fumbled around in his pocket for a minute, then handed me a series of snapshots, close-ups of his face shortly after the operation. I saw the starched white sheets, the nest of pillows, Jamie's triumphant leer and an odd glistening black line drawn across the bridge of his nose where the bandage should have been. The photos caught it from above, beneath, head-on and in profile. Jamie was looking over my shoulder. He didn't say a word, but his breathing was quick and shallow. "So what is it?" I said, swinging round on him. "What's the deal?"

One word, succulent as a flavored ice: "Leeches."

"Leeches?"

He held it a moment, center stage. "That's right, dude, latest thing. They use them to bring back the tiny blood vessels, capillaries and whatnot, the ones they can't tie up themselves. It's the sucking action," and he made a kissing noise. "Suck, suck, suck. I wore them around for three days, grossing the shit out of everybody in the hospital." He was looking into my eyes. Then he shrugged and turned away. "They wouldn't let me take them home, though—that was the pisser."

The party consisted of seven people—three women and four men, including us—sitting around a formal dining-room table eating carnitas and listening to inflammatory rap at a barely audible volume. The hosts were Hilary and Stefan, who had a house within hearing distance of the Ventura Freeway and taught with Jamie in Pacoima. Hilary's sister, Judy, was there, the end product of psychosomatic dieting and the tanning salon, along with her friend Marsha and a man in his forties with sprayed-up hair and a goatee whose name I never did catch. We drank Carta Blanca and shots of Cuervo Gold and ate flan for dessert. The general conversation ran to Jamie's nose, leeches, bowel movements and death. I don't know how we got into it exactly, but after dinner we gravitated toward a pair of mallowy couches the color of a Haas avocado and began our own anthology of final moments. I came back from the bathroom by way of the kitchen with a fresh beer, and Judy, sunk into her tan like something out of a sarcophagus at Karnak, was narrating the story of the two UCLA students, lovers of nature and of each other, who went kayaking off Point Dume.

It was winter, and the water was cold. There'd been a series of storms bred in the Gulf of Alaska and the hills were bleeding mud. There was frost in the Valley, and Judy's mother lost a bougainvillea she'd had for twenty years. That was the fatal ingredient, the cold.

The big sharks—the great whites—generally stayed well north of the Southern California coast, up near the Bay Area, the Farallons and beyond, where the seals were. That was what they ate: seals.

In Judy's version, the couple had tied their kayaks together and they were resting, sharing a sandwich, maybe getting romantic— kissing, fondling each other through their wet suits. The shark wasn't supposed to be there. It wasn't supposed to mistake the hulls of their kayaks for the silhouette of two fat rich 'hot-blooded basking seals either, but it did. The girl drowned after going faint from blood loss and the chill of the water. They never found her lover.

"Jesus," the older guy said, throwing up his hands. "It's bad enough to have to go, but to wind up as sharkshit—"

Jamie, who'd been blowing softly into the aperture of his beer bottle, looked perturbed. "But how do you know?" he demanded, settling his eyes on Judy. "I mean, were you there? Did you see it, like maybe from another boat?"

She hadn't seen it. She wasn't there. She'd read about it in the paper.

"Uh-uh," Jamie scolded, wagging his finger. "No fair. You have to have seen it, actually been there."

The older guy leaned forward, lit a cigarette and told about an accident he'd witnessed on the freeway. He was coming back from the desert on a Monday night, the end of a three-day weekend, and there was a lot of traffic, but it was moving fast. Four guys in a pickup passed him—three in the cab, the fourth outside in the bed of the truck. A motorcycle stood beside him, lashed upright in the center of the bed. They passed on the right, and they were going at a pretty good clip. Just then, feeling a little bored and left out, the guy in the back of the truck mounted the motorcycle, as a joke. He got up on the seat, leaned into the wind raking over the top of the cab and pretended he was heading into the final lap of the moto-cross. Unfortunately—and this was the morbid thrill of the exercise; there was always a pathetic adverb attached to the narrative, a "sadly" or "tragically" or "unfortunately" to quicken the audience's blood—unfortunately, traffic was stalled ahead, the driver hit the brakes and the erstwhile motocross champion careened into the cab and went sailing out over the side like an acrobat. And like an acrobat, miraculously, he picked himself up unhurt. The older guy paused, flicked the ash from his cigarette. But unfortunately—and there it was again—the next car hit him in the hips at sixty and flung him under the wheels of a big rig one lane over. Eight more cars hit him before the traffic stopped, and by then there wasn't much left but hair and grease.

Hilary told the story of the "Tiger Man," who stood outside the tiger exhibit at the L.A. Zoo eight hours a day, seven days a week, for an entire year, and then was discovered one morning on the limb of a eucalyptus that hung thirty feet over the open enclosure, in the instant before he lost his balance. She was working the concession stand at the time, a summer job while she was in college, and she heard the people round the tiger pit screaming and the tigers roaring and snarling and thought at first they were fighting. By the time she got there the tiger man was in two pieces and his insides were spread out on the grass like blue strings of sausage. They had to shoot one of the tigers, and that was a shame, a real shame.

Jamie was next. He started in on the story of Renaldo the Great as if it were an eyewitness account. "I was like at this circus in Guadalajara," he said, and my mind began to drift.

It was my turn next, and the only death I could relate, the only one I'd witnessed face to face and not in some voyeuristic video or the pages of *Newsweek* or *Soldier of Fortune*, a true death, the dulling of the eyes, the grip gone lax, the passing from animacy to quietus, I'd never spoken of, not to anyone. The face of it came back to me at odd moments, on waking, starting the car, sitting still in the impersonal dark of the theater before the trailers begin to roll. I didn't want to tell it. I wasn't going to. When Jamie was done, I was going to excuse myself, lock the bathroom door behind me, lean over the toilet and flush it and flush it again till they forgot all about me.

I was sixteen. I was on the swim team at school, bulking up, pushing myself till there was no breath left in my body, and I entertained visions of strutting around the community pool in the summer with a whistle round my neck. I took the Coast Guard–approved lifesaving course and passed with flying colors. It was May, an early searing day, and I wheeled my mother's tubercular Ford out along the ocean to a relatively secluded beach I knew, thinking to do some wind sprints in the sand and pit my hammered shoulders and iron legs against the elemental chop and roll of the Pacific. I never got the chance. Unfortunately. I came down off the hill from the highway and there was a Mexican kid there, nine or ten years old, frantic, in full blind headlong flight, running up the path toward me. His limbs were sticks, his eyes inflamed, and the urgency rode him like a jockey. "*Socorro!*" he cried, the syllables catching in his throat, choking him. "*Socorro!*" he repeated, springing up off his toes, and he had me by the arm in a fierce wet grip, and we were running.

The sand flared with reflected light, the surf broke away to the horizon beneath the blinding ache of the sky, I felt my legs under me, and there it was, the moment, the face of it, lying there in the wash like some elaborate offering to the gulls. A man, big-bellied and dark, his skin slick with the wet, lay facedown in the sand as if he'd been dropped from the clouds. The boy choked and pleaded, too wrought up even for tears, the story I didn't want to hear spewing out of him in a language I couldn't comprehend, and I bent to the man and turned him over.

He wasn't sleeping. No sleep ever looked like that. The eyes were rolled back in his head, white flecks of vomit clung to his lips and stained the dead drooping mustache, and his face was huge, bloated, as if it had been pumped up with gas, as if in a minute's time a week had elapsed and all the rot inside him was straining to get out. There was no one else in sight. I straddled that monstrous head, cleared the dark slab of the tongue, pressed the side of my face to the sand-studded chest. I might have heard something there, faint and deep, the whisper of the sea in a smooth scalloped shell, but I couldn't be sure.

"*Mi padre*," the boy cried, "*mi padre*." I was a lifesaver. I knew what to do. I knew the moment had come to pinch shut those gaping nostrils, bend my lips to the dark hole beneath the vomit-flecked mustache and breathe life into the inert form beneath me, mouth to mouth.

Mouth to mouth. I was sixteen years old. Five and a half billion of us on the planet, and here was this man, this one, this strange dark individual with the unseeing eyes and lips slick with phlegm, and I couldn't do it. I gave the boy a look, and it was just as if I'd pulled out a handgun and shot him between the eyes, and then I got to my feet in a desperate scramble—think of a kitten plucked from the sleeping nest of its siblings, all four paws lashing blindly at the air—got to my feet, and ran.

My own father died when I was an infant, killed in a plane crash, and though I studied photos of him when I was older, I always pictured him as some faceless, mangled corpse risen from the grave like the son in "The Monkey's Paw." It wasn't a healthy image, but there it was.

My mother was different. I remember her as being in constant motion, chopping things on the drainboard while the washer chugged round, taking business calls—she was an accountant—and at the same time reaching for the sponge to scrub imaginary fingerprints off the white kitchen phone, all in a simultaneous and neverceasing whirl. She died when I was thirty-two—or "passed on," as she would have had it. I wasn't there. I don't know. But as I've heard it told, digging round the crust of politesse and euphemism like an archaeologist unearthing a bone, there was no passing to it at all, no gentle progress, no easeful journey.

She died in public, of a heart attack. An attack. A seizure. A stroke. Violent and quick, a savage rending in the chest, no passing on, no surcease, no privacy, no dignity, no hope. She was shopping. At Safeway. Five-thirty in the afternoon, the place packed to the walls, the gleaming carts, this item and that, the little choices, seventeen point five cents an ounce as opposed to twenty-two point one. She writhed on the floor. Bit her tongue in two. Died. And all those faces, every one of them alive and condemned, gazing down

on her in horror, all those dinners ruined, all that time wasted at
the checkout counter.

We all knew Jamie would be the first of us to go. No one
doubted it, least of all Jamie himself. He courted it, flaunted it,
rented his videos and tried, in his own obsessive, relentless way, to
talk it to death. Every time he got in his car, even to drive to the
corner for a pack of cigarettes, it was like the start of the Indianapolis
500. He picked fights, though he was thirty years old and should
have known better, dove out of airplanes, wrecked a pair of hang
gliders. When he took up rock climbing, he insisted on free climbs
only—no gear, no ropes, no pitons, only the thin tenuous grip of
fingers and toes. I hadn't seen him in two years. He'd long since left
L.A., teaching, any sort of steady job, steady income, steady life. He
was in Aspen, Dakar, Bangkok. Once in a while I got a dirt-smeared
postcard from out of the amazing pipeline, exotic stamps, a mad
trembling hasty scrawl of which the only legible term was "dude."

This was the face of Jamie's death: Studio City, a golden winter
afternoon, Jamie on a bench, waiting for the bus. It had rained the
week before—the whole week—and the big twisting branches of
the eucalyptus trees were sodden and heavy. They have a tendency
to shear off, those branches, that's why the city keeps them trimmed
back. Or used to, when there were funds for such things. A wind
came up, a glorious dry-to-the-bone featherbed wind off the desert;
the trees threw out their leaves and danced. And a single branch,
wide around as any ordinary tree, parted company with the trunk
and obliterated my friend Jamie, crushed him, made dog meat
of him.

Am I too graphic? Should I soften it? Euphemize it? Pray to
God in His Heaven?

When the phone rang and I heard the long-forgotten but unmistakable tones of an old high school sometime acquaintance—
Victor, Victor Cashaw—I knew what he was going to say before he
knew it himself. I set down the phone and gazed through the kitchen
to the patio, where Linda, my wife, lay stretched out on a rattan
sofa, absorbed in a magazine that revealed all the little secrets of

nail acrylics and blusher and which towel to use when you wake up at his house. For all I knew, she could have been pregnant. I walked straight out the door, climbed into the car and drove down the block to Video Giant.

In a way, it was perversely gratifying to see that the *100 Faces of Death* series had grown to twenty volumes, but it was Volume IV that I wanted, only that. At home, I slipped quietly into the den— Linda was still there, still on the patio sofa, still motionless but for the beat of her eyes across the page—and inserted the cassette into the slot in the machine. It had been nine years, but I recognized Renaldo as if I'd seen him yesterday, his dilemma eternal, his sweat inexhaustible, his eyes forever glossy. I watched the lovely assistant slide toward panic, focused on the sliver of straw clenched between Renaldo's gleaming teeth. When did he realize? I wondered. Was it now? Now?

I waited till the moment came for him to drop the straw. Poor Renaldo. I froze it right there.

56–0

IT WASN'T THE CAST that bothered him—the thing was like rock, like a weapon, and that was just how he would use it—and it wasn't the hyperextended knee or the hip pointer or the yellowing contusions seeping into his thighs and hams and lower back or even the gouged eye that was swollen shut and drooling a thin pale liquid the color of dishwater; no, it was the humiliation. Fifty-six to nothing. That was no mere defeat; it was a drubbing, an ass-kicking, a rape, the kind of thing the statisticians and sports nerds would snigger over as long as there were records to keep. He'd always felt bigger than life in his pads and helmet, a hero, a titan, but you couldn't muster much heroism lying facedown in the mud at fifty-six to nothing and with the other team's third string in there. No, the cast didn't bother him, not really, though it itched like hell and his hand was a big stippled piece of meat sticking out of the end of it, or the eye either, though it was ugly, pure ugly. The trainer had sent him to the eye doctor and the doctor had put some kind of blue fluid in the eye and peered into it with a little conical flashlight and said there was no lasting damage, but still it was swollen shut and he couldn't study for his Physical Communications exam.

It was Sunday, the day after the game, and Ray Arthur Larry-Pete Fontinot, right guard for the Caledonia College Shuckers, slept till two, wrapped in his own private misery—and even then he couldn't get out of bed. Every fiber of his body, all six feet, four inches and two hundred sixty-eight pounds of it, shrieked with pain. He was twenty-two years old, a senior, his whole life ahead of him, and he felt like he was ready for the nursing home. There was a

ringing in his ears, his eyelashes were welded together, his lower
back throbbed and both his knees felt as if ice picks had been driven
into them. He hobbled, splayfooted and naked, to the bathroom at
the end of the hall, and there was blood in the toilet bowl when he
was done.

All his life he'd been a slow fat pasty kid, beleaguered and
tormented by his quick-footed classmates, until he found his niche
on the football field, where his bulk, stubborn and immovable, had
proved an advantage—or so he'd thought. He'd drunk the protein
drink, pumped the iron, lumbered around the track like some ge-
riatric buffalo, and what had it gotten him? Caledonia had gone
0–43 during his four years on the varsity squad, never coming closer
than two touchdowns even to a tie—and the forty-third loss had
been the hardest. Fifty-six to nothing. He'd donned a football helmet
to feel good about himself, to develop pride and poise, to taste the
sweet nectar of glory, but somehow he didn't feel all that glorious
lying there flat on his back and squinting one-eyed at Puckett and
Poplar's *Principles of Physical Communications: A Text,* until the
lines shifted before him like the ranks of X's and O's in the Coach's
eternal diagrams. He dozed. Woke again to see the evening shadows
closing over the room. By nightfall, he felt good enough to get up
and puke.

In the morning, a full forty hours after the game had ended,
he felt even worse, if that was possible. He sat up, goaded by the
first tumultuous stirrings of his gut, and winced as he pulled the
sweats over each bruised and puckered calf. His right knee locked
up on him as he angled his feet into the laceless high-tops (it had
been three years at least since he'd last been able to bend down and
tie his shoes), something cried out in his left shoulder as he pulled
the Caledonia sweatshirt over his head, and then suddenly he was
on his feet and ambulatory. He staggered down the hall like something out of *Night of the Living Dead,* registering a familiar face
here and there, but the faces were a blur mostly, and he avoided
the eyes attached to them. Someone was playing Killer Pussy at
seismic volume, and someone else—some half-witted dweeb he'd

gladly have murdered if only his back didn't hurt so much—had left a skateboard outside the door and Ray Arthur Larry-Pete damn near crushed it to powder and pitched right on through the concrete-block wall in the bargain, but if nothing else, he still had his reflexes. As he crossed the courtyard to the cafeteria in a lively blistering wind, he noted absently that he'd progressed from a hobble to a limp.

There was no sign of Suzie in the cafeteria, and he had a vague recollection of her calling to cancel their study date the previous evening, but as he loaded up his tray with desiccated bacon strips, mucilaginous eggs and waffles that looked, felt and tasted like roofing material, he spotted Kitwany, Moss and DuBoy skulking over their plates at one of the long tables in the back of the room. It would have been hard to miss them. Cut from the same exaggerated mold as he, his fellow linemen loomed over the general run of the student body like representatives of another species. Their heads were like prize pumpkins set on the pedestals of their neckless shoulders, their fingers were the size of the average person's forearm, their jaws were entities unto themselves and they sprouted casts like weird growths all over their bodies.

Ray Arthur Larry-Pete made the long limp across the room to join them, setting his tray down gingerly and using both his hands to brace himself as he lowered his bruised backside to the unforgiving hardwood slats of the bench. Then, still employing his hands, he lifted first one and then the other deadened leg over the bench and into the well beneath the table. He grunted, winced, cursed, broke wind. Then he nodded to his teammates, worked his spine into the swallowing position and addressed himself to his food.

After a moment, DuBoy spoke. He was wearing a neck brace in the place where his head was joined to his shoulders, and it squeezed the excess flesh of his jowls up into his face so that he looked like an enormous rodent. "How you feeling?"

You didn't speak of pain. You toughed it out—that was the code. Coach Tundra had been in the army in Vietnam at some place Ray Arthur Larry-Pete could never remember or pronounce, and he didn't tolerate whiners and slackers. *Pain?* he would yelp incredulously at the first hint that a player was even thinking of staying down. *Tell it to the 101st Airborne, to the boys taking a mortar round in the Ia Drang Valley or the grunts in the field watching their buddies get blown away and then crawling six miles through a swamp so thick it would choke a snake with both their ears bleeding down their neck and their leg gone at the knee. Get up, soldier. Get out there and fight!* And if that didn't work, he'd roll up his pantleg to show off the prosthesis.

Ray Arthur Larry-Pete glanced up at DuBoy. "I'll live. How about you?"

DuBoy tried to shrug as if to say it was nothing, but even the faintest lift of a shoulder made him gasp and slap a hand to the neck brace as if a hornet had stung him. "No . . . big thing," he croaked finally.

There was no sound then but for the onomatopoeia of the alimentary process—food going in, jaws seizing it, throats closing on the load and opening again for the next—and the light trilling mealtime chatter of their fellow students, the ones unencumbered by casts and groin pulls and bloody toilets. Ray Arthur Larry-Pete was depressed. Over the loss, sure—but it went deeper than that. He was brooding about his college career, his job prospects, life after football. There was a whole winter, spring and summer coming up in which, for the first time in as long as he could remember, he wouldn't have to worry about training for football season, and he couldn't imagine what that would be like. No locker room, no sweat, no pads, no stink of shower drains or the mentholated reek of ointment, no jock itch or aching muscles, no training table, no trainer —no chance, however slim, for glory. . . .

And more immediately, he was fretting about his coursework. There was the Phys. Comm. exam he hadn't been able to study for, and the quiz the professor would almost certainly spring in Phys. Ed., and there were the three-paragraph papers required for both Phys. Training and Phys. Phys., and he was starting to get a little paranoid about Suzie, one of the quintessentially desirable girls on campus, with all her assets on public view, and what did he have to offer her but the glamour of football? Why had she backed out on their date? Did this mean their engagement was off, that she wanted a winner, that this was the beginning of the end?

He was so absorbed in his thoughts he didn't register what Moss was saying when he dropped his bomb into the little silence at the table. Moss was wearing a knee brace and his left arm was in a sling. He was using his right to alternately take a bite of his own food and to lift a heaping forkful from Kitwany's plate to Kitwany's waiting lips. Kitwany was in a full-shoulder harness, both arms frozen in front of him as if he were a sleepwalker cast in plaster of Paris. Ray Arthur Larry-Pete saw Moss's mouth working, but the words flew right by him. "What did you say, Moss?" he murmured, looking up from his food.

"I said Coach says we're probably going to have to forfeit to State."

Ray Arthur Larry-Pete was struck dumb. "Forfeit?" he finally gasped, and the blood was thundering in his temples. "What the hell do you mean, forfeit?"

A swirl of snow flurries scoured his unprotected ears as he limped grimly across the quad to the Phys. Ed. building, muttering under his breath. What was the Coach thinking? Didn't he realize this was the seniors' last game, their last and only chance to assuage the sting of 56-0, the final time they'd ever pull on their cleats against State, Caledonia's bitterest rival, a team they hadn't beaten in modern historical times? Was he crazy?

It was cold, wintry, the last week in November, and Ray Arthur Larry-Pete Fontinot had to reach up with his good hand to pull his collar tight against his throat as he mounted the big concrete steps brushed with snow. The shooting hot-wire pains that accompanied this simple gesture were nothing, nothing at all, and he barely grimaced, reaching down automatically for the push-bar on the big heavy eight-foot-tall double doors. He nodded at a pair of wrestlers running the stairs in gym shorts, made his way past the woefully barren trophy case (*Caledonia College, Third Place Divisional Finish, 1938* read the inscription on the lone trophy, which featured a bronzed figurine in antiquated leather headgear atop a pedestal engraved with the scores of that lustrous long-ago 6-and-5 season, the only winning season Caledonia could boast of in any of its athletic divisions, except for women's field hockey and who counted that?), tested his knees on the third grueling flight of stairs, and approached the Coach's office by the side door. Coach Tundra almost never inhabited his official office on the main corridor, a place of tidy desks, secretaries and seasonal decorations; of telephones, copiers and the new lone fax machine he could use to instantaneously trade X's and O's with his colleagues at other colleges, if he so chose. No, he preferred the back room, a tiny unheated poorly lit cubicle cluttered with the detritus of nineteen unprofitable seasons. Ray Arthur Larry-Pete peered through the open doorway to find the Coach slumped over his desk, face buried in his hands. "Coach?" he said softly.

No reaction.

"Coach?"

From the nest of his hands, the Coach's rucked and gouged face gradually emerged and the glittering wicked raptor's eyes that had struck such bowel-wringing terror into red-shirt freshman and senior alike stared up blankly. There was nothing in those eyes now but a worn and defeated look, and it was a shock. So too the wrinkles in the shirt that was always pressed and pleated with military precision, the scuffed shoes and suddenly vulnerable-looking hands—even the Coach's brush cut, ordinarily as stiff and imperturbable as a falcon's crest, seemed to lie limp against his scalp. "Fontinot?" the Coach said finally, and his voice was dead.

"I, uh, just wanted to check—I mean, practice is at the regular time, right?"

Coach Tundra said nothing. He looked shrunken, lost, older in that moment than the oldest man in the oldest village in the mountains of Tibet. "There won't be any practice today," he said, rubbing his temple over the spot where the military surgeons had inserted the steel plate.

"No practice? But Coach, shouldn't we—I mean, don't we have to—"

"We can't field a team, Fontinot. I count sixteen guys out of forty-two that can go out there on the field and maybe come out of their comas for four consecutive quarters—and I'm counting you among them. And you're so banged up you can barely stand, let alone block." He heaved a sigh, plucked a torn battered shoe from the pile of relics on the floor and turned it over meditatively in his hands. "We're done, Fontinot. Finished. It's all she wrote. Like at Saigon when the gooks overran the place—it's time to cut our losses and run."

Ray Arthur Larry-Pete was stunned. He'd given his life for this, he'd sweated and fought and struggled, filled the bloated vessel of himself with the dregs of defeat, week after week, year after year. He was flunking all four of his Phys. Ed. courses, Suzie thought he was a clown, his mother was dying of uterine cancer and his father —the man who'd named him after the three greatest offensive linemen in college-football history—was driving in from Cincinnati for the game, his last game, the ultimate and final contest that stood between him and the world of pay stubs and mortgages. "You don't mean," he stammered, "you don't mean we're going to *forfeit*, do you?"

For a long moment the Coach held him with his eyes. Faint sounds echoed in the corridors—the slap of sneakers, a door heaving closed, the far-off piping of the basketball coach's whistle. Coach Tundra made an unconscious gesture toward his pant leg and for a moment Ray Arthur Larry-Pete thought he was going to expose the prosthesis again. "What do you want me to do," he said finally, "go out there and play myself?"

Back in his room, Ray Arthur Larry-Pete brooded over the perfidy of it all. A few hours ago he'd been sick to death of the game —what had it gotten him but obloquy and bruises?—but now he wanted to go out there and play so badly he could kill for it. His roommate—Malmo Malmstein, the team's kicker—was still in the hospital, and he had the room to himself through the long morning and the interminable afternoon that followed it. He lay there prostrate on the bed like something shot out in the open that had crawled back to its cave to die, skipping classes, blowing off tests and steeping himself in misery. At three he called Suzie—he had to talk to someone, anyone, or he'd go crazy—but one of her sorority sisters told him she was having her nails done and wasn't expected back before six. Her *nails*. Christ, that rubbed him raw: where was she when he needed her? A sick sinking feeling settled into his stomach—she was cutting him loose, he knew it.

And then, just as it was getting dark, at the very nadir of his despair, something snapped in him. What was wrong with him? Was he a quitter? A whiner and slacker? The kind of guy that gives up before he puts his cleats on? No way. Not Ray Arthur Larry-Pete Fontinot. He came up off the bed like some sort of volcanic eruption and lurched across the room to the phone. Sweating, ponderous, his very heart, lungs and liver trembling with emotion, he focused all his concentration on the big pale block of his index finger as he dialed Gary Gedney, the chicken-neck who handled the equipment and kept the Gatorade bucket full. "Phone up all the guys," he roared into the receiver.

Gedney's voice came back at him in the thin whistling whine of a balloon sputtering round a room: "Who is this?"

"It's Fontinot. I want you to phone up all the guys."

"What for?" Gedney whined.

"We're calling a team meeting."

"Who is?"

Ray Arthur Larry-Pete considered the question a moment, and when finally he spoke it was with a conviction and authority he never thought he could command: "I am."

At seven that night, twenty-six members of the Caledonia Shuckers varsity football squad showed up in the lounge at Bloethal Hall. They filled the place with their presence, their sheer protoplasmic mass, and the chairs and couches groaned under the weight of them. They wore Band-Aids, gauze and tape—miles of it—and the lamplight caught the livid craters of their scars and glanced off the railway stitches running up and down their arms. There were casts, crutches, braces, slings. And there was the smell of them, a familiar, communal, lingering smell—the smell of a team.

Ray Arthur Larry-Pete Fontinot was ready for them, pacing back and forth in front of the sliding glass doors like a bear at the zoo, waiting patiently until each of them had gimped into the room and found a seat. Moss, DuBoy and Kitwany were there with him for emotional support, as was the fifth interior lineman, center Brian McCornish. When they were all gathered, Ray Arthur Larry-Pete lifted his eyes and scanned the familiar faces of his teammates. "I don't know if any of you happened to notice," he said, "but here it is Monday night and we didn't have practice this afternoon."

"Amen," someone said, and a couple of the guys started hooting.

But Ray Arthur Larry-Pete Fontinot wasn't having any of it. He was a rock. His face hardened. He clenched his fists. "It's no joke," he bellowed, and the thunder of his voice set up sympathetic vibrations in the pole lamps with their stained and battered shades. "We've got five days to the biggest game of our lives, and I'm not just talking about us seniors, but everybody, and I want to know what we're going to do about it."

"Forfeit, that's what." It was Diderot, the third-string quarterback and the only one at that vital position who could stand without the aid of crutches. He was lounging against the wall in the back of the room, and all heads now turned to him. "I talked to Coach, and that's what he said."

In that moment, Ray Arthur Larry-Pete lost control of himself. "Forfeit, my ass!" he roared, slamming his forearm, cast and all, down on the nearest coffee table, which fell to splinters under the force of the blow. "Get up, guys," he hissed in an intense aside to his fellow linemen, and Moss, DuBoy, Kitwany and McCornish rose beside him in a human wall. "We're willing to play sixty minutes of football," he boomed, and he had the attention of the room now, that was for sure. "Burt, Reggie, Steve, Brian and me, and we'll play both ways, offense *and* defense, to fill in for guys with broken legs and concussions and whatnot—"

A murmur went up. This was crazy, insane, practically sacrificial. State gave out scholarships—and under-the-table payoffs too—and they got the really topflight players, the true behemoths and crackerjacks, the ones who attracted pro scouts and big money. To go up against them in their present condition would be like replaying the Gulf War, with Caledonia cast in the role of the Iraqis.

"What are you, a bunch of pussies?" Ray Arthur Larry-Pete cried. "Afraid to get your uniforms dirty? Afraid of a little contact? What do you want—to have to live with fifty-six-to-nothing for the rest of your life? Huh? I don't hear you!"

But they heard him. He pleaded, threatened, blustered, cajoled, took them aside one by one, jabbered into the phone half the night till his voice was hoarse and his ear felt like a piece of rubber grafted to the side of his head. In the end, they turned out for practice the following day—twenty-three of them, even Kitwany, who could barely move from the waist up and couldn't get a jersey on over his cast—and Ray Arthur Larry-Pete Fontinot ascended the three flights to the Coach's office and handed Coach Tundra the brand-new silver-plated whistle they'd chipped in to buy him. "Coach," he said, as the startled man looked up at him from the crucible of his memories, "we're ready to go out there and kick some butt."

The day of the game dawned cold and forbidding, with close skies, a biting wind and the threat of snow on the air. Ray Arthur Larry-Pete had lain awake half the night, his brain tumbling through all the permutations of victory and disaster like a slot machine gone amok. Would he shine? Would he rise to the occasion and fight off the devastating pass rush of State's gargantuan front four? And what about the defense? He hadn't played defense since junior high, and now, because they were short-handed and because he'd opened his big mouth, he'd have to go both ways. Would he have the stamina? Or would he stagger round the field on rubber legs, thrust aside by State's steroid-swollen evolutionary freaks like the poor pathetic bumbling fat man he was destined to become? But no. Enough of that. If you thought like a loser—if you doubted for even a minute—then you were doomed, and you deserved 56–0 and worse.

At quarter to seven he got out of bed and stood in the center of the room in his undershorts, cutting the air savagely with the battering ram of his cast, pumping himself up. He felt unconquerable suddenly, felt blessed, felt as if he could do anything. The bruises, the swollen eye, the hip pointer and rickety knees were nothing but fading memories now. By Tuesday he'd been able to lift both his arms to shoulder level without pain, and by Wednesday he was trotting round the field on a pair of legs that felt like bridge abutments. Thursday's scrimmage left him wanting more, and he flew like a sprinter through yesterday's light workout. He was as ready as he'd ever be.

At seven-fifteen he strode through the weather to the dining hall to load up on carbohydrates, and by eight he was standing like a colossus in the foyer of Suzie's sorority house. The whole campus had heard about his speech in the Bloethal lounge, and by Wednesday night Suzie had come back round again. They spent the night in his room—his private room, for the duration of Malmstein's stay at the Sisters of Mercy Hospital—and Suzie had traced his bruises with her lips and hugged the tractor tire of flesh he wore round his midsection to her own slim and naked self. Now she greeted him with wet hair and a face bereft of makeup. "Wish me luck, Suze," he said, and she clung to him briefly before going off to transform herself for the game.

Coach Tundra gathered his team in the locker room at twelve-thirty and spoke to them from his heart, employing the military conceits that always seemed to confuse the players as much as inspire them, and then they were thundering out onto the field like some crazed herd of hoofed and horned things with the scent of blood in their nostrils. The crowd roared. Caledonia's colors, chartreuse and orange, flew in the breeze. The band played. Warming up, Ray Arthur Larry-Pete could see Suzie sitting in the stands with her sorority sisters, her hair the color of vanilla ice cream, her mouth fallen open in a cry of savagery and bloodlust. And there, just to the rear of her—no, it couldn't be, it couldn't—but it was: his mom. Sitting there beside the hulking mass of his father, wrapped up in her windbreaker like a leaf pressed in an album, her scalp glinting bald through the dyed pouf of her hair, there she was, holding a feeble fist aloft. His *mom*! She'd been too sick to attend any of his games this year, but this was his last one, his last game ever, and she'd fought down her pain and all the unimaginable stress and suffering of the oncology ward just to see him play. He felt the tears come to his eyes as he raised his fist in harmony: this game was for her.

Unfortunately, within fifteen seconds of the kickoff, Caledonia was already in the hole, 7–0, and Ray Arthur Larry-Pete hadn't even got out onto the field yet. State's return man had fielded the kick at his own thirty after Malmstein's replacement, Hassan Farouk, had shanked the ball off the tee, and then he'd dodged past the entire special teams unit and on into the end zone as if the Caledonia players were molded of wax. On the ensuing kickoff, Bobby Bibby, a jittery, butterfingered guy Ray Arthur Larry-Pete had never liked, fumbled the ball, and State picked it up and ran it in for the score. They were less than a minute into the game, and already it was 14–0.

Ray Arthur Larry-Pete felt his heart sink, but he leapt up off the bench with a roar and butted heads so hard with Moss and DuBoy he almost knocked himself unconscious. "Come on, guys," he bellowed, "it's only fourteen points, it's nothing, bear down!" And then Bibby held on to the ball and Ray Arthur Larry-Pete was out on the field, going down in his three-point stance across from a guy who looked like a walking mountain. The guy had a handlebar mustache, little black eyes like hornets pinned to his head and a long wicked annealed scar that plunged into his right eye socket and back out again. He looked to be about thirty, and he wore Number 95 stretched tight across the expanse of his chest. "You sorry sack of shit," he growled over Diderot's erratic snap-count. "I'm going to lay you flat out on your ass."

And that's exactly what he did. McCornish snapped the ball, Ray Arthur Larry-Pete felt something like a tactical nuclear explosion in the region of his sternum, and Number 95 was all over Diderot while Ray Arthur Larry-Pete stared up into the sky. In the next moment the trainer was out there, along with the Coach—already starting in on his Ia Drang Valley speech—and Ray Arthur Larry-Pete felt the first few snowflakes drift down into the whites of his wide-open and staring eyes. "Get up and walk it off," the trainer barked, and then half a dozen hands were pulling him to his feet, and Ray Arthur Larry-Pete Fontinot was back in his crouch, directly across from Number 95. And even then, though he hated to admit it to himself, though he was playing for Suzie and his mother and his own rapidly dissolving identity, he knew it was going to be a very long afternoon indeed.

It was 35–0 at the half, and Coach Tundra already had his pant leg rolled up by the time the team hobbled into the locker room. Frozen, pulverized, every cord, ligament, muscle and fiber stretched to the breaking point, they listened numbly as the Coach went on about ordnance, landing zones and fields of fire, while the trainer and his assistant scurried round plying tape, bandages and the ever-present aerosol cans of Numzit. Kitwany's replacement, a huge amorphous red-faced freshman, sat in the corner, quietly weeping, and Bobby Bibby, who'd fumbled twice more in the second quarter, tore off his uniform, pulled on his street clothes without showering and walked on out the door. As for Ray Arthur Larry-Pete Fontinot, he lay supine on the cold hard tiles of the floor, every twinge, pull, ache and contusion from the previous week's game reactivated, and a host of new ones cropping up to overload his nervous system. Along with Moss and DuBoy, he'd done double duty through the first thirty minutes—playing offense and defense both—and his legs were paralyzed. When the Coach blew his whistle and shouted, "On the attack, men!" Ray Arthur Larry-Pete had to be helped up off the floor.

The third quarter was a delirium of blowing snow, shouts, curses and cries in the wilderness. Shadowy forms clashed and fell to the crunch of helmet and the clatter of shoulder pads. Ray Arthur Larry-Pete staggered around the field as if gutshot, so disoriented he was never quite certain which way his team was driving—or rather, being driven. But mercifully, the weather conditions slowed down the big blue barreling machine of State's offense, and by the time the gun sounded, they'd only been able to score once more.

And so the fourth quarter began, and while the stands emptied and even the most fanatical supporters sank glumly into their parkas, Caledonia limped out onto the field with their heads down and their jaws set in grim determination. They were no longer playing for pride, for the memories, for team spirit or their alma mater or to impress their girlfriends; they were playing for one thing only: to avoid at all cost the humiliation of 56–0. And they held on, grudging State every inch of the field, Ray Arthur Larry-Pete coming to life in sporadic flashes during which he was nearly lucid and more often than not moving in the right direction, Moss, DuBoy and McCornish picking themselves up off the ground at regular intervals and the Coach hollering obscure instructions from the sidelines. With just under a minute left to play, they'd managed (with the help of what would turn out to be the worst blizzard to hit the area in twenty years) to hold State to only one touchdown more, making it 49–0 with the ball in their possession and the clock running down.

The snow blew in their teeth. State dug in. A feeble distant cheer went up from the invisible stands. And then, with Number 95 falling on him like an avalanche, Diderot fumbled, and State recovered. Two plays later, and with eight seconds left on the clock, they took the ball into the end zone to make it 55–0, and only the point-after attempt stood between Caledonia and the unforgivable, unutterable debasement of a second straight 56–0 drubbing. Ray Arthur Larry-Pete Fontinot extricated himself from the snowbank where Number 95 had left him and crept stiff-legged back to the line of scrimmage, where he would now assume the defensive role.

There was one hope, and one hope only, in that blasted naked dead cinder of a world that Ray Arthur Larry-Pete Fontinot and his hapless teammates unwillingly inhabited, and that was for one man among them to reach deep down inside himself and distill all his essence—all his wits, all his heart and the full power of his honed young musculature—into a single last-ditch attempt to block that kick. Ray Arthur Larry-Pete Fontinot looked into the frightened faces of his teammates as they heaved for breath in the defensive huddle and knew he was that man. "I'm going to block the kick," he said, and his voice sounded strange in his own ears. "I'm coming in from the right side and I'm going to block the kick." Moss's eyes were glazed. DuBoy was on the sidelines, vomiting in his helmet. No one said a word.

State lined up. Ray Arthur Larry-Pete took a deep breath. The ball was snapped, the lines crashed with a grunt and moan, and Ray Arthur Larry-Pete Fontinot launched himself at the kicker like the space shuttle coming in for a landing, and suddenly—miracle of miracles!—he felt the hard cold pellet of the ball glancing off the bandaged nubs of his fingers. A shout went up, and as he fell, as he slammed rib-first into the frozen ground, he watched the ball squirt up in the air and fall back into the arms of the kicker as if it were attached to a string, and then, unbelieving, he watched the kicker tuck the ball and sprint unmolested across the goal line for the two-point conversion.

If it weren't for Moss, they might never have found him. Ray Arthur Larry-Pete Fontinot just lay there where he'd fallen, the snow drifting silently round him, and he lay there long after the teams had left the field and the stands stood empty under a canopy of snow. There, in the dirt, the steady drift of snow gleaming against the exposed skin of his calves and slowly obliterating the number on the back of his jersey, he had a vision of the future. He saw himself working at some tedious, spirit-crushing job for which his Phys. Ed. training could never have prepared him, saw himself sunk in fat like his father, a pale plain wife and two grublike children at his side, no eighty-yard runs or blocked points to look back on through a false scrim of nostalgia, no glory and no defeat.

No defeat. It was a concept that seemed all at once to congeal in his tired brain, and as Moss called out his name and the snow beat down, he tried hard, with all his concentration, to hold it there.

TOP OF THE
FOOD CHAIN

THE THING WAS, we had a little problem with the insect vector there, and believe me, your tamer stuff, your Malathion and pyre-thrum and the rest of the so-called environmentally safe products didn't begin to make a dent in it, not a dent, I mean it was utterly useless—we might as well have been spraying with Chanel Number 5 for all the good it did. And you've got to realize these people were literally covered with insects day and night—and the fact that they hardly wore any clothes just compounded the problem. Picture if you can, gentlemen, a naked little two-year-old boy so black with flies and mosquitoes it looks like he's wearing long johns, or the young mother so racked with the malarial shakes she can't even lift a diet Coke to her lips—it was pathetic, just pathetic, like something out of the Dark Ages. . . . Well, anyway, the decision was made to go with DDT. In the short term. Just to get the situation under control, you understand.

Yes, that's right, Senator, *DDT:* Dichlorodiphenyltrichloro-ethane.

Yes, I'm well aware of that fact, sir. But just because *we* banned it domestically, under pressure from the birdwatching contingent and the hopheads down at the EPA, it doesn't necessarily follow that the rest of the world—especially the developing world—is about to jump on the bandwagon. And that's the key word here, Senator: *developing.* You've got to realize this is Borneo we're talking about here, not Port Townsend or Enumclaw. These people don't know from square one about sanitation, disease control, pest eradication —or even personal hygiene, if you want to come right down to it.

It rains a hundred and twenty inches a year, minimum. They dig up roots in the jungle. They've still got headhunters along the Rajang River, for god's sake.

And please don't forget they *asked* us to come in there, practically begged us—and not only the World Health Organization, but the Sultan of Brunei and the government in Sarawak too. We did what we could to accommodate them and reach our objective in the shortest period of time and by the most direct and effective means. We went to the air. Obviously. And no one could have foreseen the consequences, no one, not even if we'd gone out and generated a hundred environmental-impact statements—it was just one of those things, a freak occurrence, and there's no defense against that. Not that I know of, anyway. . . .

Caterpillars? Yes, Senator, that's correct. That was the first sign: caterpillars.

But let me backtrack a minute here. You see, out in the bush they have these roofs made of thatched palm leaves—you'll see them in the towns too, even in Bintulu or Brunei—and they're really pretty effective, you'd be surprised. A hundred and twenty inches of rain, they've got to figure a way to keep it out of the hut, and for centuries, this was it. Palm leaves. Well, it was about a month after we sprayed for the final time and I'm sitting at my desk in the trailer thinking about the drainage project at Kuching, enjoying the fact that for the first time in maybe a year I'm not smearing mosquitoes all over the back of my neck, when there's a knock at the door. It's this elderly gentleman, tattooed from head to toe, dressed only in a pair of running shorts—they love those shorts, by the way, the shiny material and the tight machine-stitching, the whole country, men and women and children, they can't get enough of them. . . . Anyway, he's the headman of the local village and he's very excited, something about the roofs—*atap,* they call them. That's all he can say, *atap, atap,* over and over again.

It's raining, of course. It's always raining. So I shrug into my rain slicker, start up the 4X4 and go have a look. Sure enough, all the *atap* roofs are collapsing, not only in his village, but throughout the target area. The people are all huddled there in their running shorts, looking pretty miserable, and one after another the roofs keep falling in, it's bewildering, and gradually I realize the headman's diatribe has begun to feature a new term I was unfamiliar with at the time—the word for caterpillar, as it turns out, in the Iban dialect. But who was to make the connection between three passes with the crop duster and all these staved-in roofs?

Our people finally sorted it out a couple weeks later. The chemical, which, by the way, cut down the number of mosquitoes exponentially, had the unfortunate side effect of killing off this little wasp—I've got the scientific name for it somewhere in my report here, if you're interested—that preyed on a type of caterpillar that in turn ate palm leaves. Well, with the wasps gone, the caterpillars hatched out with nothing to keep them in check and chewed the roofs to pieces, and that was unfortunate, we admit it, and we had a real cost overrun on replacing those roofs with tin . . . but the people were happier, I think, in the long run, because let's face it, no matter how tightly you weave those palm leaves, they're just not going to keep the water out like tin. Of course, nothing's perfect, and we had a lot of complaints about the rain drumming on the panels, people unable to sleep and what-have-you. . . .

Yes, sir, that's correct—the flies were next.

Well, you've got to understand the magnitude of the fly problem in Borneo, there's nothing like it here to compare it with, except maybe a garbage strike in New York. Every minute of every day you've got flies everywhere, up your nose, in your mouth, your ears, your eyes, flies in your rice, your Coke, your Singapore sling and your gin rickey. It's enough to drive you to distraction, not to mention the diseases these things carry, from dysentery to typhoid to cholera and back round the loop again. And once the mosquito population was down, the flies seemed to breed up to fill in the gap—Borneo wouldn't be Borneo without some damned insect blackening the air.

Of course, this was before our people had tracked down the problem with the caterpillars and the wasps and all of that, and so we figured we'd had a big success with the mosquitoes, why not a series of ground sweeps, mount a fogger in the back of a Suzuki

Brat and sanitize the huts, not to mention the open sewers, which as you know are nothing but a breeding ground for flies, chiggers and biting insects of every sort. At least it was an error of commission rather than omission. At least we were trying.

I watched the flies go down myself. One day they were so thick in the trailer I couldn't even *find* my paperwork, let alone attempt to get through it, and the next they were collecting on the windows, bumbling around like they were drunk. A day later they were gone. Just like that. From a million flies in the trailer to none. . . .

Well, no one could have foreseen that, Senator.

The geckos ate the flies, yes. You're all familiar with geckos, I assume, gentlemen? These are the lizards you've seen during your trips to Hawaii, very colorful, patrolling the houses for roaches and flies, almost like pets, but of course they're wild animals, never lose sight of that, and just about as unsanitary as anything I can think of, except maybe flies.

Yes, well don't forget, sir, we're viewing this with twenty-twenty hindsight, but at the time no one gave a thought to geckos or what they ate—they were just another fact of life in the tropics. Mosquitoes, lizards, scorpions, leeches—you name it, they've got it. When the flies began piling up on the windowsills like drift, naturally the geckos feasted on them, stuffing themselves till they looked like sausages crawling up the walls. Where before they moved so fast you could never be sure you'd seen them, now they waddled across the floor, laid around in the corners, clung to the air vents like magnets—and even then no one paid much attention to them till they started turning belly-up in the streets. Believe me, we confirmed a lot of things there about the buildup of these products as you move up the food chain and the efficacy—or lack thereof—of certain methods, no doubt about that. . . .

The cats? That's where it got sticky, really sticky. You see, nobody really lost any sleep over a pile of dead lizards—though we did the tests routinely and the tests confirmed what we'd expected, that is, the product had been concentrated in the geckos because of the sheer number of contaminated flies they consumed. But lizards are

one thing and cats are another. These people really have an affection
for their cats—no house, no hut, no matter how primitive, is without
at least a couple of them. Mangy-looking things, long-legged and
scrawny, maybe, not at all the sort of animal you'd see here, but
there it was: they loved their cats. Because the cats were functional,
you understand—without them, the place would have been swimming in rodents inside of a week.

You're right there, Senator, yes—that's exactly what happened.

You see, the cats had a field day with these feeble geckos—you
can imagine, if any of you have ever owned a cat, the kind of joy
these animals must have experienced to see their nemesis, this ultra-
quick lizard, and it's just barely creeping across the floor like a bug.
Well, to make a long story short, the cats ate up every dead and
dying gecko in the country, from snout to tail, and then the cats
began to die . . . which to my mind would have been no great loss
if it wasn't for the rats. Suddenly there were rats everywhere—you
couldn't drive down the street without running over half-a-dozen of
them at a time. They fouled the grain supplies, fell in the wells and
died, bit infants as they slept in their cradles. But that wasn't the
worst, not by a long shot. No, things really went down the tube after
that. Within the month we were getting scattered reports of bubonic
plague, and of course we tracked them all down and made sure the
people got a round of treatment with antibiotics, but still we lost a
few and the rats kept coming. . . .

It was my plan, yes. I was brainstorming one night, rats scuttling
all over the trailer like something out of a cheap horror film, the
villagers in a panic over the threat of the plague and the stream of
nonstop hysterical reports from the interior—people were turning
black, swelling up and bursting, that sort of thing—well, as I say, I
came up with a plan, a stopgap, not perfect, not cheap; but at this
juncture, I'm sure you'll agree, something had to be implemented.

We wound up going as far as Australia for some of the cats,
cleaning out the SPCA facilities and what-have-you, though we
rounded most of them up in Indonesia and Singapore—approxi-
mately fourteen thousand in all. And yes, it cost us—cost us upfront

purchase money and aircraft fuel and pilots' overtime and all the rest of it—but we really felt there was no alternative. It was like all nature had turned against us.

And yet still, all things considered, we made a lot of friends for the U.S.A. the day we dropped those cats, and you should have seen them, gentlemen, the little parachutes and harnesses we'd tricked up, fourteen thousand of them, cats in every color of the rainbow, cats with one ear, no ears, half a tail, three-legged cats, cats that could have taken pride of show in Springfield, Massachusetts, and all of them twirling down out of the sky like great big oversized snowflakes. . . .

It was something. It was really something.

Of course, you've all seen the reports. There were other factors we hadn't counted on, adverse conditions in the paddies and manioc fields—we don't to this day know what predatory species were inadvertently killed off by the initial sprayings, it's just a mystery—but the weevils and whatnot took a pretty heavy toll on the crops that year, and by the time we dropped the cats, well, the people were pretty hungry, and I suppose it was inevitable that we lost a good proportion of them right then and there. But we've got a CARE program going there now, and something hit the rat population— we still don't know what, a virus, we think—and the geckos, they tell me, are making a comeback.

So what I'm saying is, it could be worse, and to every cloud a silver lining, wouldn't you agree, gentlemen?

LITTLE AMERICA

ALL HE WANTED was a quarter, fifty cents, a dollar maybe. The guy was a soft touch, absolutely—the softest. You could see it in the way he clutched the suitcase with his big-knuckled hairy old hands and kept blinking his eyes as if he'd just got out of bed or something. People were spilling out of the train, the usual crush—a scrawny black woman with the pale splash of a birthmark on her face and two angry-looking kids clinging to her dress, a tight little clump of pin-eared teenagers, guys with briefcases and haircuts hustling up the ramp with their chop-chop strides—and nobody had spotted the old man yet. Roger stood motionless, twenty feet from him, and waited. Out of the corner of his eye he saw Rohlich holding out his battered Orioles cap to a polyester wonder with sunglasses like a visor, and he saw the look of annoyance, the firm set of the jaw, the brush-off. Rohlich's voice came back to him like a bad radio over the squeal of the train's brakes and the scrape and clatter of shoes on the pavement and all the birdy jabber of the arriving and departing: "Hey, who bit you in the ass, man? All I wanted was a quarter—"

But the old man, the softest of touches, never moved. He stood rooted to the floor, just in front of the Baltimore sign, his watery old eyes roving over the crowd as if he was an explorer and he'd just discovered a new tribe. The man was old, Roger could see that, seventy at least, and he didn't have a clue as to where he was. Ducking his head and sidling across the floor with the crab walk he always used on touches—never come up to them directly, never freak them—Roger moved in. He was moistening his lips to make his pitch and thinking, *A buck, a buck at least,* when the old man's face suddenly lit with a smile. Roger looked over his shoulder. There was no one there. The old man was smiling at him.

"Hey," Roger crooned, ducking his head again and rolling it back up on his shoulders, "hello. I mean, how you doin'?"

He was wearing a suit, the old man, and nothing too shabby, either—probably mohair or something like that—and his hair was perfectly parted, a plumb line that showed a swath of naked pink scalp beneath. The skin was drawn tight under his cheekbones and there was something strange about his lips, but the milky eyes were focused now. On Roger. "Well, well," the old man said, and his voice was deep and hearty, with an echo to it, "good to see you again, a real pleasure." And he reached out his hand for a shake.

Roger took the hand, a dry old-man's hand, held it a moment and looked into his eyes. "Yeah, sure. Good to see you too." He'd begun to wonder if the guy was mental or whatever—he was probably looking for his nurse. Or his keeper. But that watch—that was a Movado, three hundred bucks, easy—and he had a college ring that looked like something. "Real good," Roger added, for emphasis.

"Yes," the old man said, and he smacked his lips and held the suitcase out for Roger to take. Roger could feel his heart going. This was too good to be true, a fantasy in three dimensions and Technicolor, too. He looked over his shoulder, scanned the place for cops and took the suitcase. "We'll be at the Sheraton again, then?" the old man asked.

Roger took a deep breath, his eyes uncontainable, a whole hive of bees buzzing round inside his chest—*Just get us out of here*—and said, "Yeah, the Sheraton. Of course. Just like last time, right?"

The old man tugged at his nose as if he was afraid it might drop off his face. He was studying his shoes. "Just like last time," he repeated.

One more look around, and then Roger hunched his shoulders over the suitcase and swung toward the street exit. "Follow me," he said.

The train always brought back memories—there was a rhythm to it, a discontinuous flow that seemed to peel back the layers of his mind like growth rings in a tree. One minute he was a boy hunched over the radio with his mother as his father's voice spoke to the whole U.S.A. from out of the clasp of the impermeable dark, and then he was a father himself, his step light on the cobbles of Beacon Hill, and then a grandfather, and finally an old man on a train, staring back at himself in the flicker of the window. The train did that to him. It was like a drug, a narcotic, a memory solution leaking drop by drop into his uncertain veins. And that was funny, too: he was on a train because he didn't like to fly. Richard Evelyn Byrd III, son of the greatest aviator of them all, and he didn't like to fly. Well, he was old now—he'd had enough of flying when he was a boy. A young man, really. He remembered the bright flaring skin of Antarctica, the whole ice shelf shaved close with a razor, felt the jolt of the landing and the hard sharp crack of the skis on the ice just as vividly as if they were beneath him now, saw again the light in his father's eyes and the perfect sangfroid with which he confronted all things, the best and the worst alike.

Leverett had put him on the train in Boston and his daughter-in-law was waiting for him in Washington. He repeated it to himself, aloud, as the car swayed and clicked over the rails. *Leverett. His daughter-in-law. Washington.* But no, that wasn't right. It was that pleasant young man from the Geographic Society, the one who'd been so nice about the rooms at the Sheraton, he was the one. Of course he was. A first-class reception all the way. And that was only as it should be—he, the son of the father, traveling all the way to the nation's capital for the unveiling of the new commemorative stamp honoring the man whose legend would never die, the last of the men in the old mold, the last hero. Yes. And he would talk to them about that—to Walter what's-his-name at the Geographic Society—about his father's museum. He had a reindeer-skin mukluk with him now, in his suitcase, from the 1929 expedition—just to show it to them, just as bait. There was a whole houseful of stuff back in Boston, a shrine, and it was a shame it wasn't on public

display, now and permanently—and why not? For lack of a few
dollars? They were financing presidents' libraries, weren't they? And
paying out welfare and food stamps and whatnot? What would the
Byrd Museum take? A million? Two? Well, he had his father's mukluk for them and that was worth a thousand words of pleading and
haggling—ten thousand.

And then the train stopped—he felt it lurch at his insides and
for an instant he thought he was up in the hard pellucid Antarctic
sky all over again, and he even felt the chill of it. But the train
stopped, and there was his suitcase, and he got off. Washington,
D.C. The capital. He recognized the station, of course he did. But
where was his daughter-in-law? Where was the car? Where was that
pleasant young fellow from the Geographic Society?

The old man's voice kept nagging at him, a fruity drone that
caught and swallowed itself and vomited it all back up again. Why
weren't they taking the car? Were they going to walk the whole way?
And his daughter-in-law, where was she? But then he'd change the
subject as if he wasn't even listening to himself and the next minute
he'd be rattling on about what a bracing day it was, just like high
summer at the South Pole, ha ha ha, and now he was laughing or
choking—it was hard to say which. Roger stayed two paces ahead
of him, head down, fingers locked around the handle of the suitcase,
and listened to him bluster and wheeze. "It's not much farther," he
said. "You'll see your daughter-in-law, she'll be there, and everybody
else, too. Here, this way," he said, and he paused to let the old man
draw even with him, and then he steered him down the alley out
back of the recycling center.

They were six blocks from the station now, and the throttle of
Roger's heart had eased back a bit, but still, with every step he had
to fight down the impulse to take the suitcase and run. That would
have been the easy way. But he would have been a fool to do it and
he knew the game was going to be a whole lot richer if he played
it right. If he could just get the old geek into the back of the warehouse, a quiet place he knew, where the newspapers were stacked
up twenty feet high, he could dig a little deeper. What else did he

have besides the watch and ring? A wallet maybe? Cash? Credit cards?

At the door to the place—a big aluminum garage door that was pried up in the corner just enough to allow a no-waist man holding his breath to slip right on through—the old guy surprised him. He didn't balk at all. Just took a glance at the trash blown up against the concrete-block wall as if it was the most ordinary thing in the world, pinched in his gut and followed Roger into the dark echoing vastness of the warehouse.

And that was it: they were safe. It was over. Anything the old man had was Roger's, right on down to his undershorts, and there was nobody to say any different. Roger led him behind a column of newsprint and set the suitcase down. "Here we are," he said, turning to face the old man, "the Sheraton."

"This isn't the Sheraton," the old man said, but he didn't seem upset at all. He was grinning and his eyes were bright. "It isn't the Ritz-Carlton, either. You're pulling my leg, aren't you?"

Roger gave him back the grin. There was a long pause, during which he became aware of the distant beep-beep-beep of a forklift somewhere on the far side of the warehouse. "Yeah, sure," Roger said finally, "I was only joking, sure I was. Can't fool you, huh?" He settled himself down on a stack of newspaper and motioned for the old man to do the same. He lit a cigarette—or the stub of a cigarette he'd picked out of an ashtray at the station. He was taking his time, enjoying himself—there was no reason to rush, or to get violent, either. The old man was out there, no doubt about it.

"So what's in the suitcase?" Roger asked casually, shaking out the match and exhaling through his nostrils.

The old guy had been sitting there, as content as if he was stretched out in his easy chair back at home, smacking his lips and chuckling softly to himself, but now his face went serious. "My father's mukluk."

Roger couldn't help himself. He let out a laugh. "Your father's who?"

"Here, let me show you," the old man said, and Roger let him take the suitcase. He propped it up on his bony old knees, popped the latches and pulled back the lid to reveal a nest of garments—socks, shirts, handkerchiefs and a tweed sportcoat. Rummaging around a moment, he finally came up with what he was looking for—some kind of shoe or boot or something, made out of fur—and held it up for Roger's inspection as if it was the Hope diamond.

"So what did you say this was?" Roger asked, taking the thing from him and turning it over in his hand.

"My father's mukluk. For the museum."

Roger didn't know what to make of this. He pulled quietly on his cigarette a moment, then handed the thing back to him with a shrug. "Is it worth anything?"

"Ha!" the old man boomed, and Roger was afraid he was going to get to his feet and try something. "Worth anything? The very mukluk Admiral Byrd wore in Little America? The very one?" The old man drew himself up, cradling the shoe to his chest. "And I tell you something—and you can tell Walter from me," he said, lowering his voice in confidentiality, "I've got plenty more where this came from. Plenty. Notebooks, parkas, reindeer pants and finnesko boots, the sun compass itself—the very one he used to make his fix on the Pole." He rocked back on his haunches. "Yes," he murmured, and he might have been talking to himself, so oblivious was he of Roger and his surroundings, "you tell Walter. All we need is maybe a million. And that's nothing these days. Nothing."

The old man was as crazy as plant life, but that only took you so far, and though Roger had nowhere to go—hadn't had anywhere to go in maybe ten years now—he was getting impatient. "You're absolutely right," he said, cutting him off in the middle of a windy speech about his museum, and he used the phrase as an excuse to lean forward and shake the dry old hand again. But this time, unlike the first, when every eye in the station was on them, Roger expertly slipped the watch over the bony wrist and dropped it in his coat pocket, and the old man didn't know a thing about it.

Or maybe he did. His expression changed suddenly, as if he was trying to remember something. The lines stood out in his face. He looked old. Old and constipated. "I'm thirsty," he suddenly announced.

"Thirsty?" Roger roared, drunk with his own success. "Hell, so am I—what say we share a pint or two, eh? Have a party. Drink to your mukluk and your museum." He stood and patted his pockets theatrically, enjoying himself all over again—he couldn't remember the last time he'd had this much fun. "But I'm a little short. You got any cash? For a drink, I mean?"

Another facial change. The jaw clenched, the eyes caught hold of him. "You're not the young man from the Geographic Society," the old man said quietly.

"The hell I'm not," Roger protested, and he was so frisky all of a sudden he spun around twice and threw out his arms like a tap dancer rising to the finale. "Sure I am, old man, sure I am—but listen, what did you say your name was?"

"Byrd. Richard Evelyn Bird. The third."

Oh, the solemnity of it, the dignity. He might have been announcing the King of Arabia or something. Roger laughed out loud. "Bird, huh? Tweet-tweet. Bird the Third." Then he let a hint of ugliness creep into his voice, and he stood over the old man now, no mistaking the posture: "I said, you got any cash for a drink, Bird the Third?"

The hand shook, the fingers fumbled in the jacket pocket, and there was the wallet, genuine calfskin, receptacle for the sort of notes and documents that separated people like the old man from Roger and Rohlich and all the other bleary-eyed, rotten-toothed bums and winos curled up on their sheets of cardboard across the city. In that moment, Roger almost felt sorry for the old retard—almost. But in the end, of course, he felt sorrier for himself, and in a quick swipe the wallet was his: five twenties, folded and joined with a paper clip; three ones; a return ticket, Washington to Boston. Photos: an old lady, a kid in a Little League outfit, some white-haired old duffer in a parka. And what was this, what was this? A Visa card, thin as a wafer, shiny as a pot of gold.

He was used to a cocktail before dinner—a Manhattan, generally, shaken, and with a twist instead of a cherry—and a good cabernet or pinot noir with his meal, but this was something he hadn't experienced before, this was something new. The young man passed him the bottle—*Gallo White Port*, the label read, *Alcohol 19% By Volume*—and he took a long gulping swallow that left his chin wet and his stomach burning. He was thirsty, nearly parched, and the liquid—it was cold, it was wet—went down easily, and after the first drink he didn't care what it was. When the bottle was gone, the young man produced another, and though he'd been hungry, though he hadn't eaten anything except the egg-salad sandwich and the apple his son had given him at the Boston station, the hunger faded and he felt better and better as the evening wore on. He was telling the young man about pemmican, how it was the highest-energy food man had yet to devise and how many calories you had to replace daily just to stay alive at seventy-five below, when all at once he felt as lucid as he ever had. He caught himself up so suddenly he almost choked. This wasn't the young man from the Geographic Society, not at all. There was the same fringe of patchy, youthful beard, the startled blue eyes and delicate raw skin, but the nose was all wrong and the mouth had a mean, hurtful look to it. And his clothes—they were in tatters, soaked through with the grease and leavings of the ages, reeking, an unforgivably human stink he could smell from all the way over here. "This isn't Washington," the old man said, understanding now that he'd gotten off at the wrong stop, that he was in some other city altogether, a place he didn't know, understanding that he was lost. "Is it?"

His face shining with drink, his ragged arms flailing at the air, the young man howled with manic glee, kicked at the newspapers heaped up round him and finally had to clutch his ribs tight to stop the laughter. He laughed till he began to cough, and he coughed till he brought something up and spat it on the floor. "You are out there, Bird," he said, straining at each word, and the laughter seized him again. "You are really out there."

So: he was lost. It had happened to him before, two or three times at least. A trick of the mind, that was all, one little mistake—getting off at the wrong stop, turning right instead of left—and the world became a strange and unfathomable place, terrain to explore all over again. He didn't mind. They'd come for him, Leverett and his wife, sweet girl, really, and the grandchildren, they'd find him. But then a little wedge of concern inserted itself along the fracture lines of his psyche, and it became a worry. Who was this man if he wasn't from the Geographic Society, and what did he want? And what was this place? Newspapers. Drifts of them, mountains, a whole continent, and all it was was newsprint.

He took the bottle when it came to him and he took a drink and passed it back, and there was a third member of their party now, another hand interposed between him and the young man who wasn't from the Geographic Society. Matted beard, nose like a bird of prey, eyes frozen into his head, and he didn't know him, not at all, but why did he look so familiar? He felt himself drifting. It was cold, damnably cold, for what—October, wasn't it? "Early winter this year," he murmured, but no one uttered a word in response.

The next time he noticed anything, it was the candle. He must have dozed. But there it was, the candle. A light in the wilderness. The bottle came back to him and the feeble light leapt out suddenly to illuminate the new man's face, and he knew him, knew him as well as he knew his own son and his own father. "You," he said out of the void, "I know you."

There was a low cackle, a dribble of hard-edged laughter from two ravaged throats. "Yeah, we know you too, Bird the Third," the young man said, and his voice had changed, the tone of it, till everything he said sounded like a school-yard taunt.

"No," the old man insisted, "not you . . . I mean"—and he looked the newcomer full in the face—"I mean you." The inspiration had flared in his brain, and he knew the man even after all these years, a great man, his father's equal almost, the only other man in the world who'd been to both poles and back again. "You're Roald Amundsen."

The laugh was ugly, almost a bark. The man showed the stubs of his teeth. He took his time, drinking, wiping his mouth with the back of his sleeve. "Shit, man, sure I am," he said, and the other one was laughing again, "and this here, your friend with the bottle, this guy's Santy Claus."

Roger was on a tear. For a full week, seven whole days and maybe more, he didn't know where he was. He hadn't had this much money, all at once, since he'd left New Jersey, when he was a kid living in that lopsided trailer with his mother and stocking the shelves at Waldbaum's. The whole thing with the old man had been unreal, the sort of score everybody dreams about but never makes, never. Oh, sure, zombies like Rohlich would tell you they were hitch-hiking once and Madonna gave them a lift or some high roller in Atlantic City handed them a C-note when all they asked for was a quarter, but this was unreal, this *happened*. Those five twenties alone could have kept him flying for a month or more, but of course they'd disappeared, dropped down the hole where all of it went sooner or later—usually sooner. He didn't know where he'd been or what he'd done, but he ached all over, so it must have been good, and he needed a drink so bad he could taste it. Or couldn't taste it. Or whatever.

And shit, it was cold. Too cold for this time of year. Cold and drizzling. When he woke up an hour or so ago he'd found himself on a wet slab of cardboard out back of the fish restaurant the yuppies flocked to—Cicero's—and he didn't know how he'd got there or what he'd done the night before, and his pockets were empty. No loose change. No nothing. He'd wandered over to the mission and passed a short dog around with the black guy they called Hoops, and now he was wet through to the skin and shivering and looking for a benefactor so he could invest in the Gallo Company and warm up where it counted most. He remembered the old guy's watch then, the black Movado, and felt around in his pockets for it. It was gone. He had a further—and dimmer—recollection of pawning it and getting ten bucks for the thing and being all pissed off about it, but then he wasn't so sure—it might have been another watch and another time.

He stayed on the street for a couple hours, it got a whole lot colder, and all he came up with was ninety-two cents. By then, his thirst was driving him crazy, so he bought a can of beer and went over to the warehouse to see who was around and maybe trade up for a hit or two of wine. He saw that somebody had tried to hammer the crease out of the door and that they'd moved a whole shitload of papers out and a whole new shitload in, but other than that nothing had changed. There was nobody around, so he made himself a little igloo out of bundled newspaper, drank his beer in two swallows and tried to stop shivering for a minute at a time.

At first he didn't hear it—or it didn't register. The place was cavernous, with a ceiling you could fly planes under and walls that went on for a block, and it was noisy, middle of the day, trucks rumbling in and out of the South Street entrance with cans and bottles, and Mr. and Mrs. Nice driving up with Sis and Bud to deliver their neat foursquare string-tied bundles of newspaper. It was noisy and he didn't hear a thing but the muted rumble of all that activity, and he wished five o'clock would come and they'd shut the place down and go home and leave him in peace, but after a while he became aware that somebody was there with him, just up the next aisle, muttering to himself in the low sweet singsong tones of the crackbrained and hopeless. Another bum. Somebody he knew maybe. A man with a short dog and maybe a bite of something scavenged from the top of the bin out back of the supermarket. He felt his spirits lift.

He pushed himself up, keeping an eye out for the watchman, and slipped up the next aisle. The papers had fallen in drifts here, sloppily stacked, and he fought his way through them in the direction of the voice, his harsh ragged breath crystallizing before him. There was a nook carved out of the wall, and he saw the back of a white head, the old withered stalk of a neck, and there he was: Bird the Third.

He was amazed. He would have thought the guy would be long gone, would have found his people, his keeper, whatever. But still, there he was, and for a moment Roger felt a surge of hope. Maybe he had something on him still, something he'd overlooked, some piece of jewelry, a pair of glasses—hell, his clothes even. But then he saw that they'd already got to him. The old retard's suit was gone, and his socks and shoes too. Somebody'd switched on him, and he was dressed in a puke-green janitor's jumpsuit and was missing a shoe—or he'd found a shoe somewhere, a torn greasy old Nike sneaker with the toes ripped out. He was pathetic. A mess. And he wasn't worth anything to anybody.

For a long while, Roger just stood there watching him. The old man was shivering, his arms wrapped around himself like coils, the bare foot discolored and bad-looking. He had that thousand-mile stare on his face, the same one you saw on some of the older guys, the Vietnam vets and whatnot. Roger's brain was working hard, and for a moment he saw himself taking the guy along to the police station and turning him in like a hero and maybe getting a reward from the guy's family or whoever. They had to be looking for him. You don't come from that world, with your haircut and your suitcase and your Movado watch, without somebody looking for you, especially if you're a little soft in the head to begin with.

It was a good idea for about eight seconds, and then it became a whole lot less good, and ten seconds further on it just plain stank. There wouldn't be any reward—maybe for Joe Average and Mr. and Mrs. Nice, maybe for them, but not for the likes of Roger. That's how things worked. There were two worlds operating here, the one where Bird the Third and all the rest of them lived, and this one, the real one, where you slept under things at ankle level and ate the crumbs they gave you. Well, fuck that. Fuck it. It was just like the credit card. He'd tried it on maybe twenty liquor stores, the ones he knew and the ones he didn't, and nobody took him for Bird the Third, no matter how much ID he showed or how hard he tried. Not the way he looked, no way. He was going to trade the thing for a bottle at this one place—*Here, you want the card, Visa Gold? Keep it*—but then the jerk behind the counter got nasty, real nasty, and confiscated the whole business, plastic, ID and all. That's how it was.

He was going to say something, goodbye or thanks for the ride or whatever, but in the end he decided against it. Somewhere, in some deep tunnel of what used to be his reality and was now somebody else's, he even felt a stab of pity and, worse, guilt. But he comforted himself with the thought that if he hadn't been there at the station, somebody else would have, and any way you looked at it Bird the Third would have wound up plucked. In the end, he just shrugged. Then he made his way off through the drifts, thinking maybe he'd just go on down to the station and check out the trains.

Oh, but it was cold. Cold to the bone. And dry. He knew the irony of it all too well—a shelf made of water, frozen and compacted over the howling eons, and not a drop to drink. It was locked in, unavailable, dry as paper. He shifted position and winced. It was his foot. He'd lost all feeling in it there for a while, but now it came back with a vengeance, a thousand hot needles radiating all the way up his leg to the thigh. That's how it was with frostbite. He'd lose his toes, he knew that, but they'd all lost toes, fingers—the great ones—even the tips of their noses. There were continents to explore, unknown corners to make known, and what was a little discomfort compared to the greatness of that?

He thought of his father in the weather shack where he'd wintered alone, the fear of that eternal blackness closing in on him like a fist, alternately freezing and asphyxiating himself on the fumes from the kerosene stove. That was greatness. That was will. That was the indomitable spirit he'd inherited. But still, it was cold, terribly, implacably, unrelentingly cold, and his foot hurt him and he felt himself drifting off to sleep. That was how it happened, that was how they died out here, numbed by the cold, seduced into sleep and forgetfulness.

He stirred, and he fought it. He beat at his thighs, hammered his hands against the meat of his arms, but he couldn't keep it up, and before long he subsided. He tried to call out, but his voice was gone, and besides, it was the coward's way—his father would never have called out. Never. No, he would have gone on into the grip of that polar night, never wavering, never halting, on and on, into the dream.

BEAT

YEAH, I WAS BEAT. We were all Beat. Hell, I'm Beat now—is, was and always will be. I mean, how do you stop? But this isn't about me—I'm nobody, really, just window-dressing on the whole mother of Bop freight-train-hopping holy higher than Tokay Beat trip into the heart of the American night. No, what I wanted to tell you about is Jack. And Neal and Allen and Bill and all the rest, too, and how it all went down, because I was there, I was on the scene, and there was nobody Beater than me.

Picture this: seventeen years old, hair an unholy mess and a little loden-green beret perched up on top to keep it in place, eighty-three cents in my pocket and a finger-greased copy of *The Subterraneans* in my rucksack along with a Charlie Parker disc with enough pops, scratches and white noise worked into the grooves to fill out the soundtrack of a sci-fi flick, hitched all the way from Oxnard, California, and there I am on Jack's front porch in Northport, Long Island, December twenty-three, nineteen fifty-eight. It's cold. Bleak. The town full of paint-peeling old monster houses, gray and worn and just plain old, like the whole horse-blindered tired-out East Coast locked in its gloom from October to April with no time off for good behavior. I'm wearing three sweaters under my Levi's jacket and still I'm holding on to my ribs and I can feel the snot crusting round my nostrils and these mittens I bummed from an old lady at the Omaha bus station are stiff with it, and I knock, wondering if there's an officially cool way to knock, a hipster's way, a kind of secret Dharma Bums code-knock I don't know about.

Knock-knock. Knockata-knockata, knock-knock-knock.

My first surprise was in store: it wasn't Jack, the gone hep satori-seeking poet god of the rails and two-lane blacktop, who answered the door, but a big blocky old lady with a face like the bottom of a hiking boot. She was wearing a dress the size of something you'd drape over a car to keep the dust off it, and it was composed of a thousand little red and green triangles with gold trumpets and silver angels squeezed inside of them. She gave me the kind of look that could peel the tread off a recapped tire, the door held just ajar. I shuddered: she looked like somebody's mother.

My own mother was three thousand miles away and so square she was cubed; my dog, the one I'd had since childhood, was dead, flattened out by a big rig the week earlier; and I'd flunked English, History, Calculus, Art, Phys. Ed., Music and Lunch. I wanted adventure, the life of the road, freewheeling chicks in berets and tea and bongos and long Benzedrine-inflected bullshit sessions that ran on into morning, I wanted Jack and everything he stood for, and here was this old lady. "Uh," I stammered, fighting to control my voice, which was just then deepening from the adolescent squeak I'd had to live with since consciousness had hit, "does, uh, Jack Kerouac live here, I mean, by any chance?"

"Go back where you came from," the old lady said. "My Jacky don't have time for no more of this nonsense." And that was it: she shut the door in my face.

My Jacky!

It came to me then: this was none other than Jack's mother, the Bop-nurturing freewheeling wild Madonna herself, the woman who'd raised up the guru and given him form, mother of us all. And she'd locked me out. I'd come three thousand miles, her Jacky was my Jack, and I was cold through to the bone, stone broke, scared, heartsick and just about a lungful of O_2 away from throwing myself down in the slush and sobbing till somebody came out and shot me. I knocked again.

"Hey, Ma," I heard from somewhere deep inside the house, and it was like the rutting call of some dangerous beast, a muted angry threatening Bop-benny-and-jug-wine roar, the voice of the man himself, "what the hell is this, I'm trying to concentrate in here."

And then the old lady: "It ain't nothing, Jacky."

Knock-knock. Knockata-knockata, knock-knock-knock. I para-diddled that door, knocked it and socked it, beat on it like it was the bald flat-topped dome of my uptight pencil-pushing drudge of a bourgeois father himself, or maybe Mr. Detwinder, the principal at Oxnard High. I knocked till my knuckles bled, a virtuoso of knocking, so caught up in the rhythm and energy of it that it took me a minute to realize the door was open and Jack himself standing there in the doorway. He looked the way Belmondo tried to look in *Breathless,* loose and cool in a rumpled T-shirt and jeans, with a smoke in one hand, a bottle of muscatel in the other.

I stopped knocking. My mouth fell open and the snot froze in my nostrils. "Jack Kerouac," I said.

He let a grin slide down one side of his mouth and back up the other. "Nobody else," he said.

The wind shot down my collar, I caught a glimpse of colored lights blinking on and off in the room behind him, and suddenly it was all gushing out of me like something I'd been chewing over and digesting all my life: "I hitched all the way from Oxnard and my name's Wallace Pinto but you can call me Buzz and I just wanted to say, I just wanted to tell you—"

"Yeah, yeah, I know," he said, waving a hand in dismissal, and he seemed unsteady on his muscatel-impaired feet, the smoke curling up to snatch at his cracked blue squinting eyes, the words slow on his lips, heavy, weighted and freighted with the deep everlasting bardic wisdom of the road, the cathouse and the seaman's bar, "but I tell you, kid, you keep drumming on the door like that you're going to end up in the hospital"—a pause—"or maybe a jazz combo." I just stood there in a kind of trance until I felt his hand—his Dharma Bum Subterranean On the Road Bop-master's gone Mexican-chick-digging hand—take hold of my shoulder and tug me forward, over the threshold and into the house. "You ever been introduced to a

true and veritable set of tight-skinned bongos?" he asked, throwing
an arm over my shoulder as the door slammed behind us.

Two hours later we were sitting there in the front room by this
totally gone Christmas tree bedecked with cherubim and little
Christs and the like, indulging in a poor boy and a joint or two of
Miss Green, my Charlie Parker record whizzing and popping on the
record player and a whole big pile of red and green construction-
paper strips growing at our feet. We were making a chain to drape
over the Beatest tree you ever saw and the music was a cool breeze
fluttering full of Yardbird breath and the smell of ambrosia and
manna crept in from the kitchen where Mémère, the Beat Madonna
herself, was cooking up some first-rate mouthwatering Canuck-style
two-days-before-Christmas chow. I hadn't eaten since New Jersey,
the morning before, and that was only some pretty piss-poor diner
hash fries and a runny solitary egg, and I was cutting up little strips
of colored paper and pasting them in little circles as Jack's chain
grew and my head spun from the wine and the weed.

That big old lady in the Christmas dress just kind of vanished
and the food appeared, and we ate, Jack and I, side by side, left our
Beat plates on the sofa, threw our chain on the tree and were just
pawing through the coats in the front hallway for another poor boy
of sweet Tokay wine when there was a knock at the door. This knock
wasn't like my knock. Not at all. This was a delicate knock, under-
stated and minimalistic, but with a whole deep continent of passion
and expectation implicit in it—in short, a feminine knock. "Well,"
Jack said, his face lit with the Beatest joy at discovering the slim
vessel of a pint bottle in the inside pocket of his seaman's pea coat,
"aren't you going to answer it?"

"Me?" I said, grinning my Beatest grin. I was in, I was part of
it all, I was Jack's confidant and compatriot, and we were in the
front hallway of his pad in Northport, Long Island, a fine hot steam-
ing mother-of-Jack-prepared meal in our gone Beat guts, and he was
asking me to answer the door, me, seventeen years old and nobody.
"You mean it?" and my grin widened till I could feel the creeping

seeping East Coast chill all the way back to my suburban-dentist-filled molars.

Jack, uncapping, tipping back, passing the bottle: "That's a chick knock, Buzz."

Me: "I love chicks."

Jack: "A gone lovely spring flower of a beret-wearing flipped long-legged coltish retroussé-nosed run-away-from-home-to-big-Jack-Kerouac chick knock."

Me: "I am crazy for gone lovely spring flower beret-wearing flipped long-legged coltish retroussé-nosed run-away-from-home-to-big-Jack-Kerouac chicks."

Jack: "Then answer it."

I pulled open the door and there she was, all the above and more, sixteen years old with big ungulate eyes and Mary Travers hair. She gave me a gaping openmouthed look, taking in my loden-green beret, the frizzed wildness of my hair sticking out from under it, my Beat Levi's jacket and jeans and my tea-reddened joyous hitching-all-the-way-from-Oxnard eyes. "I was looking for Jack," she said, and her voice was cracked and scratchy and low. She dropped her gaze.

I looked to Jack, who stood behind me, out of her line of vision, and asked a question with my eyebrows. Jack gave me his hooded smoldering dust-jacket-from-hell look, then stepped forward, took the poor boy from me and loomed over the now-eye-lifting chick and chucked her chin with a gone Beat curling index finger. "Coochie-coochie-coo," he said.

Her name was Ricky Keen (Richarda Kinkowski, actually, but that's how she introduced herself), she'd hitchhiked all the way down from Plattsburgh and she was as full of hero-worship and inarticulate praise as I was. "Dean Moriarty," she said at the end of a long rambling speech that alluded to nearly every line Jack had written and half the Zoot Sims catalogue, "he's the coolest. I mean, that's who I want to make babies with, absolutely."

There we were, standing in the front hallway listening to this crack-voiced ungulate-eyed long gone Beat-haired sixteen-year-old chick talk about making babies with Charlie Parker riffing in the background and the Christmas lights winking on and off and it was strange and poignant. All I could say was "Wow," over and over, but Jack knew just what to do. He threw one arm over my shoulder and the other over the chick's and he thrust his already-bloating and booze-inflamed but quintessentially Beat face into ours and said, low and rumbly, "What we need, the three of us hepsters, cats and chicks alike, is a consciousness-raising all-night bull session at the indubitable pinnacle of all neighborhood Bodhisattva centers and bar and grills, the Peroration Pub, or, as the fellaheen know it, Ziggy's Clam House. What do you say?"

What did we say? We were speechless—stunned, amazed, moved almost to tears. The man himself, he who had practically invented the mug, the jug and the highball and lifted the art of getting sloshed to its Beat apotheosis, was asking us, the skinny underage bedraggled runaways, to go out on the town for a night of wild and prodigious Kerouackian drinking. All I could manage was a nod of assent, Ricky Keen said, "Yeah, sure, like wow," and then we were out in the frozen rain, the three of us, the streets all crusted with ugly East Coast ice, Ricky on one side of Jack, me on the other, Jack's arms uniting us. We tasted freedom on those frozen streets, passing the bottle, our minds elevated and feverish with the fat spike of Mary Jane that appeared magically between Jack's thumb and forefinger and the little strips of Benzedrine-soaked felt he made us swallow like a sacrament. The wind sang a dirge. Ice clattered down out of the sky. We didn't care. We walked eight blocks, our Beat jackets open to the elements, and we didn't feel a thing.

Ziggy's Clam House loomed up out of the frozen black wastes of the Long Island night like a ziggurat, a holy temple of Beat enlightenment and deep soul truths, lit only by the thin neon braids of the beer signs in the windows. Ricky Keen giggled. My heart was pounding against my ribs. I'd never been in a bar before and I was afraid I'd make an ass of myself. But not to worry: we were with Jack, and Jack never hesitated. He hit the door of Ziggy's Clam House like a fullback bursting through the line, the door lurched back on its hinges and embedded itself in the wall, and even as I clutched reflexively at the eighty-three cents in my pocket Jack stormed the bar with a roar: "Set up the house, barkeep, and all you sleepy fellaheen, the Beat Generation has arrived!"

I exchanged a glance with Ricky Keen. The place was as quiet as a mortuary, some kind of tacky Hawaiian design painted on the walls, a couple of plastic palms so deep in dust they might have been snowed on, and it was nearly as dark inside as out. The bartender, startled by Jack's joyous full-throated proclamation of Beat uplift and infectious Dionysian spirit, glanced up from the flickering blue trance of the TV like a man whose last stay of execution has just been denied. He was heavy in the jowls, favoring a dirty white dress shirt and a little bow tie pinned like a dead insect to his collar. He winced when Jack brought his Beat fist down on the countertop and boomed, "Some of everything for everybody!"

Ricky Keen and I followed in Jack's wake, lit by our proximity to the centrifuge of Beatdom and the wine, marijuana and speed coursing through our gone adolescent veins. We blinked in the dim light and saw that the everybody Jack was referring to comprised a group of three: a sad mystical powerfully made-up cocktail waitress in a black tutu and fishnet stockings and a pair of crewcut Teamster types in blue workshirts and chinos. The larger of the two, a man with a face like a side of beef, squinted up briefly from his cigarette and growled, "Pipe down, asshole—can't you see we're trying to concentrate here?" Then the big rippled neck rotated and the head swung back round to refixate on the tube.

Up on the screen, which was perched between gallon jars of pickled eggs and Polish sausage, Red Skelton was mugging in a Santa Claus hat for all the dead vacant mindless living rooms of America, and I knew, with a deep sinking gulf of overwhelming un-Beat sadness, that my own triple-square parents, all the way out in Oxnard, were huddled round the console watching this same rubbery face go through its contortions and wondering where their pride and joy had got himself to. Ricky Keen might have been thinking along similar lines, so sad and stricken did she look at that moment, and I wanted to put my arms around her and stroke her hair and feel the heat of her Beat little lost body against my own. Only Jack seemed unaffected. "Beers all around," he insisted, tattooing the bar with his fist, and even before the bartender could heave himself up off his stool to comply Jack was waking up Benny Goodman on the jukebox and we were pooling our change as the Teamsters sat stoically beside their fresh Jack-bought beers and the cocktail waitress regarded us out of a pair of black staved-in eyes. Of course, Jack was broke and my eighty-three cents didn't take us far, but fortunately Ricky Keen produced a wad of crumpled dollar bills from a little purse tucked away in her boot and the beer flowed like bitter honey.

It was sometime during our third or fourth round that the burlier of the two Teamster types erupted from his barstool with the words "Communist" and "faggot" on his lips and flattened Jack, Ricky and me beneath a windmill of punches, kicks and elbow chops. We went down in a marijuana-weakened puddle, laughing like madmen, not even attempting to resist as the other Teamster, the bartender and even the waitress joined in. Half a purple-bruised minute later the three of us were out on the icy street in a jumble of limbs and my hand accidentally wandered to Ricky Keen's hard little half-formed breast and for the first time I wondered what was going to become of me, and, more immediately, where I was going to spend the night.

But Jack, heroically Beat and muttering under his breath about squares and philistines, anticipated me. Staggering to his feet and reaching down a Tokay-cradling spontaneous-prose-generating railroad-callused hand first to Ricky and then to me, he said, "Fellow seekers and punching bags, the road to Enlightenment is a rocky one, but tonight, tonight you sleep with big Jack Kerouac."

I woke the next afternoon on the sofa in the living room of the pad Jack shared with his Mémère. The sofa was grueling terrain, pocked and scoured by random dips and high hard draft-buffeted plateaus, but my stringy impervious seventeen-year-old form had become one with it in a way that approached bliss. It was, after all, a sofa, and not the cramped front seat of an A & P produce truck or

road-hopping Dodge, and it had the rugged book-thumbing late-
night-crashing bongo-thumping joint-rolling aura of Jack to recom-
mend and sanctify it. So what if my head was big as a weather
balloon and the rest of me felt like so many pounds and ounces of
beef jerky? So what if I was nauseous from cheap wine and tea and
Benzedrine and my tongue was stuck like Velcro to the roof of my
mouth and Ricky Keen was snoring on the floor instead of sharing
the sofa with me? So what if Bing Crosby and Mario Lanza were
blaring square Christmas carols from the radio in the kitchen and
Jack's big hunkering soul of a mother maneuvered her shouldery
bulk into the room every five seconds to give me a look of radiant
hatred and motherly impatience? So what? I was at Jack's. Nirvana
attained.

When finally I threw back the odd fuzzy Canuck-knitted
detergent-smelling fully Beat afghan some kind soul—Jack?—had
draped over me in the dim hours of the early morning, I became
aware that Ricky and I were not alone in the room. A stranger was
fixed like a totem pole in the armchair across from me, a skinny
rangy long-nosed Brahmin-looking character with a hundred-mile
stare and a dull brown Beat suit that might have come off the back
of an insurance salesman from Hartford, Connecticut. He barely
breathed, squinting glassy-eyed into some dark unfathomable vision
like a man trying to see his way to the end of a tunnel, as lizardlike
a human as I'd ever seen. And who could this be, I wondered,
perched here rigid-backed in Jack's gone Beat pad on the day before
Christmas and communing with a whole other reality? Ricky Keen
snored lightly from her nest on the floor. I studied the man in the
chair like he was a science project or something, until all at once it
hit me: this was none other than Bill himself, the marksman,
freighted all the way across the Beat heaving blue-cold Atlantic from
Tangier to wish Jack and his Beat Madonna a Merry Christmas and
a Happy New Year!

"Bill!" I cried, leaping up from the sofa to pump his dead
wooden hand, "this is . . . I mean, I can't tell you what an honor,"
and I went on in that gone worshipful vein for what must have been
ten minutes, some vestige of the Benzedrine come up on me sud-

denly, and Ricky Keen snapped open her pure golden eyes like two pats of butter melting into a pile of pancakes and I knew I was hungry and transported and headachy and Bill never blinked an eye or uttered a word.

"Who's that?" Ricky Keen breathed in her scratchy cracked throat-cancery rasp that I'd begun to find incredibly sexy.

" 'Who's that?' " I echoed in disbelief. "Why, it's Bill."

Ricky Keen stretched, yawned, readjusted her beret. "Who's Bill?"

"You mean you don't know who Bill is?" I yelped, and all the while Bill sat there like a corpse, his irises drying out and his lips clamped tight round the little nugget of his mouth.

Ricky Keen ignored the question. "Did we eat anything last night?" she rasped. "I'm so hungry I could puke."

At that moment I became aware of a sharp gland-stimulating gone wild smell wafting in from the kitchen on the very same Beat airwaves that carried the corny vocalizations of Bing and Mario: somebody was making flapjacks!

Despite our deep soul brother- and sisterhood with Jack and his Mémère, Ricky and I were nonetheless a little sketchy about just bursting into the kitchen and ingratiating our way into a plate of those flapjacks, so we paused to knock on the hinge-swinging slab of the kitchen door. There was no response. We heard Mario Lanza, the sizzle of grease in the pan and voices, talking or chanting. One of them seemed to be Jack's, so we knocked again and boldly pushed open the door.

If there was a climax to all that had come before, a Beat epiphany and holy epitomized moment, this was it: Jack was there at the kitchen table and his mother at the stove, yes, but there was a third person present, arrived among us like one of the bearded mystics out of the East. And who could it be with that mad calculating bug-eyed big-lipped look of Zen wisdom and froglike beauty? I knew in an instant: it was Allen. Allen himself, the poet laureate of Beatdom, come all the way from Paris for this far-out moment with Jack and his mother in their humble little Beat kitchen on the cold North

Shore of Long Island. He was sitting at the table with Jack, spinning
a dreidel and singing in a muddy moist sweet-wine-lubricated voice:

> Dreidel, dreidel, dreidel,
> I made it out of clay,
> And when it's dry and ready,
> Then Dreidel I will play.

Jack waved Ricky and me into the room and pushed us down
into two empty chairs at the kitchen table. "Flipped," he murmured
as the dreidel spun across the tabletop, and he poured us each a
water glass of sticky Mogen David blackberry wine and my throat
seized at the taste of it. "Drink up, man, it's Christmas!" Jack
shouted, thumping my back to jolt open the tubes.

That was when Mémère came into the picture. She was steam-
ing about something, really livid, her shoulders all hunched up and
her face stamped with red-hot broiling uncontainable rage, but she
served the flapjacks and we ate in Beat communion, fork-grabbing,
syrup-pouring and butter-smearing while Allen rhapsodized about
the inner path and Jack poured wine. In retrospect, I should have
been maybe a hair more attuned to Jack's mother and her moods,
but I shoved flapjacks into my face, reveled in Beatdom and ignored
the piercing glances and rattling pans. Afterward we left our Beat
plates where we dropped them and rushed into the living room to
spin some sides and pound on the bongos while Allen danced a
disheveled dance and blew into the wooden flute and Bill looked
down the long tunnel of himself.

What can I say? The legends were gathered, we cut up the
Benzedrine inhalers and swallowed the little supercharged strips of
felt inside, feasted on Miss Green and took a gone Beat hike to the
liquor store for more wine and still more. By dark I was able to feel
the wings of consciousness lift off my back and my memory of what
came next is glorious but hazy. At some point—eight? nine?—I was
aroused from my seventeen-year-old apprentice-Beat stupor by the
sound of sniffling and choked-back sobs, and found myself looking
up at the naked-but-for-a-seaman's-pea-coat form of Ricky Keen. I

seemed to be on the floor behind the couch, buried in a litter of
doilies, antimacassars and sheets of crumpled newspaper, the lights
from the Christmas tree riding up the walls and Ricky Keen standing
over me with her bare legs, heaving out chesty sobs and using the
ends of her long gone hair to dab at the puddles of her eyes.
"What?" I said. "What is it?" She swayed back and forth, rocking
on her naked feet, and I couldn't help admiring her knees and the
way her bare young hitchhiking thighs sprouted upward from them
to disappear in the folds of the coat.

"It's Jack," she sobbed, the sweet rasp of her voice catching in
her throat, and then she was behind the couch and kneeling like a
supplicant over the jean-clad poles of my outstretched legs.

"Jack?" I repeated stupidly.

A moment of silence, deep and committed. There were no
corny carols seeping from the radio in the kitchen, no wild tooth-
baring jazz or Indian sutras roaring from the record player, there
was no Allen, no Jack, no Mémère. If I'd been capable of sitting up
and thrusting my head over the back of the sofa I would have seen
that the room was deserted but for Bill, still locked in his comatose
reverie. Ricky Keen sat on my knees. "Jack won't have me," she said
in a voice so tiny I was hardly aware she was speaking at all. And
then, with a pout: "He's drunk."

Jack wouldn't have her. I mulled fuzzily over this information,
making slow drawn-out turtlelike connections while Ricky Keen sat
on my knees with her golden eyes and Mary Travers hair, and finally
I said to myself, If Jack won't have her, then who will? I didn't have
a whole lot of experience along these lines—my adventures with the
opposite sex had been limited to lingering dumbstruck classroom
gazes and the odd double-feature grope—but I was willing to learn.
And eager, oh yes.

"It's such a drag being a virgin," she breathed, unbuttoning the
coat, and I sat up and took hold of her—clamped my panting per-
spiring sex-crazed adolescent self to her, actually—and we kissed
and throbbed and explored each other's anatomies in a drifting cloud
of Beat bliss and gone holy rapture. I was lying there, much later,
tingling with the quiet rush and thrill of it, Ricky breathing softly

into the cradle of my right arm, when suddenly the front door flew back and the world's wildest heppest benny-crazed coast-to-coasting voice lit the room like a brushfire. I sat up. Groped for my pants. Cradled a startled Ricky head.

"Ho, ho, ho!" the voice boomed, "All you little boysies and girlsies been good? I been checkin' my list!"

I popped my head over the couch and there he was, cool and inexplicable. I couldn't believe my eyes: it was Neal. Neal escaped from San Quentin and dressed in a street-corner-Santa outfit, a bag full of booze, drugs, cigarettes and canned hams slung over his back, his palms hammering invisible bongos in the air. "Come out, come out, wherever you are!" he cried, and broke down in a sea of giggles. "Gonna find out who's naughty and nice, yes indeed!"

At that moment Jack burst in from the kitchen, where he and Allen had been taking a little catnap over a jug of wine, and that was when the really wild times began, the back-thumping high-fiving jumping jiving tea-smoking scat-singing Beat revel of the ages. Ricky Keen came to life with a snort, wrapped the jacket round her and stepped out from behind the couch like a Beat princess, I reached for the wine, Jack howled like a dog and even Bill shifted his eyes round his head in a simulacrum of animacy. Neal couldn't stop talking and drinking and smoking, spinning round the room like a dervish, Allen shouted "Miles Davis!" and the record player came to life, and we were all dancing, even Bill, though he never left his chair.

That was the crowning moment of my life—I was Beat, finally and absolutely—and I wanted it to go on forever. And it could have, if it wasn't for Jack's mother, that square-shouldered fuming old woman in the Christmas dress. She was nowhere to be seen through all of this, and I'd forgotten about her in the crazed explosion of the moment—it wasn't till Jack began to break down that she materialized again.

It was around twelve or so. Jack got a little weepy, sang an a capella version of "Hark the Herald Angels Sing" and tried to talk us all into going to the midnight mass at St. Columbanus' church. Allen said he had no objection, except that he was Jewish, Neal

derided the whole thing as the height of corny bourgeois sentimen-
tality, Bill was having trouble moving his lips and Ricky Keen said
that she was Unitarian and didn't know if she could handle it. Jack,
tears streaming down his face, turned to me. "Buzz," he said, and
he had this wheedling crazed biggest-thing-in-the-world sort of edge
to his voice, "Buzz, you're a good Catholic, I know you are—what
do you say?"

All eyes focused on me. Silence rang suddenly through the
house. I was three sheets to the wind, sloppy drunk, seventeen years
old. Jack wanted to go to midnight mass, and it was up to me to say
yea or nay. I just stood there, wondering how I was going to break
the news to Jack that I was an atheist and that I hated God, Jesus
and my mother, who'd made me go to parochial school five days a
week since I'd learned to walk and religious instruction on Sundays
to boot. My mouth moved, but nothing came out.

Jack was trembling. A tic started in over his right eye. He
clenched his fists. "Don't let me down, Buzz!" he roared, and when
he started toward me Neal tried to stop him, but Jack flung him
away as if he was nothing. "Midnight mass, Buzz, midnight!" he
boomed, and he was standing right there in front of me, gone Beat
crazy, and I could smell the booze on his stinking Beat breath. He
dropped his voice then. "You'll rot in hell, Buzz," he hissed, "you'll
rot." Allen reached for his arm, but Jack shook him off. I took a step
back.

That was when Mémère appeared.

She swept into the room like something out of a Japanese monster flick, huge in her nightdress, big old Jack-mothery toes sticking
out beneath it like sausages, and she went straight to the fireplace
and snatched up the poker. "Out!" she screamed, the eyes sunk back
in her head, "get out of my house, you queers and convicts and drug
addicts, and you"—she turned on me and Ricky—"you so-called
fans and adulators, you're even worse. Go back where you came
from and leave my Jacky in peace." She made as if to swing the
poker at me and I reflexively ducked out of the way, but she brought
it down across the lamp on the table instead. There was a flash, the
lamp exploded, and she drew back and whipped the poker like a

lariat over her head. "Out!" she shrieked, and the whole group, even Bill, edged toward the door.

Jack did nothing to stop her. He gave us his brooding lumber-jack Beat posing-on-the-fire-escape look, but there was something else to it, something new, and as I backpedaled out the door and into the grimy raw East Coast night, I saw what it was—the look of a mama's boy, pouty and spoiled. "Go home to your mothers, all of you," Mémère yelled, shaking the poker at us as we stood there drop-jawed on the dead brown ice-covered pelt of the lawn. "For god's sake," she sobbed, "it's Christmas!" And then the door slammed shut.

I was in shock. I looked at Bill, Allen, Neal, and they were as stunned as I was. And poor Ricky—all she had on was Jack's pea coat and I could see her tiny bare perfect-toed Beat chick feet freezing to the ground like twin ice sculptures. I reached up to adjust my beret and realized it wasn't there, and it was like I'd had the wind knocked out of me. "Jack!" I cried out suddenly, and my creaking adolescent voice turned it into a forlorn bleat. "Jack!" I cried, "Jack!" but the night closed round us and there was no answer.

What happened from there is a long story. But to make it short, I took Mémère's advice and went home to my mother, and by the time I got there Ricky had already missed her period. My mother didn't like it but the two of us moved into my boyhood room with the lame college pennants and dinosaur posters and whatnot on the walls for about a month, which is all we could stand, and then Ricky took her gone gorgeous Beat Madonna-of-the-streets little body off to an ultra-Beat one-room pad on the other end of town and I got a job as a brakeman on the Southern Pacific and she let me crash with her and that was that. We smoked tea and burned candles and incense and drank jug wine and made it till we damn near rubbed the skin off each other. The first four boys we named Jack, Neal, Allen and Bill, though we never saw any of their namesakes again except Allen, at one of his poetry readings, but he made like he didn't know us. The first of the girls we named Gabrielle, for Jack's mother, and after that we seemed to kind of just lose track and name them for the month they were born, regardless of sex, and we wound up with two Junes—June the Male and June the Female—but it was no big thing.

Yeah, I was Beat, Beater than any of them—or just as Beat, anyway. Looking back on it now, though, I mean after all these years and what with the mortgage payments and Ricky's detox and the kids with their college tuition and the way the woodworking shop over the garage burned down and how stinking close-fisted petit-bourgeois before-the-revolution pig-headed cheap the railroad disability is, I wonder now if I'm not so much Beat anymore as just plain beat. But then, I couldn't even begin to find the words to describe it to you.

THE FOG MAN

HE CAME TWICE A WEEK, rattling through the development in an army-surplus jeep, laying down a roiling smoke screen that melted the trees into oblivion, flattened hills and swallowed up houses, erased Fords, Chevies and Studebakers as if they were as insubstantial as the air itself, and otherwise transformed the world to our satisfaction. Shrubs became dinosaurs, lampposts giraffes, the black-top of the streets seethed like the surface of the swamp primeval. Our fathers stood there on their emerald lawns, hoses dripping, and they waved languidly or turned their backs to shoot a sparkling burst at the flower beds or forsythias. We took to our bikes, supercharged with the excitement of it, and we ran just behind him, the fog man, wheeling in and out of the tight billowing clouds like fighter pilots slashing across the sky or Grand Prix racers nosing in for the lead on that final excruciating lap. He gave us nothing except those moments of transfiguration, but we chased him as single-mindedly as we chased the ice-cream man in his tinkling white truck full of Drumsticks and Eskimo Pies, chased him till he'd completed his tour of the six connecting streets of the development—up one side and down the other—and lurched across the highway, trailing smoke, for the next.

And then the smoke settled, clinging to the dewy wet grass, the odor of smoldering briquettes fought over the top of the sweet narcotic smell of it, and we were gone, disseminated, slammed behind identical screen doors, in our identical houses, for the comfort and magic of the TV. My father was there, always there, propped up in his recliner, one hand over his eyes to mask an imaginary glare, the other clutched round his sweating drink. My mother was there too, legs tucked under her on the couch, the newspaper spread in her lap, her drink on the cluttered table beside her.

"The fog man was just here," I would announce. I didn't expect a response, really—it was just something to say. The show on TV was about a smiling family. All the shows were about smiling families. My mother would nod.

One night I appended a question. "He's spraying for bugs, right?" This much I knew, this much had been explained to me, but I wanted confirmation, affirmation, I wanted reason and meaning to illuminate my life.

My father said nothing. My mother looked up. "Mosquitoes."

"Yeah, that's what I thought—but how come there's so many of them then? They bit right through my shirt on the front porch."

My mother tapped at her cigarette, took a sip of her drink. "You can't get them all," she said.

It was at about this time that the local power company opened the world's first atomic power plant at Indian Point. Ten years earlier nuclear fission had been an instrument of war and destruction; now it was safe, manageable; now it would warm our houses and light our lights and power our hi-fis and toasters and dishwashers. The electric company took pains to ensure that the community saw it that way. It was called public relations.

I didn't know the term then. I was eleven years old, in my first week of my last year of elementary school, and on my way to the power plant in a school bus crammed to the yawning windows with my excitable classmates. This was known as a field trip. The previous year we'd been to a farm in Brewster and the Museum of Natural History in New York. We were starting early this year, but it was all due to the fact of this astonishing new technological force set down amongst us, this revolution in the production of electricity and the streamlining of our lives. We didn't know what to expect.

The bus rumbled and belched fumes. I sat on the hard cracked leatherette seat beside Casper Mendelson and watched the great gray concrete dome rise up out of the clutch of the trees, dominating the point and the placid broad fish-stinking river beyond it. It was impressive, this huge structure inside of which the titanic forces of the universe were pared down to size. Casper said that it could blow up, like the bomb they'd dropped on the Japanese, and that it would take all of Peterskill and Westchester with it. The river would turn to steam and there'd be nothing left but a crater the size of the Grand Canyon and we'd all be melted in our beds. I gaped out the window at the thing, awestruck, the big dome keeping a lid on all that seething complexity, and I was impressed, but I couldn't help thinking of the point's previous incarnation as an amusement park, a place of strung lights, cotton candy and carousels. Now there was this gray dome.

They led us into a little brightly lit building full of colorful exhibits, where we handled things that were meant to be handled, scuffed the gleaming linoleum floors and watched an animated short in which Johnny Atom splits himself in two and saves the world by creating electricity. The whole thing was pretty dull, aside from the dome itself and what Casper had said about it, and within the hour my classmates were filling the place with the roar of a stampede, breaking the handles off things, sobbing, skipping, playing tag and wondering seriously about lunch—which, as it turned out, we were to have back at school, in the cafeteria, after which we were expected to return to our classrooms and discuss what we'd learned on our field trip.

I remember the day for the impression that imposing gray dome made on me, but also because it was the first chance I got to have a look at Maki Duryea, the new girl who'd been assigned to the other sixth-grade section. Maki was black—or not simply black, but black and Oriental both. Her father had been stationed in Osaka during the occupation; her mother was Japanese. I watched her surreptitiously that morning as I sat in the rear of the bus with Casper. She was somewhere in the middle, sitting beside Donna Siprelle, a girl I'd known all my life. All I could make out was the back of her head, but that was enough, that alone was a revelation. Her hair was an absolute, unalloyed, interstellar black, and it disappeared behind the jutting high ridge of the seat back as if it might go on forever.

It had hung iron straight when we first climbed aboard the bus that morning, but on the way back it was transformed, a leaping electric snarl that engulfed the seat and eclipsed the neat little ball of yellow curls that clung to the back of Donna Siprelle's head. "Maki Duryea, Maki Duryea," Casper began to chant, though no one could hear him but me in the pandemonium of that preprandial school bus. Annoyed, I poked him with a savage elbow but he kept it up, louder now, to spite me.

There were no blacks in our school, there were no Asians or Hispanics. Italians, Poles, Jews, Irish, the descendants of the valley's Dutch and English settlers, these we had, these we were, but Maki Duryea was the first black—and the first Asian. Casper's father was Jewish, his mother a Polish Catholic. Casper had the soaring IQ of a genius, but he was odd, skewed in some deep essential way that set him apart from the rest of us. He was the first to masturbate, the first to drink and smoke, though he cared for neither. He caused a panic throughout the school when he turned up missing one day after lunch and was found, after a room-by-room, locker-by-locker search, calmly reading on the fire escape; he burst from his chair at the back of the classroom once and did fifty frantic squat-thrusts in front of the hapless teacher and then blew on his thumb till he passed out. He was my best friend.

He turned to me then, on the bus, and broke off his chant. His eyes were the color of the big concrete dome, his head was shaved to a transparent stubble. "She stinks," he said, grinning wildly, his eyes leaping at my own. "Maki Duryea, Maki Duryea, Maki Duryea"—he took up the chant again before subsiding into giggles. "They don't smell like we do."

My family was Irish. Irish, that's all I knew. A shirt was cotton or it was wool. We were Irish. No one talked about it, there was no exotic language spoken in the house, no ethnic dress or cuisine, we didn't go to church. There was only my grandfather.

He came that year for Thanksgiving, a short big-bellied man with close-cropped white hair and glancing white eyebrows and a trace of something in his speech I hadn't heard before—or if I had it was in some old out-of-focus movie dredged up for the TV screen, nothing I would have remembered. My grandmother came too. She was spindly, emaciated, her skin blistered with shingles, a diabetic who couldn't have weighed more than ninety pounds, but there was joy in her and it was infectious. My father, her son, woke up. A festive air took hold of the house.

My grandfather, who years later dressed in a suit for my father's funeral and was mistaken for a banker, had had a heart attack and he wasn't drinking. Or rather, he was strictly enjoined from drinking and my parents, who drank themselves, drank a lot, drank too much, took pains to secrete the liquor supply. Every bottle was removed from the cabinet, even the odd things that hadn't been touched in years—except by me, when I furtively unscrewed the cap of this or that and took a sniff or touched my tongue tentatively to the cold hard glass aperture—and the beer disappeared from the refrigerator. I didn't know what the big deal was. Liquor was there, a fact of life, it was unpleasant and adults indulged in it as they indulged in any number of bizarre and unsatisfactory practices. I kicked a football around the rock-hard frozen lawn.

And then one afternoon—it was a day or two before Thanksgiving and my grandparents had been with us a week—I came in off the front lawn, my fingers numb and nose running, and the house was in an uproar. A chair was overturned in the corner, the coffee table was slowly listing over a crippled leg and my grandmother was on the floor, frail, bunched, a bundle of sticks dropped there in a windstorm. My grandfather stood over her, red-faced and raging, while my mother snatched at his elbow like a woman tumbling over the edge of a cliff. My father wasn't home from work yet. I stood there in the doorway, numb from the embrace of the wind, and heard the inarticulate cries of those two women against the oddly inflected roars of that man, and I backed out the door and pulled it closed behind me.

The next day my grandfather, sixty-eight years old and stiff in the knees, walked two miles in twenty-degree weather to Peterskill, to the nearest liquor store. It was dark, suppertime, and we didn't know where he was. "He just went out for a walk," my mother said.

Then the phone rang. It was the neighbor two doors down. There was a man passed out in her front yard—somebody said we knew him. Did we?

I spent the next two days—Thanksgiving and the day after—camping in the sorry patch of woods at the end of the development. I wasn't running away, nothing as decisive or extreme as that—I was just camping, that was all. I gnawed cold turkey up there in the woods, lifted congealed stuffing to my mouth with deadened fingers. In the night I lay shivering in my blankets, never colder before or since.

We were Irish. I was Irish.

That winter, like all winters in those days, was interminable, locked up in the grip of frozen slush and exhaust-blackened snow. The dead dark hours of school were penance for some crime we hadn't yet committed. The TV went on at three-thirty when we got home from school, and it was still on when we went to bed at nine. I played basketball that winter in a league organized by some of the fathers in the development, and three times a week I walked home from the fungus-infested gym with a crust of frozen sweat in my hair. I grew an inch and a half, I let my crewcut grow out and I began to turn up the collar of my ski jacket. I spent most of my time with Casper, but in spite of him, as the pale abbreviated days wore on, I found myself growing more and more at ease with the idea of Maki Duryea.

She was still foreign, still exotic, still the new kid and worse, much worse, the whole business complicated by the matter of her skin color and her hair and the black unblinking depths of her eyes, but she was there just like the rest of us and after a while it seemed as if she'd always been there. She was in the other section, but I saw her on the playground, in the hallway, saw her waiting on line in the cafeteria with a tray in her hands or struggling up the steps of the school bus in a knit hat and mittens no different from what the other girls wore. I didn't have much to say to any of the girls really, but I suppose I must have said things to her in passing, and once, coming off the playground late, I found myself wedged up against her on the crowded school bus. And then there was the time the dancing teacher, with a casual flick of her wrist, paired me off with her.

Everything about dancing was excruciating. It was not kickball, it was not basketball or bombardment. The potential for embarrassment was incalculable. We were restless and bored, the gymnasium was overheated against the sleet that rattled at the windows, and the girls, entranced, wore peculiar little smiles as Mrs. Feldman demonstrated the steps. The boys slouched against one adamantine wall, poking one another, shuffling their feet and playing out an elaborate ritual to demonstrate that none of this held the slightest interest for them, for us, though it did, and we were nervous about it despite ourselves. Alone, of all the two classes combined, Casper refused to participate. Mrs. Feldman sent him to the principal's office without so much as a second glance, chose partners arbitrarily for the remainder of the class and started up the ancient phonograph and the arcane scratchy records of songs no one knew and rhythms no one could follow, and before I was fully cognizant of what was happening I found myself clutching Maki Duryea's damp palm in my own while my arm lay like a dead thing across the small of her back. She was wearing a sweater thick enough for Arctic exploration and she was sweating in the choking humid jungle atmosphere of the gymnasium. I could smell her, but despite what Casper had said the heat of her body gave off a luxurious yeasty soporific odor that held me spellbound and upright through the droning eternity of the record.

The dance, the big dance that all this terpsichorean instruction was leading up to, was held on February 29, and Mrs. Feldman, in an evil twist of fate, decided to honor custom and have the girls invite the boys as their partners. We did perspective drawing in art class—great lopsided vistas of buildings and avenues dwindling in the distance—while the girls made up the invitations with strips of ribbon, construction paper and paste. My mind was on basketball, ice fishing, the distant trembling vision of spring and summer and liberation from Mrs. Feldman, the gym and the cafeteria and all the rest, and I was surprised, though I shouldn't have been, when Maki's invitation arrived. I didn't want to go. My mother insisted. My father said nothing.

And then the telephone began to ring. My mother answered each call with quiet determination, immovable, unshakable, whispering into the phone, doodling on a pad, lifting the drink or a cigarette to her lips. I don't know what she said exactly, but she was talking to the other mothers, the mothers of sons who hadn't been invited to the dance by Maki Duryea, and she was explaining to them precisely how and why she could and would allow her son to go to the dance with a Negro. In later years, as the civil-rights movement arose and Malcolm X and Martin Luther King fell and the ghettoes burned, she never had much to say about it, but I could feel her passion then, on the telephone, in the cool insistent rasp of her voice.

I went to the dance with Maki Duryea. She wore a stiff organdy dress with short sleeves that left her looking awkward and underdressed and I wore a tie and sportcoat and arranged my hair for the occasion. I held her and I danced with her, though I didn't want to, though I snapped at her when she asked if I wanted a brownie and a cup of punch, though I looked with envy and longing to the streamer-draped corner where Casper alternately leered at me and punched Billy Matechik in the shoulder; I danced with her, but that was it, that was as far as I could go, and I didn't care if the snow was black and the dome blew off the reactor and Johnny Atom came and melted us all in our sleep.

It was a late spring and we tried to force it by inaugurating baseball season while the snow still lingered atop the dead yellow grass and the frozen dirt beneath it. We dug out balls and mitts and stood in the street in T-shirts, gooseflesh on our arms, shoulders quaking, a nimbus of crystallized breath suspended over our heads. Casper didn't play ball—foot, hand, base or basket—and he stood hunched in his jacket, palming a cigarette and watching us out of his mocking gray eyes. I caught cold and then flu and stayed in bed a week. On the first of April I went trout fishing, a ritual of spring, but the day was gloomy and lowering, with a stiff wind and tem-

peratures in the twenties. I cast a baited hook till my arm lost all
sensation. The trout might as well have been extinct.

Since the time of the dance I'd had nothing to do with Maki
Duryea. I wouldn't even look at her. If she'd suddenly exploded in
flames on the playground or swelled up to the size of a dirigible I
wouldn't have known. I'd taken a steady stream of abuse over the
dance episode, and I was angry and embarrassed. For a full month
afterward I was the object of an accelerated program of ear snapping
and head knuckling, the target of spitballs and wads of lined note-
book paper with crude hearts scrawled across their rumpled interi-
ors, but we were innocent then, and no one used the epithets we
would later learn, the language of hate and exclusion. They turned
on me because I had taken Maki Duryea to the dance—or rather,
because I had allowed her to take me—and because she was different and their parents disapproved in a way they couldn't yet define.
I resented her for it, and I resented my mother too.

And so, when the rumors first began to surface, I took a kind
of guilty satisfaction in them. There had been trouble at Maki's
house. Vandals—and the very term gave me a perverse thrill—vandals had spray-painted racial slurs on the glistening black surface of
their macadam driveway. My mother was incensed. She took her
drink and her cigarettes and huddled over the phone. She even
formed a committee of two with Casper's mother (who was one of
the few who hadn't phoned over the dance invitation), and they met
a time or two in Casper's living room to drink a clear liquid in high-
stemmed glasses, tap their cigarettes over ashtrays and lament the
sad state of the community, the development, the town, the country,
the world itself.

While our mothers were wringing their hands and buzzing at
one another in their rasping secretive voices, Casper took me aside
and showed me a copy of the local newspaper, flung on the lawn
not five minutes earlier by Morty Solomon as he weaved up the
street on his bicycle. I didn't read newspapers. I didn't read books.
I didn't read anything. Casper forced it into my hands and there it
was, the rumor made concrete: VANDALS STRIKE AGAIN. This time,
a cross had been burned on the Duryea lawn. I looked up at Casper

in amazement. I wanted to ask him what that meant, a cross—a cross was religious, wasn't it, and this didn't have anything to do with religion, did it?—but I felt insecure in my confusion and I held back.

"You know what we ought to do?" he said, watching me closely.

I was thinking of Maki Duryea, of her hair and her placid eyes, thinking of the leaping flames and the spray paint in the driveway. "What?"

"We ought to egg them."

"But—" I was going to ask how we could egg them if we didn't know who did it, but then I caught the startling perverse drift of what he was suggesting and in my astonishment I blurted, "But why?"

He shrugged, ducked his head, scuffed a foot on the carpet. We were in the hallway, by the telephone stand. I heard my mother's voice from the room beyond, though the door was closed and she was talking in a whisper. The voice of Casper's mother came right back at her in raspy collusion. Casper just stared at the closed door as if to say, *There, there's your answer.*

After a moment he said, "What's the matter—you afraid?"

I was twelve now, twelve and a half. How could anyone at that age admit to fear? "No," I said, "I'm not afraid."

The Duryea house lay outside the confines of the development. It was a rental house, two stories over a double garage in need of paint and shingles, and it sat on a steep rutted dirt road half a mile away. There were no streetlights along that unfinished road and the trees overhung it so that the deepest shadows grew deeper still beneath them. It was a warm, slick, humid night at the end of May, the sort of night that surprises you with its richness and intensity, smells heightened, sounds muffled, lights blurred to indistinction. When we left Casper's it was drizzling.

Casper bought the eggs, two dozen, at the corner store out on the highway. His parents were rich—rich compared to mine, at any rate—and he always seemed to have money. The storekeeper was a tragic-looking man with purple rings of puffed flesh beneath his eyes and a spill of gut that was like an avalanche beneath the smeared white front of his apron. Casper slipped two cigars into his pocket while I distracted the man with a question about the chocolate milk—did it come in a smaller size?

As we started up the dirt road, eggs in hand, Casper was strangely silent. When a dog barked from the driveway of a darkened house he clutched my arm, and a moment later, when a car turned into the street, he pulled me into the bushes and crouched there, breathing hard, till the headlights faded away. "Maki Duryea," he whispered, chanting it as he'd chanted it a hundred times before, "Maki Duryea, Maki Duryea." My heart was hammering. I didn't want to do this. I didn't know why I was doing it, didn't yet realize that the whole purpose of the exercise was to invert our parents' values, trash them, grind them into the dirt, and that all ethical considerations were null in the face of that ancient imperative. I was a freedom fighter. The eggs were hand grenades. I clutched them to my chest.

We hid ourselves in the wild tangle of shrubs gone to seed outside the house and watched the steady pale lighted windows for movement. My hair hung limp with the drizzle. Casper squatted over his ankles and fingered his box of eggs. I could barely make him out. At one point a figure passed in front of the window—I saw the hair, the mat of it, the sheen—and it might have been Maki, but I wasn't sure. It could have been her mother. Or her sister or aunt or grandmother—it could have been anybody. Finally, when I was as tired of crouching there in the bushes as I've ever been tired of being anywhere, even the dentist's, the lights flicked off. Or no, they didn't just flick off—they exploded in darkness and the black torrent of the night rushed in to engulf the house.

Casper rose to his feet. I heard him fumbling with his cardboard carton of eggs. We didn't speak—speech would have been superfluous. I rose too. My eggs, palpable, smooth, fit the palm of my hand as if they'd been designed for it. I raised my arm—baseball, football, basketball—and Casper stirred beside me. The familiar motion, the rush of air: I will never forget the sound of that first egg loosing itself against the front of the house, a wetness there, a softness, the birth of something. No weapon, but a weapon all the same.

The summer sustained me. Hot, unfettered, endless. On the first day of vacation I perched in an apple tree at the end of the cul-de-sac that bordered the development and contemplated the expanse of time and pleasure before me, and then it was fall and I was in junior high. Maki Duryea had moved. I'd heard as much from Casper, and one afternoon, at the end of summer, I hiked up that long rutted dirt road to investigate. The house stood empty. I climbed the ridge behind it to peer in through the naked windows and make sure. Bare floors stretched to bare walls.

And then, in the confusion of the big parking lot at the junior high where fifty buses deposited the graduates of a dozen elementary schools, where I felt lost and out of place and shackled in a plaid long-sleeved shirt new that morning from the plastic wrapping, I saw her. She sprang down from another bus in a cascade of churning legs and arms and anxious faces, a bookbag slung over one shoulder, hair ironed to her waist. I couldn't move. She looked up then and saw me and she smiled. Then she was gone.

That night, as I slapped a hard black ball against the side of the house, thinking nothing, I caught a faint electrifying whiff of a forgotten scent on the air, and there he was, the fog man, rattling by the house in his open jeep. My bike lay waiting at the curb and my first impulse was to leap for it, but I held off. There was something different here, something I couldn't quite place at first. And then I saw what it was: the fog man was wearing a mask, a gas mask, the sort of thing you saw in war movies. He'd collected the usual escort of knee-pumping neighborhood kids by the time he'd made his second pass down the street in front of our house, and I'd moved to the curb now to study this phenomenon, this subtle alteration in the texture of things. He looked different in the mask, sinister somehow, and his eyes seemed to glitter.

The fog obliterated the houses across from me, the wheeling children vanished, the low black roiling clouds melted toward me across the perfect sweep of the lawn. And then, before I knew what I was doing, I was on my bike with the rest of them, chasing the fog man through the mist, chasing him as if my life depended on it.

SITTING ON TOP
OF THE WORLD

PEOPLE WOULD ASK HER what it was like. She'd watch them from
her tower as they weaved along the trail in their baseball caps and
day packs, their shorts, hiking boots and sneakers. The brave ones
would mount the hundred and fifty wooden steps hammered into
the face of the mountain to stand at the high-flown railing of the
little glass-walled shack she called home for seven months a year.
Sweating, sucking at canteens and bota bags, heaving for breath in
the undernourished air, they would ask her what it was like. "Beautiful," she would say. "Peaceful."

But that didn't begin to express it. It was like floating unteth-
ered, drifting with the clouds, like being cupped in the hands of
God. Nine thousand feet up, she could see the distant hazy rim of
the world, she could see Mount Whitney rising up above the cren-
ellations of the Sierra, she could see stars that haven't been discovered yet. In the morning, she was the first to watch the sun emerge
from the hills to the east, and in the evening, when it was dark
beneath her, the valleys and ridges gripped by the insinuating fingers
of the night, she was the last to see it set. There was the wind in
the trees, the murmur of the infinite needles soughing in the uncountable branches of the pines, sequoias and cedars that stretched
out below her like a carpet. There was daybreak. There was the
stillness of 3:00 A.M. She couldn't explain it. She was sitting on top
of the world.

Don't you get lonely up here? they'd ask. Don't you get a little
stir-crazy?

And how to explain that? Yes, she did, of course she did, but it didn't matter. Todd was up here with her in the summer, one week on, one week off, and then the question was meaningless. But in September he went back to the valley, to his father, to school, and the world began to drag round its tired old axis. The hikers stopped coming then too. At the height of summer, on a weekend, she'd see as many as thirty or forty in the course of a day, but now, with the fall coming on, they left her to herself—sometimes she'd go for days without seeing a soul.

But that was the point, wasn't it?

She was making breakfast—a real breakfast for a change, ham and eggs from the propane refrigerator, fresh-dripped coffee and toast—when she spotted him working his way along one of the switchbacks below. She was immediately annoyed. It wasn't even seven yet and the sign at the trailhead quite plainly stated that visitors were welcome at the lookout between the hours of ten and five *only*. What was wrong with this guy—did he think he was exempt or something? She calmed herself: maybe he was only crossing the trail. Deer season had opened—she'd been hearing the distant muted pop of gunfire all week—and maybe he was only a hunter tracking a deer.

No such luck. When she glanced down again, flipping her eggs, peering across the face of the granite peak and the steep snaking trail that clung to it, she saw that he was coming up to the tower. Damn, she thought, and then the kettle began to hoot and her stomach clenched. Breakfast was ruined. Now there'd be some stranger gawking over her shoulder and making the usual banal comments as she ate. To them it might have been like Disneyland or something up here, but this was her home, she lived here. How would they like it if she showed up on their doorstep at seven o'clock in the morning?

She was eating, her back to the glass door, hoping he'd go away, slip over the lip of the precipice and disappear, vanish in a puff of smoke, when she felt his footfall on the trembling catwalk that ran round the outside of the tower. Still, she didn't turn or look up. She was reading—she went through a truckload of books in the course of a season—and she never lifted her eyes from the page. He could gawk round the catwalk, peer through the telescope and hustle himself back on down the steps for all she cared. She wasn't a tour guide. Her job was to watch for smoke, twenty-four hours a day, and to be cordial—if she was in the mood and had the time—to the hikers who made the sweaty panting trek in from the trailhead to join her for a brief moment atop the world. There was no law that said she had to let them in the shack or show them the radio and her plotting equipment and deliver the standard lecture on how it all worked. Especially at seven in the morning. To hell with him, she thought, and she forked up egg and tried to concentrate on her book.

The problem was, she'd trained herself to look up from what she was doing and scan the horizon every thirty seconds or so, day or night, except when she was asleep, and it had become a reflex. She glanced up, and there he was. It gave her a shock. He'd gone round the catwalk to the far side and he was standing right in front of her, grinning and holding something up to the window. Flowers, wildflowers, she registered that, but then his face came into focus and she felt something go slack in her: she knew him. He'd been here before.

"Lainie," he said, tapping the glass and brandishing the flowers, "I brought you something."

Her name. He knew her name.

She tried a smile and her face froze around it. The book on the table before her upset the saltshaker and flipped itself shut with a tiny expiring hiss. Should she thank him? Should she get up and latch the door? Should she put out an emergency call on the radio and snatch up the kitchen knife?

"Sorry to disturb you over breakfast—I didn't know the time," he said, and something happened to his grin, though his eyes—a hard metallic blue—held on to hers like pincers. He raised his voice to penetrate the glass: "I've been camping down on Long Meadow Creek and when I crossed the trail this morning I just thought you might be lonely and I'd surprise you"—he hesitated—"I mean, with some flowers."

Her whole body was frozen now. She'd had crazies up here before—it was an occupational hazard—but there was something unnerving about this one; this one she remembered. "It's too early," she said finally, miming it with her hands, as if the glass were impervious to sound, and then she got up from her untouched ham and half-eaten eggs and deliberately went to the radio. The radio was just under the window where he was standing, and when she picked up the mike and depressed the talk button she was two feet from him, the thin wall of glass all that separated them.

"Needles Lookout," she said, "this is Elaine. Zack, you there? Over."

Zack's voice came right back at her. He was a college student working on a degree in forestry, and he was her relief two days a week when she hiked out and went down the mountain to spend a day with her son, do her shopping and maybe hit a bar or movie with her best friend and soul mate, Cynthia Furman. "Elaine," he said, above the crackle of static, "what's up? See anything funny out there? Over."

She forced herself to look up then and locate the stranger's eyes—he was still grinning, but the grin was slack and unsteady and there was no joy in the deeps of those hard blue eyes—and she held the black plastic mike to her lips a moment longer than she had to before answering. "Nothing, Zack," she said, "just checking in."

His voice was tinny. "Okay," he said. "Talk to you. Over and out."

"Over and out," she said.

And now what? The guy wore a hunting knife strapped to his thigh. His cheeks were caved in as if he were sucking candy, and an old-fashioned mustache, thick and reddish, hid his upper lip. Instead of a baseball cap he wore a wide-brimmed felt hat. Wyatt Earp, she thought, and she was about to turn away from the window, prepared to ignore him till he took the hint, till he counted off the hundred and fifty wooden steps and vanished down the path and out of her life, when he rapped again on the glass and said, "You got something to put these in—the flowers, I mean?"

She didn't want his flowers. She didn't want him on her platform. She didn't want him in her thirteen-by-thirteen-foot sanctuary, touching her things, poking around, asking stupid questions, making small talk. "Look," she said finally, talking to the glass but looking through him, beyond him, scanning the infinite as she'd trained herself to do, no matter what the problem, "I've got a job to do up here and the fact is no one's allowed on the platform between the hours of five in the afternoon and ten in the morning"—now she came back to him and saw that his smile had collapsed—"you ought to know that. It says so in plain English right down there at the trailhead." She looked away; it was over, she was done with him.

She went back to her breakfast, forcing herself to stare at the page before her, though her heart was going and the words meant nothing. Todd had been with her the first time the man had come. Todd was fourteen, tall like his father, blond-headed and rangy. He was a good kid, her last and final hope, and he seemed to relish the time he spent with her up here. It was a Saturday, the middle of the afternoon, and they'd had a steady stream of visitors since the morning. Todd was in the storage room below, reading comics (in its wisdom, the Forestry Service had provided this second room, twenty-five steps down, not simply for storage but for respite too—it was a box, a womb, with only a single dull high-placed window to light it, antithesis and antidote to the naked glass box above). Elaine was at her post, chopping vegetables for soup and scanning the horizon.

She hadn't noticed him coming—there'd been so many visitors she wasn't attuned to them in the way she was in the quiet times. She was feeling hospitable, lighthearted, the hostess of an ongoing party. There'd been a professor up earlier, an ornithologist, and they'd had a long talk about the golden eagle and the red-tailed hawk. And then there was the young girl from Merced—she couldn't have been more than seventeen—with her baby strapped to her back, and two heavyset women in their sixties who'd proudly made the two-and-a-half-mile trek in from the trailhead and were giddy with the thin air and the thrill of their own accomplishment. Elaine had offered them each a cup of tea, not wanting to spoil their fun and point out that it was still two and a half miles back out.

She'd felt his weight on the platform and turned to give him a smile. He was tall and powerful across the chest and shoulders and he'd tipped his hat to her and poked his head in the open door. "Enjoying the view?" he said.

There was something in his eyes that should have warned her off, but she was feeling sociable and buoyant and she saw the generosity in his shoulders and hands. "It's nothing compared to the Ventura Freeway," she deadpanned.

He laughed out loud at that, and he was leaning in the door now, both hands on the frame. "I see the monastic life hasn't hurt your sense of humor any—" and then he paused, as if he'd gone too far. "Or that's not the word I want, 'monastic'—is there a feminine version of that?"

Pretty presumptuous. Flirtatious, too. But she was in the mood, she didn't know what it was—maybe having Todd with her, maybe just the sheer bubbling joy of living on the crest of the sky—and at least he wasn't dragging her through the same old tired conversation about loneliness and beauty and smoke on the horizon she had to endure about a hundred times a week. "Come in," she said. "Take a load off your feet."

He sat on the edge of the bed and removed his hat. He wore his hair in a modified punk style—hard irregular spikes—and that surprised her: somehow it just didn't go with the cowboy hat. His jeans were stiff and new and his tooled boots looked as if they'd just been polished. He was studying her—she was wearing khaki shorts and a T-shirt, she'd washed her hair that morning in anticipation of the crowd, and her legs were good—she knew it—tanned and shaped by her treks up and down the trail. She felt something she hadn't felt in a long time, an ice age, and she knew her cheeks were flushed. "You probably had a whole slew of visitors today, huh?" he said, and there was something incongruous in the enforced folksiness of the phrase, something that didn't go with his accent, just as the haircut didn't go with the hat.

"I've counted twenty-six since this morning." She diced a carrot and tossed it into the pan to simmer with the onions and zucchini she'd chopped a moment earlier.

He was gazing out the window, working his hands on the brim of his hat. "Hope you don't mind my saying this, but you're the best thing about this view as far as I can see. You're pretty. Really pretty."

This one she'd heard before. About a thousand times. Probably seventy percent of the day-trippers who made the hike out to the lookout were male, and if they were alone or with other males, about ninety percent of those tried to hit on her in some way. She resented it, but she couldn't blame them really. There was probably something irresistible in the formula: young woman with blond hair and good legs in a glass tower in the middle of nowhere—and all alone. Rapunzel, let down your hair. Usually she deflected the compliment—or the moves—by turning officious, standing on her authority as Forestry Service employee, government servant and the chief, queen and despot of the Needles Lookout. This time she said nothing. Just lifted her head for a quick scan of the horizon and then looked back down at the knife and the cutting board and began chopping green onion and cilantro.

He was still watching her. The bed was big, a double, one of the few creature comforts the Forestry Service provided up here. There was no headboard, of course—just a big flat hard slab of mattress attached to the wall at window level, so you could be lying in bed and still do your job. Presumably, it was designed for couples. When he spoke again, she knew what he was going to say before the words were out of his mouth. "Nice bed," he said.

What did she expect? He was no different from the rest—why would he be? All of a sudden he'd begun to get on her nerves, and when she turned her face to him her voice was cold. "Have you seen the telescope," she said, indicating the Bushnell Televar mounted on the rail of the catwalk—beyond the window and out the door.

He ignored her. He rose to his feet. Thirteen by thirteen: two's a crowd. "You must get awfully lonely up here," he said, and his voice was different now too, no attempt at folksiness or jocularity, "a pretty woman like you. A beautiful woman. You've got sexy legs, you know that?"

She flushed—he could see that, she was sure of it—and the flush made her angry. She was about to tell him off, to tell him to get the hell out of her house and stay out, when Todd came rumbling up the steps, wild-eyed and excited. "Mom!" he shouted, and he was out of breath, his voice high-pitched and hoarse, "there's water leaking all over the place out there!"

Water. It took a moment to register. The water was precious up here, irreplaceable. Once a month two bearded men with Forestry Service patches on their sleeves brought her six twenty-gallon containers of it—in the old way, on the backs of mules. She husbanded that water as if she were in the middle of the Negev, every drop of it, rarely allowing herself the luxury of a quick shampoo and rinse, as she had that morning. In the next instant she was out the door and jolting down the steps behind her son. Down below, outside the storage room where the cartons were lined up in a straight standing row, she saw that the rock face was slick with a finely spread sheen of water. She bent to the near carton. It was leaking from a thin milky stress fracture in the plastic, an inch from the bottom. "Take hold of it, Todd," she said. "We've got to turn it over so the leak's on top."

Full, the carton weighed better than a hundred and sixty pounds, and this one was nearly full. She put her weight behind it, the power of her honed and muscular legs, but the best she could do, even with Todd's help, was to push the thing over on its side. She was breathing hard, sweating, she'd scraped her knee and there was a stipple of blood on the skin over the kneecap. It was then that she became aware of the stranger standing there behind her. She looked up at him framed against the vastness of the sky, the sun in his face, his big hands on his hips. "Need a hand there?" he asked.

Looking back on it, she didn't know why she'd refused—maybe it was the way Todd gaped at him in awe, maybe it was the old pretty-woman/lonely-up-here routine or the helpless-female syndrome—but before she could think she was saying "I don't need your help: I can do it myself."

And then his hands fell from his hips and he backed away a step, and suddenly he was apologetic, he was smooth and funny and winning and he was sorry for bothering her and he just wanted to help and he knew she was capable, he wasn't implying anything—

and just as suddenly he caught himself, dropped his shoulders and slunk off down the steps without another word.

For a long moment she watched him receding down the trail, and then she turned back to the water container. By the time she and Todd got it upended it was half empty.

Yes. And now he was here when he had no right to be, now he was intruding and he knew it, now he was a crazy defining new levels of the affliction. She'd call in an emergency in a second—she wouldn't hesitate—and they'd have a helicopter here in less than five minutes, that's how quick these firefighters were, she'd seen them in action. Five minutes. She wouldn't hesitate. She kept her head down. She cut and chewed each piece of meat with slow deliberation and she read and reread the same paragraph until it lost all sense. When she looked up, he was gone.

After that, the day dragged on as if it would never end. He couldn't have been there more than ten minutes, slouching around with his mercenary grin and his pathetic flowers, but he'd managed to ruin her day. He'd upset her equilibrium and she found that she couldn't read, couldn't sketch or work on the sweater she was knitting for Todd. She caught herself staring at a fixed point on the horizon, drifting, her mind a blank. She ate too much. Lunch was a ceremony, dinner a ritual. There were no visitors, though for once she longed for them. Dusk lingered in the western sky and when night fell she didn't bother with her propane lantern but merely sat there on the corner of the bed, caught up in the wheeling immensity of the constellations and the dream of the Milky Way.

And then she couldn't sleep. She kept thinking of him, the stranger with the big hands and secretive eyes, kept scanning the catwalk for the sudden black shadow of him. If he came at seven in the morning, why not at three? What was to prevent him? There was no sound, nothing—the wind had died down and the night was clear and moonless. For the first time since she'd been here, for the first time in three long seasons, she felt naked and vulnerable, exposed in her glass house like a fish in a tank. The night was everything and it held her in its grip.

She thought about Mike then, about the house they'd had when he'd finished his degree and started as an assistant professor at a little state school out in the lost lush hills of Oregon. The house was an A-frame, a cabin with a loft, set down amidst the trees like a cottage in a fairy tale. It was all windows and everywhere you looked the trees bowed down and stepped into the house. The previous owner, an old widower with watery eyes and yellow hair climbing out of his ears, hadn't bothered with blinds or curtains, and Mike didn't like that—he was always after her to measure the windows and order blinds or buy the material for drapes. She'd balked. The openness, the light, the sense of connection and belonging: these were the things that had attracted her in the first place. They made love in the dark—Mike insisted on it—as if it were something to be ashamed of. After a while, it was.

Then she was thinking of a time before that, a time before Todd and graduate school, when Mike sat with her in the dormitory lounge, books spread out on the coffee table before them, the heat and murmur of a dozen other couples locking their mouths and bodies together. A study date. For hours she clung to him, the sofa like a boat pitching in a heavy sea, the tease of it, the fumbling innocence, the interminable foreplay that left her wet and itching while the wind screamed beyond the iced-over windows. That was something. The R.A. would flash the lights and it was quarter of one and they would fling themselves at each other, each step to the door drenched in hormones, sticky with them, desperate, until finally he was gone and she felt the loss like a war bride. Until the next night.

Finally—and it must have been two, three in the morning, the Big Dipper tugged down below the horizon, Orion looming overhead—she thought of the stranger who'd spoiled her breakfast. He'd sat there on the corner of the bed; he'd stood beyond the window with his sad bundle of flowers, devouring the sky. As she thought of him, in that very moment, there was a dull light thump on the steps, a faint rustle, movement, and she couldn't breathe, couldn't move. The seconds pounded in her head and the rustling —it was like the sweep of a broom—was gone, something in the night, a pack rat, the fleeting touch of an owl's wing. She thought

of those hands, the eyes, the square of those shoulders, and she felt
herself being drawn down into the night in relief, and finally, in
gratitude.

She woke late, the sun slanting across the floor to touch her
lips and mask her eyes. Zachary was on the radio with the news that
Oakland had clinched the pennant and a hurricane was tearing up
the East Coast. "You sound awful," he said. "I didn't wake you,
did I?"

"I couldn't sleep."

"Stargazing again, huh?"

She tried out a laugh for him. "I guess," she said. There was a
silence. "Jesus, you just relieved me. I've got four more days to put
in before I come back down to the ground."

"Just don't get mystical on me. And leave me some granola this
time, will you? And if you run out, call me. That's my breakfast we're
talking about. And lunch. And sometimes, if I don't feel like
cooking—"

She cut him off: "Dinner. I know. I will." She yawned. "Talk
to you."

"Yeah. Over and out."

"Over and out."

When she set the kettle on the grill there was gas, but when
she turned her back to dig the butter out of the refrigerator, the
flame was gone. She tried another match, but there was nothing.
That meant she had to switch propane tanks, a minor nuisance. The
tanks, which were flown in once a year by helicopter, were located
at the base of the stairway, one hundred and fifty steps down. There
was a flat spot there, a gap cut into the teeth of the outcrop and
overhung on one side by a sloping twenty-foot-high wall of rock. On
the other side, the first step was a thousand feet down.

She shrugged into her shorts, and because it was cold despite
the sun—she'd seen snow as early as the fifth of September, and
the month was almost gone now—she pulled on an oversized
sweater that had once belonged to Mike. After she'd moved out
she'd found it in a pillowcase she'd stuffed full of clothes. He hadn't

wanted it back. It was windy, and a blast knifed into her when she threw open the door and started down the steps. Big pristine tufts of cumulus hurried across the sky, swelling and attenuating and changing shape, but she didn't see anything dark enough—or big enough—to portend a storm. Still, you could never tell. The breeze was from the north and the radio had reported a storm front moving in off the Pacific—it really wouldn't surprise her to see snow on the ground by this time tomorrow. A good snowfall and the fire season would be over and she could go home. Early.

She thought about that—about the four walls of the little efficiency she rented on a dead street in a dead town to be near Todd during the winter—and hoped it wouldn't snow. Not now. Not yet. In a dry year—and this had been the third dry year in a row—she could stay through mid-November. She reached the bottom of the steps and crouched over the propane tanks, two three-hundred-gallon jobs painted Forestry Service green, feeling depressed over the thought of those four dull walls and the cold in the air and the storm that might or might not develop. There was gooseflesh on her legs and her breath crowded the air round her. She watched a ground squirrel, its shoulders bulky with patches of bright gray fur, dart up over the face of the overhang, and then she unfastened the coupling on the empty tank and switched the hose to the full one.

"Gas problems?"

The voice came from above and behind her and she jumped as if she'd been stung. Even before she whirled round she knew whose voice it was.

"Hey, hey: didn't mean to startle you. Whoa. Sorry." There he was, the happy camper, knife lashed to his thigh, standing right behind her, two steps up. This time his eyes were hidden behind a pair of reflecting sunglasses. The brim of the Stetson was pulled down low and he wore a sheepskin coat, the fleecy collar turned up in back.

She couldn't answer. Couldn't smile. Couldn't humor him. He'd caught her out of her sanctuary, caught her out in the open, one hundred and fifty steep and unforgiving steps from the radio, the

kitchen knife, the hard flat soaring bed. She was crouching. He tow-
ered above her, his shoulders cut out of the sky. Todd was in school.
Mike—she didn't want to think about Mike. She was all alone.

He stood there, the mustache the only thing alive in his face.
It lifted from his teeth in a grin. "Those things can be a pain," he
said, the folksy tone creeping into his voice, "those tanks, I mean.
Dangerous. I use electricity myself."

She lifted herself cautiously from her crouch, the hard muscles
swelling in her legs. She would have risked a dash up the stairs, all
hundred and fifty of them, would have put her confidence in her
legs, but he was blocking the stairway—almost as if he'd anticipated
her. She hadn't said a word yet. She looked scared, she knew it.
"Still camping?" she said, fighting to open up her face and give him
his smile back, insisting on banality, normalcy, the meaningless drift
of meaningless conversation.

He looked away from her, light flashing from the slick convexity
of the sunglasses, and kicked at the edge of the step with the silver-
tipped toe of his boot. After a moment he turned back to her and
removed the sunglasses. "Yeah," he said, shrugging. "I guess."

It wasn't an answer she expected. He guessed? What was that
supposed to mean? He hadn't moved a muscle and he was watching
her with that look in his eyes—she knew that look, knew that stance,
that mustache and hat, but she didn't know his name. He knew hers
but she didn't know his, not even his first name. "I'm sorry," she
said, and when she put a hand up to her eyes to shade them from
the sun, it was trembling, "but what was your name again? I mean,
I remember you, of course, not just from yesterday but from that
time a month or so ago, but . . ." She trailed off.

He didn't seem to have heard her. The wind sang in the trees.
She just stood there, squinting into the sun—there was nothing else
she could do. "I wasn't camping, not really," he said. "Not that I
don't love the wilderness—and I do camp, backpack and all that—
but I just—I thought that's what you'd want to hear."

What she'd want to hear? What was he talking about? She stole
a glance at the tower, sun flashing the windows, clouds pricked on

the peak of the roof, and it seemed as distant as the stars at night. If only she were up there she'd put out an emergency, she would, she'd have them here in five minutes. . . .

"Actually," and he looked away now, his shoulders slumping in that same hangdog way they had when she'd refused his help with the water carton, "actually I've got a cabin up on Cedar Slope. I just, I just thought you'd want to hear I was camping." He'd been staring down at the toe of his boots, but suddenly he looked up at her and grinned till his back fillings glinted in the light. "I think Elaine's a pretty name, did I tell you that?"

"Thank you," she said, almost against her will, and softly, so softly she could barely hear it herself. He could rape her here, he could kill her, anything. Was that what he wanted? Was that it? "Listen," she said, pushing it, she couldn't help herself, "listen, I've got to get back to work—"

"I know, I know," he said, holding up the big slab of his hand, "back to the nest, huh? I know I must be a pain in the—in the butt for you, and I'll bet I'm not the first one to say it, but you're just too good-looking a woman to be wasted out here on the squirrels and coyotes." He stepped down, stepped toward her, and she thought in that instant of trying to dart past him, a wild thought, instinctual and desperate, a thought that clawed its way into her brain and froze there before she could move. "Jesus," he said, and his voice was harsh with conviction, "don't you get lonely?"

And then she saw it, below and to the right, movement, two bobbing pink hunter's caps, coming up the trail. It was over. Just like that. She could walk away from him, mount the stairs, lock herself in the tower. But why was her heart still going, why did she feel as if it hadn't even begun? "Damn," she said, directing her gaze, "more visitors. Now I really have to get back."

He followed her eyes and looked down to where the hunters sank out of view and then bobbed back up again, working their way up the path. She could see their faces now—two men, middle-aged, wispy hair sticking out from beneath the fluorescent caps. No guns. Cameras. He studied them a moment and then looked into her eyes, looked deep, as if he'd lost something. Then he shrugged, turned his back and started down the path toward them.

She was in good shape, the best shape of her life. She'd been up the steps a thousand times, two thousand, but she'd never climbed them quicker than she did now. She flew up the stairs like something blown by the wind and she felt a kind of panic beating against her ribs and she smelled the storm coming and felt the cold to the marrow of her bones. And then she reached the door and slammed it shut behind her, fumbling for the latch. It was then, only then, that she noticed the flowers. They were in the center of the table, in a cut-glass vase, lupine, groundsel, forget-me-not.

It snowed in the night, monstrous swirling oversized flakes that clawed at the windows and filled her with despair. The lights would only have made her feel vulnerable and exposed, and for the second night running she did without them, sitting there in the dark, cradling the kitchen knife and listening for his footfall on the steps while the sky fell to pieces around her. But he wouldn't come, not in this weather, not at night—she was being foolish, childish, there was nothing to worry about. Except the snow. It meant that her season was over. And if her season was over, she had to go back down the mountain and into the real world, real time, into the smog and roar and clutter.

She thought of the four walls that awaited her, the hopeless job—waitressing or fast food or some such slow crucifixion of the spirit—and she thought of Mike before she left him, saw him there in the black glass of the window, sexless, pale, the little butterfly-wing bifocals perched on the tip of his nose, pecking at the type-writer, pecking, pecking, in love with Dryden, Swift, Pope, in love with dead poets, in love with death itself. She'd met a man at a party a month after she'd left him and he was just like Mike, only he was in love with arthropods. Arthropods. And then she came up to the tower.

She woke late again and the first thing she felt was relief. The sun was out and the snow—it was only a dusting, nothing really—

had already begun to recede from the naked high crown of the rock. She put on the kettle and went to the radio. "Zack," she called, "Needle Rock. Do you copy?"

He was there, right at her fingertips. "Copy. Over."

"We had some snow up here—nothing much, just a dusting really. It's clear now."

"You're a little late—Lewis already checked in from Mule Peak with that information. Oversleep again?"

"Yeah, I guess so." She was watching the distant treetops shake off the patina of snow. A hawk sailed across the window. She held the microphone so close to her lips it could have been a part of her. "Zack—" She wanted to tell him about the crazy, about the man in the Stetson, about his hands, wanted to alert him just in case, but she hesitated. Her voice was tiny, detached, lost in the electronic crackle of time and space.

"Lainie?"

"Yes. Yes, I'm here."

"There's a cold front coming through, another storm behind it. They're saying it could drop some snow. The season's still on—Reichert says it will be until we get appreciable precipitation—but this one could be it. It's up to you. You want to come out or wait and see?"

Reichert was the boss, fifty, bald, soft as a clam. The mountains were parched—six inches of powdery duff covered the forest floor and half the creeks had run dry. The season could last till November. "Wait and see," she said.

"Okay, it's your choice. Lewis is staying too, if it makes you feel better. I'll keep in touch if anything develops on this end."

"Yeah. Thanks."

"Over and out."

"Over and out."

It clouded up late in the afternoon and the sky closed in on her again. The temperature began to drop. It looked bad. It was early for snow yet, but they could get snow any time of the year at this altitude. The average was twenty-five feet annually, and she'd seen storms drop four and five feet at a time. She talked to Zack at four and he told her it looked pretty grim—they were calling for a seventy-percent chance of snow, with the snow level dropping to three thousand feet. "I'll take my chances," she told him. There was a pair of snowshoes in the storage room if it came to that.

The snow started an hour later. She was cooking dinner—brown rice and vegetables—and she'd opened the bottle of wine she'd brought up to commemorate the last day of the season. The flakes were tiny, pellets that sifted down with a hiss, the sort of configuration that meant serious snow. The season was over. She could drink her wine and then think about packing up and cleaning the stove and refrigerator. She put another log on the woodstove and buttoned up her jacket.

The wine was half gone and she'd sat down to eat when she noticed the smoke. At first she thought it must be a trick of the wind, the smoke from her own stove twisting back on her. But no. Below her, no more than five hundred feet, just about where the trail would be, she could see the flames. The wind blew a screen of snow across the window. There hadn't been any lightning—but there was a fire down there, she was sure of it. She got up from the table, snatched her binoculars from the hook by the door and went out on the catwalk to investigate.

The wind took her breath away. All the universe had gone pale, white above and white beneath: she was perched on the clouds, living in them, diaphanous and ghostly. She could smell the smoke on the wind now. She lifted the binoculars to her eyes and the snow screened them; she tried again and her hair beat at the lenses. It took her a moment, but there, there it was: a fire leaping up out of the swirling grip of the snow. A campfire. But no, this was bigger, fallen trees stacked up in a pyramid—this was a bonfire, deliberate, this was a sign. The snow took it away from her. Her fingers were numb. When the fire came into focus again she saw movement there, a shadow leaping round the flames, feeding them, reveling in them, and she caught her breath. And then she saw the black stabbing peak of the Stetson and she understood.

He was camping.

Camping. He could die out there—he *was* crazy, he *was*—this thing could turn into a blizzard, it could snow for days. But he was camping. And then the thought came to her: he was camping for her.

Later, when the tower floated out over the storm and the coals glowed in the stove and the darkness settled in around her like a blanket, she disconnected the radio and put the knife away in the drawer where it belonged. Then she propped herself in the corner of the bed, way out over the edge of the abyss, and watched his fire raging in the cold heart of the night. He would be back, she knew that now, and she would be ready for him.

FOR THE BEST IN PAPERBACKS, LOOK FOR THE

In every corner of the world, on every subject under the sun, Penguin represents quality and variety—the very best in publishing today.

For complete information about books available from Penguin—including Puffins, Penguin Classics, and Arkana—and how to order them, write to us at the appropriate address below. Please note that for copyright reasons the selection of books varies from country to country.

In the United Kingdom: Please write to *Dept. EP, Penguin Books Ltd, Bath Road, Harmondsworth, West Drayton, Middlesex UB7 0DA.*

In the United States: Please write to *Penguin Putnam Inc., P.O. Box 12289 Dept. B, Newark, New Jersey 07101-5289* or call 1-800-788-6262.

In Canada: Please write to *Penguin Books Canada Ltd, 10 Alcorn Avenue, Suite 300, Toronto, Ontario M4V 3B2.*

In Australia: Please write to *Penguin Books Australia Ltd, P.O. Box 257, Ringwood, Victoria 3134.*

In New Zealand: Please write to *Penguin Books (NZ) Ltd, Private Bag 102902, North Shore Mail Centre, Auckland 10.*

In India: Please write to *Penguin Books India Pvt Ltd, 11 Panchsheel Shopping Centre, Panchsheel Park, New Delhi 110 017.*

In the Netherlands: Please write to *Penguin Books Netherlands bv, Postbus 3507, NL-1001 AH Amsterdam.*

In Germany: Please write to *Penguin Books Deutschland GmbH, Metzlerstrasse 26, 60594 Frankfurt am Main.*

In Spain: Please write to *Penguin Books S. A., Bravo Murillo 19, 1° B, 28015 Madrid.*

In Italy: Please write to *Penguin Italia s.r.l., Via Benedetto Croce 2, 20094 Corsico, Milano.*

In France: Please write to *Penguin France, Le Carré Wilson, 62 rue Benjamin Baillaud, 31500 Toulouse.*

In Japan: Please write to *Penguin Books Japan Ltd, Kaneko Building, 2-3-25 Koraku, Bunkyo-Ku, Tokyo 112.*

In South Africa: Please write to *Penguin Books South Africa (Pty) Ltd, Private Bag X14, Parkview, 2122 Johannesburg.*